Thinly Veiled: The 80's

I0553361

VOLUME 8

THE CASTLE OF HORROR ANTHOLOGY

CASTLE BRIDGE MEDIA
DENVER, COLORADO, USA

CASTLE BRIDGE MEDIA
Denver, Colorado
Edited by Jason Henderson and In Churl Yo
Designed by In Churl Yo
Cover Photo Mark Murphy Photos/Shutterstock

© 2022 Castle Bridge Media and Individual Authors

ISBN: 979-8-9859702-3-4

⇒ TABLE OF CONTENTS ⇐

INTRODUCTION

A Chat on Thinly Veiled with Publishers Jason Henderson and In Churl Yo

Castle of Horror Volume 8: Thinly Veiled: The 80s is a special collection for Castle Bridge because it's the first time we've returned to a concept because of its popularity. This time rather than the usual prose introduction, In Churl and Jason sat down instead to chat. The following transcript has been edited for clarity.

In Churl: So this is Volume 8 of the Castle of Horror Anthology.

Jason: Unbelievable. And we've always had themes. Women Running from Houses. Holidays. Summer. But Thinly Veiled—that one really resonates. Thinly Veiled was this concept where we asked people to take a known property and "thinly veil" it while writing a horror story. And the writers and readers got it *instantly*. What is it about Thinly Veiled?

In Churl: The idea of making horror out of the familiar, what's the appeal of it? One of the things you've said before is that it's fun, right? It's like a game.

Jason: Yes. People have written reviews where they say one of their favorite things is to read through and see how quickly they can identify the brand that's being riffed on. To get the clues together and go, oh, this is *Family Ties*. (Although we don't have a *Family Ties* story this time.)

In Churl: That's one thing, but the other is the subversion—the idea of taking these properties that we cherish so much and creating something completely new and unexpected out of them. And there's the subversion of horror as well; we know that horror is often something you find when you're in the woods, or you're in a haunted house, or whatever. You expect horror in those settings. But if you take something like *Back to the Future*, something we grew up loving that has a place in our hearts, and you make Doc Brown a serial killer, you subvert it. And I think people are drawn to that because you've taken something we care deeply about and inserted this horror trope into it and made it scary. So it doesn't just impact our minds, it impacts our hearts. Yeah. You know, it just feels--

Jason: --subversive in a way. It feels transgressive, yeah.

In Churl: We have a more visceral reaction to those kinds of stories. I think those are the two things that cause people to love Thinly Veiled: it's fun, but it also has this emotional impact.

Jason: Do you want to talk about what's coming up for the Castle of Horror Anthology?

In Churl: Well, we know for sure that later in the year we'll have our first LGBTQ+ collection.

Jason: That one's not edited by us, I should add. For the reader, anytime we're doing a collection that reflects a community that we're not part of, we go outside to find an editor who does.

In Churl: More on that soon. Plus, we've got a YA collection coming. And there's any number of directions you can go with YA—romance, adventure, sci-fi, but of course all with a horror twist.

Jason: And more Thinly Veiled, I imagine.

In Churl: Plenty of worlds left to explore for Thinly Veiled. I mean *so many* ideas. The 90s. I think that's the last decade. But: elections. Superheroes. Saturday morning cartoons. The Sunday funny papers. So many. So. Many.

Jason: I want to do all of those things. Let's talk 80s. So in this book we've got: Charles R Rutledge with a riff on ███████ where a certain Hawaii-based detective faces a Cthulhu-style threat in "The Shadow Over Waikiki;"

5

Alethea Kontis gives us a humorous SF tale about a clone of Elvis acting as a troubleshooter in a world where soap opera stars have been cloned over and over again in "The Way of the Restless;" In Churl Yo gives us a zombified take on ██████ that manages to put most of the action of the original movie into the background with "The Dead Die Hard;" Katya de Becerra's "Howl" takes a Jackson-esque look at the spooky Yorkshire community found in ██████; in "Guests for Dinner," Henry Herz shows us that ██████ could have been a much spookier show; Jim Towns' tongue-in-cheek "HELL Copter" is a perfect reflection of 80s machismo, especially around a certain helicopter show; "Novelty" from Will McDermott is a hilarious look at the possible dangers of koosh balls; Bryan Young's "Late Night Reruns" tells a blood-curdling story of a boy who might be receiving help from another dimension; "The Donjon" from John Pritchard is like a version of cult favorite ██████ transported into a Hammer period adventure; Dennis K. Crosby's "Jump" is a tense look at police work, spirits and death; "Notes from Project CyberPolice" brings searing corporate humor to ██████; Rob Nisbet in "Do Androids Dream?" offers a dark continuation of ██████; "Life Form" from Heath Shelby asks if the fuzzy visitor in the sitcom ██████ could be a Bigfoot; and Jason Henderson's "Floodwater" brings a serial killer and a dangerous flood to the girls of ██████.

In Churl: I hope people love it. Definitely we want to hear from them.

Jason: Definitely. Can you believe that with this volume of the Castle of Horror Anthology, Castle Bridge Media has published over 100 horror short stories? What a milestone! It's been such an honor to have had the privilege of working with all of these amazing writers who bring their unique voices and talents to our anthology series, and to share those stories with the world. Each work is like a priceless gem on a jewelry box.

In Churl: I couldn't have said it better myself. And we're just getting started. I can't wait to read the next volume. It can't happen soon enough.

Jason: And the next! ♜

THE SHADOW OVER WAIKIKI

By Charles R. Rutledge

Oahu, Hawaii—1987

AMOS MORGAN PARKED THE FERRARI behind the police barricade and stepped out into the cool morning air. The sun was barely up and the sky above Keehi Harbor was as red as blood. Appropriate, Morgan thought, given the circumstances. Morgan walked up to the crime scene tape and showed a uniformed officer his ID.

"Lieutenant Santos is expecting me," Morgan said.

The officer nodded. "Yeah, he said you'd be along. Go down this walkway and turn left."

Morgan did as instructed and made his way down a wooden walkway to a narrow strip of rocky shore. In the distance he could see Keehi Marina and beyond that, the looming bulk of Sand Island. As he reached the end of the walkway, he saw Honolulu Police Lieutenant Dennis Santos crouched on the rocks beside a form covered in a blue tarp.

Santos looked up as he heard the boards creaking under Morgan's weight. He wore one of his customary floral Hawaiian shirts and his trademark Panama hat.

"Thanks for coming, Morgan," Santos said. He was a transplanted New Yorker and still sounded like it. "Like I told you on the phone, a jogger and his dog found this woman. She had your business card on her but no ID. Need you to take a look at her."

7

Morgan gave a short nod. "Okay."

Santos said, "She's been in the water at least two days, but she doesn't look as bad as she could."

Morgan gritted his teeth as Santos pulled the tarp back just enough to show the woman's head. Like Santos had said, not as bad as it could be. Her face was swollen and puffy, but he could still recognize her features.

Morgan said, "Eve Donner. She hired me two weeks ago to find out if her husband was cheating on her."

"Was he?" Santos said.

"Yeah. What happened to her, Lieutenant?"

Santos stood up and stretched for a moment. "I'll tell you, but keep your mouth shut about it. She was gutted. Slit down the abdomen from throat to stomach. Ligature marks on her wrists and ankles show she was bound."

Morgan said, "Jesus. You think she was alive when it was done?"

"Have to wait for the Medical Examiner's report, but it looks likely. She was topless when we found her, but still wearing some jean shorts. No wallet, but a plastic case with some small bills and your card in one pocket. Here's the thing, Morgan. She's not the first. We've had two other deaths like this in the last ten days."

Morgan said, "Are you thinking serial killer?"

"Looks like it. I'm only telling you this because you're involved. We've kept it from the press about as long as we can. When it hits, at least you'll know what's going on."

"Thanks, Lieutenant. I appreciate it."

Santos said, "What can you tell me about her?"

Morgan said, "Not much really. It was a two-day job. Like I said, she thought her husband was fooling around. I followed him and the second night he went to a motel with his secretary. I took pictures and showed them to Eve. Just another sad day in paradise."

"Husband strike you as capable of something like this?"

"I never got that close to him."

Santos shrugged. "Had to ask. We'll check him out. I guess that's all I need from you right now. Call me if you think of anything."

"You can count on it."

Morgan turned and went back up the walkway. He'd only met Eve Donner twice, but she'd seemed like a nice woman caught in a small, sad life. He had solved her case so quickly he had insisted she take back half of his retainer. Not smart business practice maybe, but it had seemed the right thing to do.

Morgan glanced back toward Santos. The Lieutenant was walking slowly around the strip of shore, looking at the ground as the light improved. It was his problem now. There was no reason for Morgan to be involved. Private investigators didn't hunt for serial killers, no matter what the movies said.

And yet.

The police would follow the usual path. Talk to her husband. Talk to the girlfriend. Spread out from there to question friends and acquaintances and co-workers. Even now they were probably getting Eve's address and preparing to go to her apartment. They'd follow all the leads they had. But Morgan had one they didn't.

Morgan didn't have an office and Eve hadn't wanted to meet at her apartment for obvious reasons, so she had suggested they meet at Ke'ehi Lagoon Park. It wasn't that far from her apartment, and it wasn't far from where Morgan was standing at that moment.

He got back in the Ferrari and headed north on Puuhale Road and hung a left onto Nimitz Highway. Ten minutes later he was parking near a picnic table at the park. Residents often used the lagoon for canoe practice because the water tended to be calm. It was early still and there were only a couple of guys paddling around in an outrigger.

Morgan walked across the grass and into the sand near the waterline. There were a few stone benches there with a good view of the lagoon and the city across the water. Eve had told him she often came to this spot to sit and think. The park would be mostly deserted at night. A good place for someone looking for a victim.

The sand around the bench was churned with footprints, and Santos had estimated Eve had been in the water a couple of days, so not likely any physical evidence would remain. Morgan still made a slow circuit of the area. As he walked from the lagoon back to the bench, he caught the glint of something metallic in the sand.

Morgan crouched and brushed the sand away, revealing a thin, intricately worked bracelet. It looked to be made of white gold and it was far too large for Eve Donner's wrists. Probably unconnected. He put it in his pocket anyway. If it wasn't related to Eve's death, he could turn it in to lost and found later.

Morgan felt a sudden 'crawling' sensation at the back of his neck. He had felt it before back in Viet Nam just before someone died from a sniper bullet. It was a feeling of being watched. He spun back toward the lagoon but there was nothing in that direction. And how could there be? He took one more look around and decided he had seen all there was to see. He got back into the Ferrari and headed for home.

9

It took him a little over half an hour in morning traffic to get back to Raven's Aerie, the estate of Texas billionaire Buford Raven. He had been living there for the last couple of years in the guest house. Ostensibly, Morgan was part of security at the estate, but really, Raven just let him live there because he had saved the billionaire's life when Raven had been kidnapped a while back.

Estate security was actually overseen by a former British soldier named Antony Q. Rollins. Rollins was waiting in front of the main house when Morgan pulled in. He was a short man who still dressed with military precision. His taste in clothes tended toward khakis with razor sharp creases. He was flanked by his two German Shepherd guard dogs, Aries and Deimos.

Rollins started talking as Morgan got out of the car. "Morgan, I told you last night I would need the Ferrari today. It has to go in for scheduled maintenance. Now there are any number of other cars you could use for…"

Morgan said, "Sorry, Rollins. The police called me before sunrise, and I had to go to a crime scene. I just forgot."

"The police? What has happened?"

Morgan gave Rollins a brief account of his morning. The small man listened with his full attention. For all his bluster he was good at his job, and Morgan respected his opinions. Not that he would ever admit that.

"Good God, Morgan," Rollins said. "First the Honolulu Strangler and now this."

"Yeah, doesn't seem like the sort of thing that should happen in paradise."

"Are you going to look into it?" said Rollins.

"I'm staying clear of the police investigation, but I did think of one thing." He dug the bracelet out of his pocket. "Have you ever seen anything like this?"

Rollins took the bracelet and studied it for a moment. "Where did you get this?"

"I found it in the sand when I was at Ke'ehi Lagoon."

Rollins said, "This is very very old. Might I borrow it? I can probably tell you more about if after I've had a chance to consult some of my books."

"Feel free," Morgan said. "And I really do appreciate your help."

The little man was already lost in thought, wandering back toward the main house with the two dogs in his wake, the Ferrari and all else forgotten as he studied the bracelet. Though he could be a bit of a blowhard sometimes, Morgan knew Rollins was an expert on many strange and obscure subjects.

The morning's events had left Morgan feeling pensive. He walked across the lawn to the guest house, admiring the well-trimmed lawns and landscaped grounds. According to Rollins, the massive main house was of the Spanish-Colonial style and had been built in 1933.

Morgan only stopped by the guest house long enough to change into swim trunks. Then he went across the lawn to the ocean facing side of the main house and made his way down to the tidal pool. Hopefully a swim would clear the cobwebs floating in his brain. He waded into the surf and began swimming along the stone retaining wall that separated the 'turtle pond' from the sea.

About an hour later, Morgan was beginning to think about the possibility of lunch when he was again struck by the sensation of something crawling between his shoulder blades. Feeling something close to panic, Morgan swam into the shallows, then stood and gazed out toward the ocean. Nothing but clouds and a stray sea bird to be seen.

Morgan hurried back to the beach. He grabbed his towel and headed for the guest house to shower. As he stepped inside the house, he noticed the red light blinking on his answering machine. He pressed the play button. A message from Rollins, asking him to come to the main house.

Morgan took a quick shower and then crossed to the big house. He found Rollins in the small man's study. Books and papers were spread across his desk. Rollins looked up from his studies as Morgan entered.

"Ah, Morgan," Rollins said. "I have a little information for you."

"That was fast," Morgan said.

"I said a little. Look here."

Rollins turned one of the large books on the desk so Morgan could see it upside right. There were two black and white photographs of jewelry. One piece was a tiara and the other a bracelet similar to the one Morgan had found.

"Holy cow, Rollins. The carving work on these things looks just like the bracelet."

"Filigree," Rollins corrected. "Not carving."

"Okay. Where did these two come from?"

"Their origin isn't known precisely. These pieces are housed in a museum at Miskatonic University in Massachusetts. They apparently belonged to one of the local families."

"I'm not seeing any connection between the bracelet and Eve Donner's death."

Rollins said, "I wouldn't rule it out too quickly. I think you should talk to my friend Alicia Finlay. She's an associate professor of anthropology at Honolulu University. She might be able to tell you more about the bracelet. I can give her a call if you like."

"That would be great. Thanks."

Rollins picked up the phone. He apparently reached Professor Finlay first try and talked to her for less than a minute.

Rollins hung up and said, "Alicia said she could talk to you between classes if you can be at the campus in about an hour. Take the Jeep. Now, I really must go and see to the Ferrari."

#   #   #

"Where did you say you found this, Mr. Morgan?" Professor Alicia Finlay said.

"At Ke'ehi Lagoon Park," Morgan said.

They were in Professor Finlay's office at Honolulu university. Finlay was an attractive woman in her late 30s with red hair and pale eyes. She had ushered him in and snatched the bracelet as soon as he produced it. She examined it under a lighted magnifying lens, making a lot of *oooh* and *aaah* sounds.

Finlay said, "As Anthony told you, this is very old. I haven't seen many specimens of this sort of jewelry, but it does pop up from time to time. Most of it seems to have come from the Polynesian islands, though back in the 1920s quite a bit of it turned up in New England of all places."

"Yeah, Rollins...er...Anthony said there were two examples in Massachusetts."

"Yes, apparently a sea captain named Marsh had brought some islanders back to a fishing town there called Innsmouth, and they had some of the jewelry. That's why there are specimens at Miskatonic."

Morgan said, "We're a lot closer to the islands than that."

"Very true, and a few pieces of this type have turned up here on Oahu. Some of the local fisher folk sold a few rings and such over the years."

"Where would they have gotten them, do you suppose?" said Morgan.

Finlay shook her head. "No way of knowing. Keep in mind, indigenous Hawaiian people are thought to be Polynesians who came here from the Society Archipelago about 800 years ago, so it's possible the gold items were handed down. Then again, according to certain legends, the jewelry wasn't made by the islanders. They got it from a race of beings who lived under the sea."

"Like mermaids?"

Finlay said, "Slightly more sinister than that. Come over here and look at the bracelet under the lens."

Morgan did as she said and gave the bracelet his first actual close inspection. Magnified, he could see the detail was even more impressive than he had thought. It seemed to show a bunch of tiny people in various activities. But no, they weren't people. They were roughly humanoid, but they had bodies more like frogs than men and their heads were something like those of fish. Finlay was right. There was something disturbing about these 'fish men'.

Finlay said, "You see it now?"

Morgan said, "I do. What are they?"

"No one really knows. I've heard them referred to as Deep Ones, but that was by a professor who specialized in fringe science. I'm just a plain old anthropologist. I steer clear of anything that smacks of pseudo-science. Makes the tenure committee nervous."

"So as far as you know, these Deep Ones aren't real?"

Finlay said, "No. How could they be? Just legends. Probably a good thing too."

"Why do you say that?" said Morgan.

"According to some of those legends they were fond of human sacrifices."

Finlay had to get to her next class, so Morgan thanked her and made his way back to the visitor's parking lot. It was midmorning now, another beautiful sunny day on Oahu. Morgan's mood was anything but sunny.

Morgan still didn't know if the bracelet was in any way connected to Eve Donner's murder. He decided to take the night to think about it, and after that he would call Santos and tell him what he'd learned. In the meantime, he would get Rollins to lock the bracelet in the safe at the main house.

\#   \#   \#

Morgan came awake with a start. It was full dark and there were no lights in the room. He had fallen asleep on the couch while reading and now he had no idea what time it was. He reached behind him to switch on a lamp. Nothing happened. A power outage?

He heard the front door rattle. He had locked it when he came in out of habit. It rattled again and Morgan sat up, adrenalin bringing him fully awake. He got off the couch and moved to where he could see the door. There was just enough ambient light from the windows that he could make it out in the gloom. Someone was trying to turn the knob.

The door rattled again and then it shook as something slammed against it. Whatever it was hit the door again and the frame splintered. The door flew open, and a large, bulky figure filled the doorway. Morgan was aware of a strong smell like the seabed when the tide rolls back. An almost overpowering

13

stench of dead fish and rotting seaweed.

The figure lurched into the living room. All Morgan could see was the outline of whoever it was against the dim light filtering in the door. There was something…disturbing about the shape of the visitor.

"The bracelet," a liquid, gargling voice said.

"Look," Morgan said. "I don't know who you are, but…"

"The bracelet," the voice repeated.

"It isn't here," said Morgan.

The shape snarled and came lurching toward Morgan. Some instinct warned him not to try and fight it barehanded. He whirled and stumbled down a hall to his bedroom. His Army .45 was in a drawer in his nightstand along with a flashlight. He heard whoever it was right behind him. Their feet made wet smacking sounds on the carpet.

Morgan reached the bedroom and rolled across the bed to the far side. He jerked the nightstand drawer open and fumbled for the flashlight and the .45. He got his hands on both and swung the light up and pointed it at the door. What he saw almost made him drop both light and gun.

The shape in the doorway wasn't human. It stood on two legs, but its feet were flat and elongated, with splayed toes tipped with claws. Its body was bulbous and covered with scales. It had long arms and webbed, clawed fingers. Its face was a parody of a man's, with bulging eyes, two wet, ragged holes where the nose should have been, and a wide mouth full of sharp teeth.

Morgan couldn't have told you how, but he knew at once it wasn't a man in a costume. It was some sort of creature. The thing's breathing sounded like its lungs were full of water and Morgan could see something like gills flexing at either side of its neck. It was one of the things shown on the bracelet. A Deep One.

The thing came into the room and Morgan pulled the trigger. In his panic he had forgotten to chamber a round, but now he did so. This time the gun fired. The shot went wide and hit the wall beside the door, but Morgan's second shot struck the monster in the chest. The thing kept coming.

He fired twice more. The creature gave a gurgling growl, but it turned and staggered back through the door. Morgan took several deep breaths, then went after it. He followed the thing back through the living room and out the front door. There was faint moonlight now and Morgan watched as the creature lumbered down the sloped lawn toward the sea.

Morgan's legs suddenly refused to support his weight and he sank to his knees. What the hell had he just seen? What the living hell?

Morgan heard footsteps and he managed to turn and bring the flashlight up. Rollins stood there holding his own semi-automatic handgun.

"Oh. My. God!" Rollins said, enunciating every word.

#   #   #

"So what do you think it was?" Morgan said.

Rollins said. "I have no idea. I didn't get as good a look at it as you did. You're certain it wasn't someone in some sort of costume?"

They were back in Rollins' study, and it was almost sunrise. They had checked the electric line on the guest house and found it had been ripped from the wall. Whatever the thing was, it appeared to be smart enough to kill the power.

Morgan said, "No, it couldn't have been a person. The anatomy was all wrong. Besides, at least three of my rounds hit it and all we found was a little blood. Those were .45 slugs, and they should have done more damage."

Morgan didn't like to think about just how *wrong* the creature had looked. It had a weird, rolling gait and for one moment, before it reached the water, it had switched to running on all fours. It wasn't an image he would forget anytime soon.

Rollins said, "Yes, I suppose that's true. But I'm not ready to believe in Alicia's Deep Ones just yet."

Morgan shrugged. "Truthfully I don't know what to believe. Or what to do. I can't just call Lieutenant Santos and tell him a sea monster came looking for a bracelet that might or not be connected to Eve Donner's murder."

Rollins said, "Do you think our intruder might return?"

"It's possible, and that's another reason to try and find out more about it. It might come back, and it might bring help. When I was talking to Professor Finlay, she said she had learned about the Deep Ones from another professor. One who specialized in fringe science. Do you know who she meant?"

Rollins said, "I suspect she was talking about Jeremy Derleth. He was forced out of the university a few years ago because of some of his more bizarre theories."

"He sounds like someone I should talk to. Could you check with Finlay and see if she has a current address or phone number for him?"

"I'll do so just as soon as it's a decent hour."

As things turned out, Rollins couldn't get hold of Alicia Finlay until late afternoon, so it was approaching dusk as Morgan drove the newly tuned Ferrari north along Mokolua Drive. Finlay had indeed had an address for Derleth. She hadn't had a number however, and Derleth wasn't in the phone book, so Morgan hoped he'd find him at home.

Derleth's house was a small, white, wood-frame affair with a flagstone walkway leading up to a screened front door. It was hidden from the houses on either side by thick growths of trees and bushes. A beat-up silver Honda was parked in front. That was a good sign.

15

There wasn't room to fit his car in the driveway, so he parked a block away in front of a house for sale. When Morgan got out of the car he could hear the ocean a few hundred yards away, though other small houses across the street obscured it from view. He made his way to Derleth's place, walked up to the front door, and knocked.

A few moments later the door swung inward and a tall, thin man with bushy gray hair and beard peered out. Morgan said, "Professor Derleth? My name is Morgan. I'm a private investigator and I wondered if I could ask you a few questions."

"Concerning what?"

Morgan said, "Concerning the Deep Ones."

Derleth frowned. "I don't know who put you up to this, but I'm not in the mood for jokes." He started to close the door.

"No, no," Morgan said. "No one sent me, I'm very serious. Look." He held out the bracelet.

Derleth said, "I think you had better come inside."

Morgan stepped into the house. If he had expected the professor's place to be a wreck, he was disappointed. The living room was neat, though dominated by walls lined with bookshelves.

"Come back to my office," Derleth said.

Morgan followed Derleth down a short hall. The house had been built with two small bedrooms and Derleth had converted one of them into an office. Here, there was more of the chaos Morgan expected. Books and papers everywhere. A small desk was jammed into one corner and Derleth seated himself behind it. Morgan moved a pile of books off the room's only other chair and sat.

Derleth placed the bracelet on the center of his desk and turned on a desk lamp. He grabbed a magnifying lens from a drawer an used it to give the bracelet a long look.

"Beautiful workmanship," Derleth said. "What do you know about the Deep Ones, Mr. Morgan?"

"Not much. Alicia Finlay told me this was one of their bracelets."

"I see. And she sent you to me. Do you mind if I ask what your interest is?"

"I'll level with you, professor. I'm investigating a murder and this bracelet was found at a spot where the victim might have been abducted."

Derleth said, "I haven't seen anything in the news about a murder."

"The police are keeping it quiet. It was pretty gruesome."

"Can you explain how? I assure you this isn't morbid curiosity on my part. It could be important."

Morgan considered that for a moment. Santos had warned him to keep

16

his mouth shut. Then again, the Lieutenant had also said news of the murder would hit the press soon enough, and Derleth might have useful information.

"According to the police, the woman was probably bound and then cut open. Probably while she was still alive."

Derleth nodded. "Yes, that would fit the pattern of a religious sacrifice."

"Religious?"

"The Deep Ones worship old and bloody gods, Mr. Morgan. Dagon. Mother Hydra. Great Cthulhu. Ritual sacrifice is often part of that worship. It usually is a means to an end as well."

"How do you mean?"

Derleth leaned back in his chair. "Those entities I mentioned, be they gods or whatever, they actually answer the prayers of their supplicants. Back in the nineteenth century here in Hawaii, both colonial and indigenous people sometimes made pacts with Dagon for better fishing, better weather, or personal gain. The Deep Ones often acted as intermediaries. They would provide gold and other gifts to the humans who would swear loyalty to the Great Old Ones."

"So someone could be looking to benefit from these sacrifices?" Morgan said.

"I can think of little other reason for them to occur. I have to say, you're taking all of this rather eldritch information very well. Most people are more incredulous when I tell them about the Deep Ones and their gods."

"That's because I've seen one of them. It came looking for that bracelet."

Derleth leaned forward. "Are you serious? You saw one of them?"

Morgan gave a brief account of his run-in with the fish man.

When Morgan finished, Derleth said, "Do you want my advice, Mr. Morgan? Go outside right now. Walk across the street to the beach and throw that bracelet into the sea."

"It's my only lead, professor."

"And keeping it could lead to your death. Some of these relics have religious and personal importance to the Deep Ones. It won't stop trying to get it back. And they can do things you can't begin to imagine. Call upon forces no one can fight."

"You've seen them too," Morgan said.

"Yes, I've seen them. I won't tell you where. It's best you never try to go there. Take my advice. Throw this thing in the sea. Once it's in the water its owner will be able to find it."

That seemed to be the end of the conversation. Morgan said, "Thank you for your time, professor. I'll consider what you told me."

"I hope you do. I'll walk you out. Let me give you my phone number. Next time you can call first."

'Yeah, Professor Finlay didn't have your number."

Derleth smiled. "She'll have it after I call her and tell her not to send people to my house."

Morgan stepped out into darkness. Night had fallen while he'd been talking to Derleth. He walked to the edge of the driveway. From this viewpoint he could see the glimmer of waves breaking beyond the houses across the street. Should he do what Derleth said and ditch the bracelet? He held it for a moment, watching the water.

Then he put it back in his pocket. He walked back to where he had left the Ferrari. He didn't see a shadow detach itself from the others until it was too late.

#   #   #

Morgan awoke to a throbbing head and the realization that he was bound hand and foot. He was in a seated position, leaning against a large rock. His hands were tied in front of him, and his ankles were wrapped tightly.

He looked around him and saw he was on what appeared to be a small, rocky islet. Morgan knew there were over 120 small, uninhabited islands, islets, and atolls in the Hawaiian archipelago. He could be anywhere.

The only light came from a hissing kerosene lamp which sat about six feet away. A figure stepped into the yellow light and then Morgan heard a familiar voice.

"You should have taken my advice, Mr. Morgan," Jeremy Derleth said.

Morgan said, "Derleth. What's going on?"

"Isn't it obvious?" Derleth said. He tossed something onto the ground. It landed with a clank in front of the lamp and Morgan saw it was a large, heavy bladed knife. "I'm sorry about this Morgan, but I owe the Deep Ones three more sacrifices."

"You killed Eve Donner," Morgan said.

"Yes, and the other two victims as well. Six is the number I must reach before I get my reward. The bracelet was mine too. Part of my 'down payment' from the Deep Ones. I foolishly dropped it when I was abducting the Donner woman, and R'yn K'rin was trying to retrieve it for me when you stumbled across it. They have an affinity for their gold. As I told you, under the water R'yn K'rin could find it, and even on land he had a sense of its general location."

Morgan tested the ropes around his wrist. They were tight and very strong. "Look, Derleth. Someone knew I was coming to see you. People will come looking."

"I'm sure they will, but I'll tell them the truth. I answered your questions

18

and you left. I've no idea what happened to you between my house and that lovely car of yours. I might buy one of those when the Deep Ones bring me my gold."

"You're doing this for money?" Morgan said.

"What else? I was thrown out of the university for my 'wild' theories. Theories you know now to be absolutely correct. No other college would hire me. My life and career were over. But I had learned from my studies how to summon the Deep Ones. I made a pact with them. They needed the sacrifices for one of their rituals."

"What kind of ritual?" Morgan said. He didn't have much hope of freeing himself, but he wanted to keep Derleth talking.

Derleth reached into his pocket and pulled out a pocket flashlight. "I'm not really sure, but it involves that."

He shined the light on an object that had been invisible in the darkness outside the range of the lamp. It was an obelisk of some sort, about nine feet tall and it looked to have been cut from a single stone. The harsh light made tiny symbols visible on the obelisk's surface. It was completely covered in carved runes of some kind.

Derleth said, "I brought the victims here for the Deep Ones' ceremonies. Unfortunately, the tides took the bodies back to Oahu rather than washing them out to sea."

Morgan heard loud sloshing sounds and he looked toward the shore. Three misshapen figures emerged from the dark water and stepped into the circle of baleful light.

Derleth said, "The Deep Ones have arrived. I'm sure R'yn K'rin will be pleased to see you. Your gun actually damaged him a bit. He'll probably want to wield the knife himself this time."

As the creatures came closer, Morgan saw one of them was carrying the limp figure of an unconscious woman. Apparently, he wasn't going to die alone.

"It looks like they've saved me finding one of my last two sacrifices," Derleth said.

The fish man placed the woman on the ground and joined his two brethren. All three of the weird figures stood staring at the obelisk. Then they turned back to Derleth.

Derleth said, "These two tonight and then we'll just need one more."

The Deep Ones said nothing, but they moved closer to Derleth. Morgan realized what was going to happen at the same time Derleth did. He could see it in the older man's eyes.

Derleth held his hands up. "Wait. No. You don't have to do this. I can find another sacrifice. God, no. Please don't kill me."

19

Two of the fish men grabbed Derleth and dragged him toward the obelisk. The third came over to the kerosene lamp and picked up the knife Derleth had brought. He pointed the knife at Morgan and gave a good impression of a smile. This had to be R'yn K'rin, the one Morgan had shot.

R'yn K'rin waddled over to the obelisk. Derleth was still begging, as his two captors pushed him up against the stone pillar and pinned his arms up over his head. They apparently weren't going to bother binding him. Morgan gritted his teeth as R'yn K'rin drove the sharp knife into Derleth's stomach and ripped the blade upward, disemboweling him. Derleth only screamed once. Then the two Deep Ones turned him, so his blood fountained all over the obelisk.

When they had finished with Derleth, they dragged his body aside and allowed it to fall to the rocky ground. Still holding the knife, R'yn K'rin walked back to where Morgan sat helpless. His stride seemed almost jaunty. Guess he was looking forward to some payback for the .45 slugs.

The Deep One reached down and grabbed Morgan by the biceps and jerked him to his feet. Morgan almost fell over since his ankles were still bound but he managed to stay partly upright as R'yn K'rin dragged him toward the obelisk.

They passed close to the lantern and Morgan reached down and caught it by the handle. He swung the lantern as hard as he could, hitting R'yn K'rin in the head with the glass part of the cylinder. The lantern broke open, covering the Deep One with kerosene which burst into flame as the rest of the lamp ruptured.

Morgan pulled away as R'yn K'rin screeched in agony. The Deep One dropped the knife as he used his webbed hands to try and stifle the flame, but he only succeeded in spreading it. Morgan snatched up the knife and the ropes around his ankles parted with one swipe. His legs were asleep from being bound but he forced himself to get up.

One of the other Deep Ones came running over, arms spread to grab Morgan. He pushed inside the thing's reach and drove the point of the knife through one of its eyes. The Deep One fell. The third one stood staring at Morgan for a moment, then turned and ran into the waves. Morgan could barely see it as the flames on the dead R'yn K'rin began to die.

Still Morgan had time to spot the small motorboat that had doubtless brought Derleth to this island. Morgan limped over to the woman prisoner. She wasn't moving, but he put a hand to her throat and her pulse was strong. She had probably been drugged.

A tinge of red was just beginning to show on the horizon. It would be dawn soon. Morgan wasn't sure in which direction Oahu lay but he didn't care. He would put the woman in the boat and get off this damnable chunk of rock. If the last of the Deep Ones returned with friends, he wanted to be well away. Maybe it was time to think of moving back to the mainland. To somewhere far from the ocean. He'd heard Arizona was nice. ♜

THE WAY OF THE RESTLESS

By Alethea Kontis

ELECTRONIC DOORBELLS JANGLING, ELVIS SASHAYED into the diner, took a stool at the antiseptic orange counter, and ordered a cherry pie.

"Ain't got cherry today hon." Cayenne absentmindedly wiped the cracked enamel with a damp rag; she didn't take her eyes off the iVizion soap for a second. Nikki and Victor were apparently on the outs. Again. Heated argument. Always the way of the restless: on again, off again for the last few centuries. Elvis knew a bit about that. Sure, Dot had always made a scene, shrieked mercilessly, and thrown whatever was at hand, but the day she'd left for good she'd just turned and walked away without a word. The way they were going at it, Nikki and Victor would be back together again before the end of the daymonth.

No one could have guessed that soap operas would be the biggest outlet for legalized cloning. Elvis wasn't sure if that was a good thing or a bad thing, not that he had any right to complain. He caught his reflection in the glass of the pie case and resisted the urge to snarl. Had some distant grandmother not been ready, willing, and fertile when they'd finally dug up The King all those years ago, he wouldn't even be here.

He spread his fingers on the slick counter before him, orange as ration crackers. Orange as surplus flight suits. Dot's flight suit. Nope. Not going there. "Sweet potato then," he said, when Nikki took a dramatic breath. Something slightly less orange.

Cayenne's eyes remained glued. "Case is stale, shug. Go pull a fresh one out of the back?"

"Anything for you darlin'," he drawled. Straight to business then. He was fine with that. Elvis dismounted and made his way through the swinging doors to the back office.

Jane was smoking. Jane was always smoking. Being a Phytollan refugee, Jane had managed to swindle a medicinal scrip for nicotine and a license to smoke in public. Elvis suspected it was more of an affectation than a need, but he had to admit that her skin did look healthier when the tint ran more green than blue. And of course, Jane could swindle anything, any day of the week. That's what she had him for.

Swindler, driver, persuader, seducer, anarchist, requisitionist, treasure hunter, bounty hunter, collector, seller. Elvis had acquired more than a few job titles during his time with Jane. Good thing he didn't bother with business cards. Nobody on Jane's payroll did. Not that he knew anyone else on her payroll or wanted to. He could, however, guess Miles Draven was behind that box of Cubans so proudly displayed on her desk. Draven was good. He was better.

Elvis extracted the small velvet pouch, soft like skin, from one of the many pockets in his black leather pants and tossed it onto the ledger Jane refused to look up from. She took a long drag on her cig and exhaled slowly out her three nostrils before setting her pen down. She sniffed the bag--how she could smell anything beyond that cloud of smoke was beyond him-- and then slid the contents into her palm. The mother of pearl on the cameo glittered beneath her unforgiving desk lamp. "Catherine Rainey," she said with a voice like gravel. "Nice to meet you."

"The Library of Robinson 7 is now vacant."

"Take the ghost out of the ghost town and what do you get?" Jane mused. "Some would call it genocide."

"I call it a job well done," said Elvis. "You wanted a planet, you got one."

Jane closed her fingers over the Librarian's shining face. "Did she give you any trouble?"

Sensor rats. Laser spray. Acid cannons. That unrelenting, cold winter gray. Elvis shrugged. "Nothing out of the ordinary." Nothing but that soft voice, repeating the same sad tale over and over again. He shoved that memory back, swept it under the fluorescent orange carpet in the bowels of his mind. "The hard data storage is still intact. Her access memory might be damaged, though; she was rambling when I got there. Spent enough time rerouting systems to realize it was on a cycle. I recorded the message to a beacon and left it there transmitting so no one'd be the wiser, but I suggest that your customer to plants their flag soon." A lost city. An entire

23

planet up for grabs. He wondered which refugee camp had been the highest bidder in that room. He had a sudden image of a city full of Janes, walking around carefree in their blue-green birthday suits, sucking down a bilious atmosphere of nicotine and schadenfreude. Jane, who had said something. "Sorry. What?"

"What. Was. The. Message," she said slowly.

"I wasn't paying that much attention," he lied. "Something about her daughter."

Jane said nothing, didn't even nod, but Elvis took the bounce of the cig between her thin lips as acknowledgement. Mission accomplished. On to the next thing. "I've got something, but you're not going to like it," she said, waiting on the platform when his ship of thought landed.

She was usually right. The announcement still piqued his interest, though. He'd hate whatever she was about to ask him to do, but it would no doubt leave him with at least a Buchanan Cycle's worth of bar tabs in decent stories. "I'll take it."

"Fine," said Jane to her ledgers. "Skeezix is your contact."

Aw, *Hezmat*, Elvis cursed in Venutian. Skeezix. No-good, thieving, tweaked-out son of a port skank. Backstabbing, bastard mutt of a blinking alien whose chameleon hide was more trouble than it was worth, and whose meter-long tongue was as silver as it was forked. Elvis hadn't seen Skeezix since...since that last run with *her*. He was surprised anyone had let him live this long.

Jane raised a thin eyebrow. "And he's currently in the diner eating your pie."

Nice to know some things hadn't changed. Elvis burst back through the swinging door in time to watch Skeezix lick the last of the whip cream off the plate with that acrobatic tongue.

"Thanks, E." Skeezix burped, his dull orange lips betraying the pumpkiny sweetness that had just passed through them. "Cayenne, my loveliest, you've outdone yourself. Haven't had something that good in a daymonth of forevers. Still can't top that messberry cobbler Dot used to make, though." He had obviously been hoping for a reaction from Elvis, and he got one. "Wow. I guess I can see now why that expression became famous. Dot's still a sore spot, huh? You know, you should really give her a call. You two were--"

"What's the job, Skeezix." The last person he'd confess his deep dark secrets to would be a snitch.

"No time to cut chase. I see how it is," said Skeezix. "Well, this is easy leezy. Art heist. In and out job."

"What do you need me for, then?"

"Not me," said Skeezix, "my employer. I'm just a messenger, same as you, only shorter and better looking. And full of pie." Elvis refused to react, so Skeezix went on. "Frame is in a safe in the cargo hold of your basic Grub-run interstellar transport. I imagine there will be quite a few other goodies in there too." He waggled his eyebrows, but Elvis didn't bite there either. He flipped open the electronic assistant on his wrist and punched a few buttons. "Well, don't get distracted. You're only there for the art. I'm downloading the location and lot number onto your EA. You're the systems guy. Should be the breeze for you."

Elvis confirmed the transfer and nodded. "Where do I make the drop?"

"Where else?"

Elvis looked at his EA again. "You're kidding me." He remembered that warehouse in the Colt Islands all too well. Skeezix's main hideyhole, back in the day. Back on the day that Dot had strung him up and left him there, the heartless wench.

Skeezix grinned a disturbing pointed-toothed smile the width of his face. "Good times."

"Let's just get on with it," said Elvis. "How far can you take me?"

Skeezix laid a clawed hand on his shoulder and Elvis felt the world bend around him as they blinked out of the diner. When they "landed," he swallowed multiple times in quick succession as his stomach did backflips. He hated when Skeezix blinked him without warning, but he instantly stopped lamenting his stolen pie. As much as he despised it, he stared at Skeezix, willing his bearings to right themselves. When they did, he realized that the snitch's orange blush had faded into the gunmetal gray of the cargo hold around them.

"Delivery in thirty seconds or less," said Skeezix. "Have fun!"

"Whoa," said Elvis as the world slowly stopped spinning. "You can't just leave me here." To which Skeezix responded by blinking out and proving him wrong. Elvis cursed in Wyvernese. Skeezix's face may change with the weather, but Elvis had no doubt his belly stayed yellow. He shook his head. Some people never changed. He wasn't sure if that was a good thing or a bad thing either.

The first thing he did was use his EA watch to hack into the comms system. It took him less than five minutes of listening to realize that the ship he was on was transporting more than just nonsentient cargo. However, it only took him a moment of shuddering vibrations to realize that the ship he was on was currently taking off. Elvis cursed again, this time in Candician. He was only fluent in three languages, but he could get by in a solid dozen and boasted invectives in at least twice that. It was always good to know what the customer was calling you behind your back.

One thing at a time. There was no stopping the ship now, and no point. First, he needed to find the painting and liberate it from the safe. He'd worry about how to get out of there when there was an out to actually get to. Elvis brought up the location numbers and cross-checked them on the ship's manifest, running the program in diagnostic mode to avoid detection. It took him longer to locate the shipping container than it did to disarm the securities and crack the safe. Like Skeezix had said in his own rare brand of tweaked-out vocabulary, it was easy leezy. Perhaps too easy leezy.

Elvis coded the locks back into place, resealed the container, and dragged the waist high polymer crate back to his listening post at the comms unit. He had passed the hibernation chambers on the way to find the artifact and, now that he had the luxury to be, he was curious as to their contents. Based on the mode of transport and the level of secrecy around them he had his own idea as to the origins, so he was not surprised when it was confirmed. Eddys. Anarchist groups who frequented the fringes of the galaxies, refusing to ally themselves with any defined place or government. The only commonality was that they were all misfits, on the basis of which some incredibly strong bonds between sects had been created. So strong, in fact, that certain planets felt threatened and paid a great sum to see the Eddy groups "taken care of." If he'd had the means, he'd get them out, hand them all weapons, and set them free on their captors.

Don't get distracted, Skeezix's voice echoed in his head. *You're only here for the art.* Elvis sneered. Oh, like hell. He was here for himself. He pulled up the codes for the hibernation chambers--a bit more strenuous task this time--and checked the numbers against his watch. Something was off. He altered his approach, reentered the sequence, and checked again. No... the numbers were right. The calculations were the same. But the results the ship's computer was spewing forth were not in Grub units of relative time.

Elvis had become a bit of an expert on time pieces after the accident, and the emergency installation of Dot's artificial gearheart. Her atomic ticker, that's what she'd called it. That had been the beginning of the end, and he knew it. He had never forgiven himself for putting her in harm's way. He couldn't let her keep taking the risks she kept taking without company or comment, and boy did she let him have it. Perhaps she had thought it flattering at first, but she never had been the fragile flower. Dot Stringer was a star on the brink of nova vaccu-sealed in a can of worms and whoop-ass with "Trouble" stamped on the label and woe to any man who opened it.

Gods, how he'd loved her.

He shook it off. The proper shift equations always had to be downloaded into the gearheart prior to any jump so that it could equalize immediately upon landing. A blink like the one Skeezix had pulled on him earlier had the potential to kill her. And so Elvis had become familiar with possibly even more alien units of time than he knew curses. He wasn't positive what these units were, but they were not Grub units. And if they were not Grub units, then they must belong to the only other race of beings on the ship...the beings in the hibernation chambers that currently appeared to be decompressing. It seemed that the Eddys had beaten him to the punch and already planned their own mutiny.

Aw, *Hezmat*.

The relief that he was no longer escorting scores of innocent anarchists to their death was suddenly buried under self-preservation. He laid the polymer crate flat on the floor and casually sat on top of it. He waited patiently while faction after faction of Eddys awoke, struggled in lungfuls of the hold's stale air, mustered, and armed themselves. And when the leader strode up to him, he raised his hands in surrender.

"Impressive," said Elvis. "That was the quickest hibernation recovery I believe I've ever witnessed."

"Training goes a long way," said the leader, "as does the right combination of stimulants." He lowered his wave weapon at Elvis's head. "Tell me why I shouldn't kill you."

"I'm just here for the art," Elvis said automatically, and then thought better of it. He snapped the fingers of one surrendering hand and pointed at the leader. "I can give you the coordinates of a newly-vacant planet in the Robinson System."

"How do I know you're not lying?"

Elvis shrugged. "You don't."

The leader motioned with his gun. "Punch in the coordinates. We'll see when we get there."

"When I turn out to be right, I'll need free passage back off the rock. I want a ship and--he knocked on the crate beneath him--this box. The planet's yours." As was whatever fallout came later when the high bidders showed up to claim it. Or when the Asteroid Spiders came out of hibernation. Surely nothing a seasoned Eddy general hadn't been through before.

The leader lowered his weapon. "If there's a ship to be had, friend, it's yours."

There were, in fact, ships to be had on Robinson 7. Elvis had already picked one out. A cherry red rocket, far classier than that ancient, energy-swilling Star-V. Dot refused to trade in. The keys were already in his pocket.

"Then I believe you have a ship to take over," said Elvis.

He stayed in the hold for that part. He didn't watch them execute the crew, but he did feel the vibration of the wave weapons, and he fell off the crate when they opened a starboard airlock and the ship shifted beneath

27

him. In the light of the now-empty hibernation chambers, he could make out something etched just over the seam. Words. He squinted. No...just one word. A word he was definitely familiar with, in one of the languages that he just so happened to speak fluently. He ran his thumb over the ragged edges.

ELVIS.

It took him far too long to find something with which to break the seal and pry open the crate. Once he had he found another crate inside, and then layers upon layers of protective wrapping. The actual frame was much smaller than the polymer crate had led him to believe. He held it out before him and looked into an older version of himself, in a white jumpsuit on black velvet. He stared at it for a long time, marking the differences in the face of the ancient singer, examining the freeform shapes behind him like clouds of space dust that resolved themselves into a guitar, a neutron clock, an old film reel, a pair of sunglasses. This was more than just coincidence. Had to be. But why?

Elvis closed his eyes and tried to let the pieces fall into place, but he was distracted into holding himself steady while the ship began its planetary descent. Dot had always hated descent. "What's the point of flying if you have to land?" she'd say. Her earrings would rattle together like the open doors of the hibernation chamber, only at a higher pitch. She would hold his hand in one of hers and place the other one over her heart. Sometimes she'd leave her flight suit unzipped low enough to distract them both during the unpleasant experience. She liked to be watched, and she liked to know that it was him doing the watching. It would be a lifetime before he'd be able to get those pink, rhinestone-studded fingernails out of his mind, clashing against that ridiculous orange flight suit, sliding across her smooth skin, over her atomic ticker, and down...

Elvis opened his eyes and examined the painting again. He ran a hand across the soft velvet, soft like her skin, and over the face of the neutron clock. Neutron clock. Atomic ticker. It wasn't much of a stretch. Elvis picked up the frame and carefully crawled into the hibernation chamber where the light was better. He swept his hand one way across the clock, and then back the other way. The first essentially obliterated the face of the clock. The second revealed enough detail to make out the roman numerals. Only because he was looking for it did he find the tiny, five-pointed shape beside the number five. Star-V.

Elvis cursed in Fannish, Perkinese, Balsin, and Catawani, just for good measure.

When the Eddy ship finally landed, Elvis shook the leader's hand in farewell beneath the ominous skies. "There's one more thing I need," he said. The nanomaintained landscaping in front of the library had contained rainbow peonies, black-eyed susans, and a few other flowers he didn't know the names of. Not that he needed to know. Dot liked flowers, and the less ceremoniously presented the better. Ripped from a bed in a former ghost town should suit her just fine. He also relished the idea of giving her a black eye with some other woman's name on it. Dot liked irony too.

"Anything for you, my friend," said the leader.

"Not for me," Elvis corrected. "For a girl. My girl."

The leader smiled, grabbed the soldier that was standing closest to him, and hauled her up to his side. "I understand," he said, and with that she kissed him with a vigor that gave Elvis the perfect opportunity to walk away. Those two would be fighting again by the end of the week; if not themselves, then someone else. Off gain, on again; that was the way of the restless.

Elvis decided it was a good thing. ♜

THE DEAD DIE HARD

By In Churl Yo

MOLLY GURANO WANTED NOTHING MORE than to slap the smug look off the face of the man standing across from her—a man who was technically still her husband, a New York City police detective, and father to her two children. Only that last designation, not even the cop one, had kept her from knocking Sean McCade's sorry ass all the way back to the East Coast. That, and he was looking a lot better than she remembered.

At least he came across the country to be with them at Christmas. At least he was here at her company party trying to make an effort. That was a big deal. Sean hated California. He hated her job. He probably even hated being in this shiny new skyscraper her company had spent hundreds of millions constructing for its U.S. headquarters.

Damn him.

She counted to three in her head before speaking again. "This is an Asian company. They figure a woman who's married has got one foot—"

"You *are* married, Molly," Sean replied. "Married to me."

"We're not having this conversation again. We did this in June."

"We never finished this conversation in June."

"I had an opportunity. One I had to take."

"Sure. No matter the consequences, no matter what it did to our marriage, you had to—"

"It didn't do anything to our marriage, except maybe change your idea of what our marriage should be," she countered, sensing how rapidly their conversation was escalating now.

"You don't have a *clue* what I think our marriage should be."

"I know *exactly*—"

Gun shots. Not from small arms but rapid, automatic rifle fire. Screams. Yelling. She knew what those sounds meant, and Sean knew it, too. He knew it better than anybody.

Molly watched him pull a sidearm from his shoulder holster hanging up in the nearby bathroom and glide toward the office door, cracking it open just enough to observe the chaos happening in the hallway outside. Men with machine guns were herding everyone they found out into the main reception area, and they were coming this way.

"The phones are dead," she whispered, returning the receiver to its cradle.

"We have to go," he whispered back. "The staircase—"

"Wait." If Molly had this right, there were only two possible reasons why someone would be bold enough to attack her company's HQ in the middle of Los Angeles, one of the most heavily policed cities in the country. Neither were great. One was worse. "Sean, you've got to trust me on this. We need to split up."

"What?! I'm not leaving you—"

"There's no time to argue, as much as I do love arguing with you. I need for you to head upstairs now, find a way to contact the authorities, and generally be a huge pain in the ass to the bad guys with guns. I know you're an expert at that last one. Besides, we'll need the distraction."

"Thanks. What are you going to be doing?"

"There's something downstairs. Something those men can never have. I've got to make sure that doesn't happen."

"Molly—"

"No. No more fighting, Sean. We've got to go. *Now.*"

Sean knew better than to try and drag this out. He'd never win now that his wife had made up her mind. Besides, she was right. They were out of time. The men had just entered the neighboring office to remove a couple of sales executives who were caught in the middle of a poorly timed, drunken, party hook up. They would have been taken next, except...

Molly allowed the metal stairwell door to close softly behind them, and she put her ear against it, wondering whether anyone had seen them slip away. Ten seconds ticked by, a lifetime, before she allowed herself to breathe again.

Sean nodded at her and turned to head upstairs when Molly pulled him back toward her at the last moment, kissing him harder than she had planned to. A flood of emotions came at her then, emotions that she had spent the better part of a year trying to keep at bay, and it almost carried her away. Sean was definitely better than she had remembered, but now was not the time. Sadly, it hadn't been for a long while.

"Be careful out there, partner," he whispered.

"You, too, cowboy."

Molly kicked off her high heels and forced herself to go down the stairs without looking back. She couldn't afford to think about Sean now. She couldn't afford to think about their kids, or her co-workers, or anyone else, even if she was doing this for all of them. She had to focus on the task at hand, which was what, exactly?

As Director of Corporate Affairs, Molly had her hand in pretty much everything the Nakamura Corporation produced, from large-scale construction projects to high-grade petroleum refining, from bioengineering to aerospace—a well-rounded, highly diversified portfolio of ventures that she found both satisfying and endlessly interesting. It kept her sharp and her mind engaged. Since she moved out here to California, Molly had been forced to become an expert on a wide array of subjects in a very short period. That was one way of looking at it.

Another was to say that the sum of her knowledge was wide but shallow, but then, it had to be. Nakamura had its hand in so many different pies baking around the globe, it would be hard for any one person to possibly fathom everything there was to know about them all. So, Molly knew of the project down on the 20th floor and what was inside the vault on the 30th of Nakamura Plaza. She just didn't know everything, but there were rumors, whispers shared between colleagues in elevators or break rooms when they thought no one else was listening. Most of the time Molly had simply ignored them. Now she couldn't stop thinking about them.

The balls of Molly's stockinged feet slapped hard against the concrete treads as she flew further down the stairwell, almost too quickly to maneuver around the landing, barely avoiding a painful collision with a wall of cinder blocks that would have laid her out good. She cursed. If she was going to do this, if she was going to beat the bad guys, Molly needed to not only be fast but also smart. Fast might get you the lead but smart would deliver you across the finish line, and in this race, she had no interest in coming in second. The stakes were simply way too high for her not to win.

The descent felt like it took forever, but only minutes had passed since she and Sean had separated from each other. Molly had reached the 20th floor winded, her heart throbbing in her ears, and she leaned against the door until the adrenaline passed enough that she felt in control of her breath again. So much for those weekly aerobics classes, huh? She pivoted around and saw the keypad in front of her at eye level.

Only two floors in the entire building had restricted access like this. Molly had never been to either of them, not that she wasn't allowed. She just never had a legitimate reason to, and pop in visits were highly frowned upon. Those floors weren't exactly a part of the company tour for new employees either. In fact, only a select few in the entire building had access to them, which of course was by design.

The lock required a six-digit code, and she entered a combination of her daughter's and son's birthdays into the keypad. A soft buzz and click indicated that the bolt had successfully released its hold, and Molly opened the door and walked inside where…

Something was wrong.

Emergency lighting bathed the darkened hallway in a pale red hue. She walked slowly until her eyes adjusted, then moved toward the reception area where the elevators and main entry door sat, usually guarded by a team of armed personnel. Instead, the room was empty, and their absence, coupled by the resulting silence, spooked her to no end. Had she been too late?

"Hello? Anyone?"

Molly didn't expect to hear an answer. She just wanted to fill the overarching quiet for a moment, a small reprieve to keep her imagination from conjuring up something even more disturbing within the shadows, before she approached another keypad nearby and entered her code again. This time a series of loud clanks followed, and the large, heavy metal door behind the guard stand swung open. The heart of the 20th floor waited just beyond.

Only this heart was empty. Another room. Another set of security doors. There was nothing between these four walls except for Molly, and when the door behind her clanked shut, she found herself sealed inside with no keypad or door handle visible anywhere, trapped like a rat in a security trap. But was it?

Molly ran her fingers around the smooth edges of the second door, searching for a hidden panel or mechanism that might open it. She took her time, knowing there had to be some way past this room. She just had to find it.

"You're wasting your time, Ms. Gurano," a nasally voice cautioned her.

She reckoned a hidden speaker somewhere. Maybe a hidden camera, too. Molly scanned the corners of the room but found nothing. "Thanks for the advice," she replied. "Do I know you?"

"Yes. Well… not really, but I know you. You're Molly Gurano, Director of Corporate Affairs. I saw your face on the orientation video."

"That's right. You work at Nakamura."

"Yes. You're very pretty, but uh, you probably knew that already."

33

Molly took a beat to absorb the statement. She couldn't afford to alienate her new friend, not if she wanted to get inside. Not if she wanted to end this. But maybe she could use it to her advantage. "Can you tell me your name?"

"Cedric... *Doctor.* That is, Doctor Cedric Ellis. I'm in charge, Ms. Gurano. Of the lab."

"It's Molly. Can I call you Cedric?"

Silence. She could practically hear the wheels turning in his head from here. "Why are you here, Molly? This is a restricted area."

"I have access. I'm on the list."

"What happened to the guards then? Why are we on internal power?"

"I promise to answer all your questions, Dr. Ellis, but you must let me in *now.* Please."

There was no Plan B, not that Molly had a plan coming into this. All she knew was that eventually men with guns would show up, assuming the lab was their actual objective. She also assumed that if they were going to all this trouble, then unlike her, they probably had a way to get inside it. One way or another, she wasn't going to be alone in here for much longer. The question was whether it was at gunpoint or not. She preferred not.

"Okay."

Molly looked up at the invisible speaker in the ceiling. "Okay?" she repeated, unsure.

The second security door hissed then slid open, a pitch black revealed on the other side. She poked her head in but couldn't discern anything within it at all.

"An elevator is headed down to this floor," Dr. Ellis announced.

"Really? How do you know that?"

"I know things. I'm very smart. You should probably hurry."

Molly took a deep breath. *In for a penny.*

As soon as she went inside, the door behind her closed, sealing Molly in darkness. She couldn't see her hand in front of her face yet could sense objects all around the room. She could feel them and resisted the urge to reach out for one. A pop followed by some static sizzled overhead as fluorescent lights flickered on, bathing the room in a blue, sterile hue.

Once her eyes adjusted, Molly could see that she was surrounded by rows of hazmat suits, the bright yellow and orange kind, hung up at stations partitioned against the walls.

"You'll need to put one on," said Dr. Ellis.

"Seriously?"

"I'm afraid so. Once we switched over to internal power, the entire lab went into lockdown. Standard procedure requires anyone who enters the

34

facility now to wear an isolation suit. You're a size four, right? Dr. Kim's a four too, I think. Her suit is in the left corner."

Molly bit her lip again and walked over to the locker. She could almost feel the intruders coming up on her heels as she hurried to get inside the bulky suit.

"Normally, you'd have to change into a onesie, tape some rubber gloves on your hands, and test the suit for leaks first but—"

"I'm not doing that."

"I know. Besides, there isn't time."

She didn't know exactly what he meant by that but had a pretty good guess. The men with guns were here. Now.

"Molly, put the headset on before you zip up so we can continue communicating."

The suit fit well enough, but it was a little stuffy. Molly hoped she wouldn't have to be inside it long. "I'm ready," she said into the microphone.

"Not yet. Not unless you want to asphyxiate. See the red coiled tubes extending from the ceiling near the back door? The nozzle at the end of one of them should clip onto the attachment at your waist," Dr. Ellis explained, "delivering oxygen into your suit and creating positive pressure against the air outside of it. Go ahead. I'll wait."

As soon as the hose connected, Molly's suit inflated, and she could breathe much easier. She lifted her arm and presented a thumbs up, assuming Dr. Ellis was still watching her.

The back door clanked open, proving he was, and she walked through, the coiled hose trailing behind her attached to a track in the ceiling. Immediately she faced yet another door, but Molly wasn't surprised. The room was the size of a closet and likely served as an airlock, which made sense to her. Knowing that something so potentially dangerous was housed inside the lab, she understood Nakamura had to make sure if something unforeseen were to happen that it could never accidentally find its way out into the world. But what if someone tried to bring it out?

"Molly. Welcome to the lab." A man in an identical suit stood up from behind a computer station and waved at her.

"Dr. Ellis," she said while walking toward him. "You're... *alone?*"

"Well, it's Christmas. And I uh, I hate my family."

She nodded. "I assume you know there are people outside who are trying very hard to get into this lab as we speak."

"Yes."

"Why?"

"I thought you were going to tell *me*."

"What I know is that several heavily armed men crashed the Nakamura

Christmas party this evening and have probably taken everyone in the entire building hostage, including CEO Takashi," Molly replied. "They either did that for the bearer bonds the company keeps inside the vault for collateral or for whatever secrets we've got squirreled away in this lab. I chose the lab. Now I need you to tell me why that was a good choice."

"I can't. Please don't ask me that."

"Cedric, you can either answer me now or answer the guys with guns later. I don't think they'll ask as nicely. Your choice."

Dr. Ellis plopped back into his chair and leaned back. She could hear him taking a deep breath. "I see your point," he replied, "but I could lose my job, my *career*."

"Would it make you feel any better if I told you that I know we received a hazardous biological shipment here six weeks ago?"

"Marginally. What else do you know?"

Molly tried to recall the rest of the memo the COO had sent her. She had only been able to scan through it a couple of times before she had to move on to other business. By the time she was ready to get back to it, the document had already been shredded. "It came from Brazil. Something contagious."

"You know more than I would have guessed, Molly."

"Only because I had to prepare Nakamura's media response based on several potential worst-case scenarios. Top-level stuff. Nothing too deep. Nothing specific. More of a case study, really. I didn't think much of it until today."

"Well, that's fine. I won't get into any specifics with you then either."

"Please, don't. Most of it would probably go over my head anyway. I just need to know two things, Dr. Ellis. First, could bad people do bad things with it?"

He sat upright in his chair now. "Yes. Definitely. What's the second?"

"Can you destroy it?"

Dr. Ellis snorted. "You're talking about months of research. We've only just begun to scratch the surface... I mean, we don't even fully understand the damn thing yet."

"All the more reason to get rid of it."

"You don't know what you're asking. With enough careful manipulation, this virus could potentially unlock any number of groundbreaking cures. Lupus. Necrosis. Even Cancer. It's not hyperbole to say it might even one day dramatically extend the human lifespan well beyond its current limits. We're not talking about something that's worth billions of dollars or even trillions. This could be priceless. We just need to figure out how it works."

"And what if the virus was released in its current form in a highly populated area?" Molly asked. "What if it were used as a weapon? What

36

then? What price would we have to pay then?"

"Well. You said it yourself, Molly," said Dr. Ellis. "That's all conjecture. These people may only be common thieves after bearer bonds. They probably have no idea the virus even—"

A boom, so loud it stunned them. Then the room shook. Violently. Both Molly and Dr. Ellis lost their balance in the aftershock, falling hard onto the floor, the lights flickering briefly before calm returned and the Nakamura Plaza ceased its gentle swaying.

Dr. Ellis scrambled back to his workstation. "They've broken through the exterior door."

"So much for conjecture," Molly whispered.

"They obviously have no clue how virulent the pathogen is or else they wouldn't try blowing the damn place up, which means that we're either dealing with psychopaths or idiots, neither of which is good. Come on. We've got some work to do."

She followed him down an adjacent hallway to a locked door, where Dr. Ellis entered his own code into a keypad that gave them access to a room that looked like an actual laboratory filled with microscopes and beakers.

"The wall. Over there," said Dr. Ellis while pointing. "You see those round cubbies? Press the green button in the center of one then, using the handle, pull out the glass cylinder inside. It'll be like those uh, pneumatic tube containers you use at bank drive thru lanes. Once you've got it free, bring it over to me. Carefully."

Molly did as she was told and when she handed it to him asked, "What is this thing anyway?"

"The virus," he replied nonchalantly, before sliding the container into an industrial-looking contraption clad in thick metal. Dr. Ellis closed the lid and started the machine up. "We're going to torch all the samples using this medical incinerator. Go grab another one."

After a brief bout of shock, disbelief, and anger from Molly, they managed to work quickly through more than a dozen containers. "This is the last one, Dr. Ellis. Are you sure they're all destroyed?"

"The incinerator burns at around 1,000 degrees Celsius, so uh, pretty sure."

"That's it then. We did it," she announced once the burning cycle completed, a look of relief settling on her face.

Dr. Ellis shook his head. "Not exactly. There's still one sample left."

The look quickly dissipated. "Well, where is it? There can't be a trace of it anywhere."

A loud buzz, like a saw or a drill, caught their attention. They looked toward the airlock where the noise was coming from, and Molly imagined the room with no door handle full of men with guns—and tools—working furiously.

"You seem like a nice person, Molly. Do you have kids?"

"I don't think—what does that have to do with anything?"

"Nothing. Everything. Eh, forget it. Follow me." Dr. Ellis led her toward another door in the back of the room, entered another code, then swung it open while motioning her inside. As soon as she stepped across the threshold, he slammed the door shut behind her. Molly looked around the small closet and immediately understood what had happened.

"Dr. Ellis? Cedric?" she yelled while banging her fist against the door. "What exactly do you think you're doing?"

"I had to. I'm sorry. It's for your own good."

"Open the door."

"Listen to me, Molly. I've set the lock on a timer. The bolt will release in twenty minutes. By then those men should be inside the lab. I'll do my best to distract them while you get away. You should be able to slip out behind them."

"But I can help you."

"It's too dangerous. The last sample, it's uh, it's in a host. A rhesus. We have her locked up in the main lab under observation."

"Please tell me you're kidding," she said.

"She's been... aggressive lately. Unpredictable. I don't want you getting hurt. Or worse. Tell me, Molly. Do you think we could have been friends? Close friends? I do."

"Sure, Cedric. Sure. But if you were really my friend, you'd let me out of here."

No response.

"Cedric? Dr. Ellis?"

Nakamura Corporation's main laboratory was the largest, most secure room on the entire 20th floor. A state of the art, closed system ventilation and quarantine suite integrated into the building's substructure that rivaled any the Centers for Disease Control had at their facility, insuring everything within it remained isolated and safe from the outside world. It's where the team tested most of its theories. It's where they purposefully exposed lab animals to the virus to study its effects on them. Most of those studies ended in death. All were disturbing.

Dr. Ellis adhered as best he could to protocol when he entered the main lab, but time was precious now, and he couldn't afford to waste any of it, so he bypassed anything he felt was redundant and forced the dedicated airlock door open.

He immediately ran to the supply closet to retrieve what he needed, a tranquilizing pistol and six darts filled with a potent cocktail of ketamine and diazepam.

"Hello, Margaux."

Margaux didn't answer, except in the way she had been lately by screeching, violently pounding against the cage and reaching at him through the bars, as if attacking him, destroying him, was her only purpose in life. It wasn't normal. Neither was her appearance. The tiny primate had shed most of its fur, and the exposed flesh had deteriorated, a thin membrane of gray, rotted-looking skin pulled taut over her bony frame.

"You should be thanking me for this," said Dr. Ellis, as he loaded the pistol and aimed it Margaux. The first dart, which under normal circumstances should have put the animal down, only enraged her. The monkey discarded the projectile and violently thrashed its body over and over against the cage wall without regard to pain or injury. The second dart had pretty much the same effect.

As Dr. Ellis loaded the third dart, he couldn't help but be fascinated by Margaux's physical transformation and the power the virus had imbued upon her. If only that power could have been harnessed, but they had missed their opportunity. There would be no miracle cures, no Nobel Prizes, no talk shows. Four more darts should put a definitive end to those dreams. He sighed. *If only.* But Molly was right. The virus was dangerous. He raised the gun toward Margaux to finish it.

"Stop. Put it down."

A wiry European-looking fellow with long, blonde hair dressed in black slid into the lab then, holding an automatic rifle with its barrel aimed squarely at Dr. Ellis. "Put the gun down," the man repeated in what sounded like a German accent.

"Absolutely," Dr. Ellis replied, tossing the tranquilizer pistol to the floor before raising his hands above his head. "I'm no hero."

"I cannot hear you. Take the suit off. *Now.*"

Dr. Ellis reluctantly unzipped his hazmat suit, stepped out of it, and reassumed his previous position with both hands raised high while attempting not to feel ridiculous standing there wearing nothing but an adult-sized onesie.

"Why are you trying to kill that monkey?"

"It's... complicated," Dr. Ellis replied.

The German decided then that he didn't really care anymore. "Where is the virus?"

"Destroyed. We burned it—all of it—right before you arrived."

"That would be very bad for you if true."

"It's true. Nothing that awful should be loose in the world. Do you even know what this virus is? What it does to the human body?"

"No. I don't care what it does. I only care how much they will pay me for it. Now tell me, where is the virus?"

Dr. Ellis tried not to look at Margaux but glanced at her anyway. The tranquilizer was having a mild effect on the rhesus, keeping her deceptively still. The subtle glance didn't go unnoticed.

"I see not all of the virus has been destroyed after all," the German said. "Open the cage."

"Why not just shoot me instead?"

"Open it. Now."

There was no way around the impending animal attack. Dr. Ellis knew Margaux would pounce as soon as the latch was released, so he tried to position himself to the side of the cage hoping the German would prove to be the better target, which was exactly what happened.

A loud screech. A blur. Gun shots. Dr. Ellis sprinted for the door as fast as he could. He toggled the switch for the headset that still dangled around his neck and yelled, "Molly, listen! If you can hear me, *run!*"

Inside the locked storage closet Molly pressed the tiny headset speaker against her ear. "Dr. Ellis? What's happening?" she asked, only there was no response. "Cedric, please answer!"

The remaining minutes felt like forever to her. She sat in silence willing the bolt to release. When it finally did, Molly almost couldn't bring herself to open the door. Outside, the lab room was quiet. She stood next to the incinerator and listened—for anything. A sound. A footstep.

Nothing.

Should she go looking for Dr. Ellis? Maybe she could still help him.

Molly stepped out into the hallway. At one end sat the main airlock where she first entered the lab. At the other, far in the distance, she saw a shadow and then... *movement.* Something was walking toward her with an uneven, unnatural gait. It made her uncomfortable just looking at it. It seemed human but also distinctly not. She remembered Dr. Ellis' last words to her and willed herself to turn her back to it. She forced her legs to move. She ran.

The suit made her move like a Weeble, her body wobbling back and forth as she slowly progressed toward airlock door, and all the while she could feel the predator advancing behind her, stalking her, but Molly dared not look back. She focused all her attention ahead toward her goal.

Her gloved fingers grasped the handle, and she pulled it hard, desperately hoping the latch would open. The door swung free, and Molly didn't hesitate to dart inside, the sound of shuffling footsteps behind in the hallway coming nearer. Her peripheral vision was crap inside the suit though, and she ran square into someone inside the airlock, tumbling them both to the ground.

A man in a dark, expensive suit sporting a neatly trimmed beard and mustache gawked at her with disdain. "Who are *you*?" he asked.

Molly looked back at him and screamed, "The door! Close the door!"

He saw the strange figure down the hallway approaching fast behind her and called out, "Klaus?"

The being once known as Klaus hesitated, a glimmer flashing across its eyes for the briefest moment before disappearing, a raspy skreich wailing from it that echoed through the lab.

Molly kicked the door closed and unzipped her suit. "Does that door lock?" she sputtered.

"No, we disabled it. What happened to Klaus?"

"We've got to go. In case you didn't notice, that isn't Klaus anymore."

The man in the suit did some quick calculations in his head. "Friedrich!" he yelled. Two men with machine guns appeared from the reception area through the gaping hole they'd created with explosive charges to get in, running to join them in the changing room. *"Bewache die Tür, nichts kommt durch!"*

They took defensive positions on either side of the airlock door, guns at the ready. Molly had just finished taking off her pressure suit when the man in charge grabbed her by the arm and hissed, "You, madam, are coming with me. I need information."

He led her to the elevators, waited for a car to arrive, and once inside pushed the button for the 30th floor. "First, you will tell me who you are and why you are here," he demanded before the doors had a chance to close.

Molly wrestled out of his grasp. "I'll tell you my name if you tell me yours," she replied, trying to gauge the man's temperament. He smiled back at her while pulling out a small pistol.

"My name is Heinz Kruger. I am the one who is in charge here. If you'd like to make it out of this alive, I suggest that you cooperate."

Static crackled from Molly's headset, and she heard a tinny voice from the small speaker cry, "Molly?"

"Dr. Ellis? Are you okay? Can you hear me?!"

No answer. Molly tried to reach him again without success. "We've got to go back. We have to get him out of there," she exclaimed.

"Not until you tell me everything you know," said Heinz as the elevator chimed and the doors opened to the 30th floor. "*Molly.*"

The reception area that greeted them was Nakamura Plaza's largest gathering area, complete with extensive water features and enough greenery to put any theme park to shame. Molly remembered being so impressed by the spectacle on the day of her in person interview that she would have almost taken any job they offered her. In hindsight, that might not have been such a good idea.

Today the room was decorated with lights and garland, a giant flocked and dressed Douglas fir sitting at a place of honor illuminated by red and green spotlights. A table lined with chafing dishes, salads and desserts sat along the back wall. Sitting between them at gunpoint were Molly's fellow Nakamura employees strewn about the room. Some of them gasped when they saw her enter.

"In there," Heinz ordered, pointing the way with a flick of his gun. Molly marched to a corner office belonging to one of the company's vice presidents and sat across from the desk from him in a guest chair. "Now, start by telling me who you are."

"Molly Gurano, Director of Corporate Affairs," she answered.

"What were you doing in the lab, Ms. Gurano?"

"I was delivering some papers to Dr. Ellis when the power went out and got locked inside."

"I see. Tell me, what do you know about what happens inside the lab?"

"There's not much to tell. I'm more of a public relations gal. They don't include me in anything that goes on in there. That way if someone in the media tries to ask me questions, I don't have to lie to them. You're better off asking the CEO."

"Alas, your Mr. Takashi wasn't very cooperative, so he won't be joining us for the rest of his life." Molly tried to suppress the shock that rose within her, a feeling that only worsened as Heinz leveled the barrel of his gun at her. "Clearly, you are lying, so I will make you the same offer I made to him, Ms. Gurano. I am going to count to three. There will not be a four. Tell me what you were doing in the lab, or you will be joining your CEO very soon. One. Two—"

"We destroyed the virus."

"Klaus would beg to differ."

"There was a monkey. A host. Dr. Ellis stuck me inside a storage closet and went to kill it by himself. That's all I know. I promise."

Molly watched Heinz process this and appreciated the fact that he appeared to be a thinker first and foremost, otherwise she would've likely already been dead by now—though that could of course still change at any moment. He looked at her and was about to speak when they heard a woman scream in the reception area.

They ran out of the office toward the elevators, Heinz pulling Molly there forcefully by her arm. In the open elevator car, they discovered a man in a chair sporting a Santa hat with a message scribbled on his shirt, his eyes leveled in a blank and lifeless stare.

Heinz straightened the shirt and read, "Now I have a machine gun. Ho-ho-ho."

"A security guard we missed?" one of Heinz's men asked.

"They're usually tired old men growing fat on a pension. No, this is something different."

As they began to debate in German, Molly felt a wave of relief move across her. Sean was alive—this was clearly his handiwork—and he was still out there doing his job. Alone.

"His bag is also missing," the man continued now in English.

"But he had the detonators," Heinz stated.

Molly sensed the mood change quickly from annoyed to worried to angry, but then Sean had that effect on people. Maybe there was some hope left to be had after all.

Then a wave of automatic gunfire erupted across the room.

"Now what?" Heinz spat.

Molly spun around and watched in horror as her co-workers were being attacked—not by men with guns, who were trying to protect them, but by something darker and more feral. These creatures, who had traveled up from the lab through the rear stairwell, were biting the others, consuming some of them, and growing in number. The infection was spreading practically in real time as people were changing right before their eyes. Nothing Heinz's men did slowed any of them down, and even they, despite all their firepower and training, eventually succumbed as well.

"Klaus has been busy," Heinz said. "Friedrich, too." He watched his former comrades in arms devour the remains of a bearded executive wearing an expensive suit and a Rolex watch.

"We've got to get out of here," Molly begged. There were dozens of infected around them now, and one of them was looking right at her. "We've got to go, go, go."

"For once we agree. This way, Ms. Gurano."

They retreated to the elevators. Thank God the car with the man Sean had killed was still waiting. Inside, Heinz pushed the 35th floor button. Molly could hardly believe her eyes.

"What are you doing? We need to leave the building," she said.

"No one is going anywhere until I have secured a sample of the virus."

"Are you insane?! Can't you see what's going on here?"

"Yes, it's quite breathtaking, isn't it?"

Molly looked out at the reception area, into the soulless faces of so many people she once considered friends but were now something different, something other, as the elevator doors closed on their slow advance not a moment too soon, and the car began its ascent.

The 35th floor was still under construction. They stepped off the car and were surrounded everywhere by unfinished metal framing, exposed wiring, and stacks of drywall waiting to be hung. Heinz walked a quick circle and, once he was confident that they were safe, turned to Molly and asked, "Tell me, how did you and Dr. Ellis destroy the virus?"

"We burned it," she replied. "Why?"

He nodded and held up a finger at her as if telling her to be quiet, then lifted a two-way radio to his mouth and said, "Is our mysterious party crasher listening?"

"I was about to call you, Heinz," Sean responded. "I figured that since I waxed Paulie and Gunter and his friend here that you and Klaus and Friedrich might be a little lonely, so I wanted to give you a call."

"That's very kind of you. You are most troublesome… for a security guard."

"*Bzzzt.* Sorry, Heinz. Wrong guess. Would you like to go for Double Jeopardy, where the scores can really change?"

Undeterred, Heinz moved on.

"You have me at a loss. You know my name, but who are you? Just another American who saw too many movies as a child? Another orphan of a bankrupt culture who thinks he's John Wayne? Rambo? Marshal Dillon?"

"I was always kind of partial to Roy Rogers actually," said Sean. "I really liked those sequined shirts."

"Be that as it may, Mr. Cowboy, are you aware of what happened on the 20th floor this evening?"

The radio went silent, but Molly knew Sean was probably out of his mind right now, wanting to ask a million questions about her. She knew he was in danger of becoming overwrought by worry. But she also knew how strong he could be.

"Allow me to enlighten you," Heinz continued. "The lab on the 20th floor housed a lethal virus that has infected everyone in the building. Only we lucky few have been spared, so that we may act against it."

"Boy, you must be awfully desperate to spin a yarn that ridiculous, Heinz. I've heard better stories from low rent hustlers trying to shake down their own grandma."

"I assure you that what I'm telling you is true. Everyone who works for Nakamura is either infected or dead. Those who carry the virus transform into mindless creatures who attack anyone they come across." Heinz handed the radio to Molly and whispered, "Tell him."

"This is Molly Gurano, Director of Corporate Affairs at Nakamura. Everything this man has said is, unbelievably, true."

Sean didn't miss a beat with his response: "Except for the part where he said that everyone in the company was infected or dead, right?"

"I'm okay," she assured him. "We all are. For now."

"Great, let's get the hell out of Dodge then while the getting's good. There's a getaway limo in the garage with a driver and a stocked bar. I'll let you even be prom king, Heinz."

Heinz took the radio back. "Unfortunately, Mr. Cowboy, there are plans in place that still need attending here. Plans that cannot be altered, that sadly you must now become a part of."

"Why me, pal? You throwing me a surprise party?"

"You have my detonators. I want them back."

"How about an old-fashioned prisoner exchange then? The detonators for Ms. Gurano. That sound good to you?"

"Fine. No tricks. Meet us on the 35th floor. We'll be waiting."

Heinz eyed Molly suspiciously for a moment before he turned and stepped toward the large floor-to-ceiling windows that lined the outside walls. There he became lost in his thoughts and the view of the silent, dark cityscape that surrounded them. Things had not gone exactly to plan, but the virus had always been the one variable he'd never been able to fully control. It forced him to adapt, and yet despite all his best efforts the odds of successfully completing this operation were dwindling rapidly, especially now that he must rely on other people to see things through to their eventual end.

Molly began pacing the room. Her internal clock was telling her that Sean should have been here by now, or maybe it was her heart that was speaking. The only thing she knew for certain was that the longer they stayed inside Nakamura Plaza, the worse their chances of survival became.

Where are you, Sean?

A loud clank, the sound of a metal door being swung open, answered her. Molly watched her husband sprint out of a nearby stairwell still wearing nothing but the undershirt and slacks he had on when they'd separated earlier, only now they were soiled completely in grit and blood. A look of concern was smeared across his face.

Sean turned around and peppered the still open door with bullets from the automatic rifle slung over his shoulder. "Honey, I'm home!" he yelled. "Hope you don't mind but I brought some company over for dinner!"

Klaus appeared, leaned his grotesque body against the door frame, and let out a piercing shriek. The other infected creatures stumbled into the room beside him, following their instinctual, unsatiable urge to feed.

"This way!" Heinz screamed and led them to a second set of stairs in the far back corner of the room. When they entered the stairwell, Sean rammed the barrel of his spent rifle across the door handle and twisted the butt across the door frame, making it impossible to open.

"That ought to slow them down," said Sean.

Heinz held out his hand. "Give me the detonators. Quickly."

Molly watched both men work as they connected the small detonator tubes to wiring that had already been set inside the false ceiling. A complex series of explosives ringed the perimeter of the building and were now primed and set to go off. Heinz dropped the wireless detonator into his jacket pocket.

"We must go to the roof," Heinz said.

"Wait a minute. We're not going anywhere until you tell us what you have planned," Molly protested. "You have your detonators. You said we could go."

"Go where, madam? Have you somehow overlooked the horde of infected monstrosities tightening their macabre noose upon us? This all must end. Now."

Sean put his hand on Molly's shoulder and offered her a reassuring look. "It's alright, honey. I think I know what Heinz has cooking. Besides, I bet you can see all the way to the ocean from up there."

As soon as they stepped out into the open air, Molly shivered. Anyone who said California was all sunshine and beaches never experienced a cold snap here in December. The temperature sat in the lower forties, which was on the low side for this time of year. A light breeze made it feel even colder. As she exhaled to steel herself for what was to come, Molly watched her breath dissipate into the cool night air.

"Over there," Heinz said and pointed to the large, flat open area that sat at the center of the roof. "We will wait on the helipad."

Sean gave Molly a silent signal and pointed to the handgun he had tucked inside his pants at the small of his back. She nodded, then asked aloud, "Wait for what?"

"The infected. Somehow, they have tracked us this far. I don't believe they will stop until they finally have us," Heinz replied. "We must do what you and Dr. Ellis did. We must burn them all using the explosives we've placed, leave no trace of the virus behind, and make our escape."

Molly wasn't convinced. "You said before that you needed a sample. Why, so you can sell it? I'm sure there's someone out there who's willing to pay big bucks to get their hands on that virus. How exactly are you planning on getting that sample once everything's incinerated? This isn't about saving the world. It's about saving your payday. Turns out that after all your posturing, all your little speeches, you're nothing but a common thief."

"I am an *exceptional* thief," he replied, "and since I'm moving up to armed assault, you should be more polite." Heinz aimed his handgun at Sean and pulled the trigger. The force of the bullet spun him around as Molly screamed, her husband's body landing face down on the cold, hard ground.

"You see, Ms. Genaro, it does me no good if the virus spreads beyond this building. My buyers would not be willing to pay so high a price for something that would no longer be... exclusive to them," explained Heinz. "So, it must all be destroyed, and the only way to achieve that is to lead the creatures here, which you two will accomplish for me as bait. Meanwhile, I will circle back and capture one for myself."

Then almost as if on cue, Klaus appeared on the rooftop, his followers close behind.

"If it's any consolation," said Heinz, "this will all be over quickly." He offered Molly a quick bow before slinking away down an adjacent stairwell.

Molly pulled Sean's body into her lap, tears streaming from her eyes. She no longer cared about monsters, or viruses, or thieves. Now there was only a tumult of regret left for her, far too much of it and far too late for her to do anything about it.

"Does this mean you still love me?" Sean whispered.

Molly wiped her eyes and laughed. "I never, ever stopped loving you."

"I don't want to spoil the moment here, babe, but we should probably skedaddle. Things are about to get hot up here."

"Can you stand?"

"Help me."

Molly placed her hands under each of his arms and pulled Sean until he was upright again, although he was clearly still in a large amount of pain. The bullet had entered at his right shoulder, just avoiding the brachial artery and any major organs, and went clean through. She put his arm over her neck and carried him away from the infected that were creeping slowly toward them.

Molly tried the door that Heinz had used to get away but found it locked.

"Getting a little crowded out here," Sean quipped.

A quick look by Molly confirmed they were gradually being surrounded. It was the closest she had ever been to them, and she felt a visceral reaction that filled her to the core with dread, as if these creatures were insatiable, inevitable even, and wouldn't stop until they had them.

Many of them had gaping gunshots wounds. Some were missing entire limbs. Their skin appeared sallow and gray, and yet they continued to march toward them, unencumbered by their physical, mortal limitations. Their eyes carried no hint of life at all, only the impervious glare of a predator locked on to its helpless prey, and they did not speak. The creatures moaned instead, the sound of it both forbidding and sad.

"Sean, I've got a crazy idea."

47

"Welcome to the club!"

She carried him over to the railing and left him there, then ran over to a nearby firehose coiled up on a metal wheel and unspooled it over toward him. Molly wrapped the hose around them both and tied the end in a knot. They climbed over the railing and stood at the edge of the roof looking down at 36 floors of open air between them and the ground below.

"You weren't kidding, sister," said Sean. "I promise, I will never even think about going up in a tall building again."

Klaus reached the hose behind them and began to tug on it.

"Oh, God. Please don't let us die," Sean whispered, as they flung their bodies out into space. A searing hot cloud of vapor pushed them even further out, and a flash of brilliance followed by a deafening boom left them stunned as they fell and then swung like a pendulum hard against the glass windows on the 32nd floor. A cloud of smoke and debris rained down on them.

Molly slowly gathered her wits but found her husband limp and unresponsive. She kicked off away from the window over and over until they had sufficient momentum before retrieving Sean's gun and firing several rounds into the cracked pane. The pair crashed through it in a shower of broken glass and landed on the floor inside the building.

Before she could even catch her breath, they both began sliding toward the gaping hole where the window used to be. The large metal wheel that once housed the firehose had been blown off the roof in the explosion and was falling to the ground below, pulling them down with it. Molly frantically pulled at the hose, working to loosen the knot, until just as they reached the edge, she was able to untangle it, and the hose released its grip on them and disappeared, whipping about like an angry snake before receding away into the darkness.

Molly dragged Sean away from the edge and once they were safe, rested her head on his chest. The soft rise and fall of his breathing comforted her. He was still alive. He was broken and bleeding but alive. The monsters were gone now. There was some hope to be had after all.

"Molly…"

She reached down and felt the headset around her neck that she'd still been wearing all this time. Her hand shaking, Molly pressed the transmit button at her waist and whispered, "Cedric? Is… that you?"

"Molllllyyyyy…"

"Dr. Ellis, where are you?"

"Partyyyyyyyy. Parrrrrrrrtyyyy," the voice hissed back at her.

This wasn't over yet.

Molly stood, looked down at Sean, and made her decision.

She held her husband's gun in her right hand, then thumbed the release toggle and caught the magazine with her left, just as Sean had trained her. Only two bullets remained inside. Molly jammed the magazine back into the butt of the pistol, then racked the slide back, chambering a round.

She held the gun using two hands with her arms outstretched, allowing the weapon to guide her into the stairwell where she slowly descended to the 30th floor and the place where all of this had started a million years ago. Molly was going back to Nakamura's main reception hall, back to the site of her company's Christmas party.

The room was dark. The roof explosion had likely blown out every circuit breaker in the building. Only emergency lighting offered faint illumination. Even the pumps for the water features were dead. The great hall was uncomfortably dim and far too quiet.

Then Molly heard it. A noise that sounded like…*chewing*.

She turned and crept toward it.

"Cedric, it's me. It's Molly."

The chewing stopped. Back in the far corner sitting at a table, Molly saw a figure half in shadow. She could feel its stare fixed upon her, even without seeing its face. Suddenly an arm swung in the air, and something landed at her feet with a wet thud. The object bobbed about the floor for a moment before settling to a rest.

At first, Molly thought her mind was playing tricks with her, but then she recognized that what she was seeing was real. A scream lodged in her throat as terror seized her.

Heinz. His face. His *eyes*.

Molly stepped back from the disembodied head. She wished she could say that he got what he deserved, but no one deserved that. Not even Heinz.

"Mollllllyyyyy…"

The figure rose from the table. Molly tried to steady her breathing as she raised her weapon at it. Once it stepped out of the shadow into the muted light, she knew immediately that it was Dr. Ellis. Or rather, that it used to be Dr. Ellis. Tears began welling in her eyes.

"I'm so sorry," she whispered.

"Sorrrrrrryyyy…"

"How are you able…? None of the other infected could talk."

Dr. Ellis staggered closer to her. "I smarrrrrrt. I knooow thiiiiiings."

Half his face was gone, his jaw line and teeth exposed. A tangle of loose and rotted flesh dangled over the gaping wound, as if something had chewed it over. Several bullet holes were pocked deeply across his torso, no doubt courtesy of the late, great Heinz, but they had done nothing to slow Dr. Ellis down.

"Mollllllyyyyy… Prettyyyyyy…"

Now hardly an arm's length away, he swiped his wretched hand at the gun, then tried to grab her, but Molly was able to pull away. Dr. Ellis hissed and pursued her more aggressively now, clawing after her until he grabbed a sleeve on her blouse and held on.

Molly fired the gun point blank into his leg, forcing Dr. Ellis to lose his balance and let go, but he recovered quickly.

"Cedric, please. I want to help you."

"Hellllllp…"

"Yes, how can I help you?"

Maybe she imagined it. Maybe she wished it. But for the briefest moment, there was a flash of recognition in his eyes, a spark, and then Dr. Ellis let out a great wail which caused Molly to cry out, too.

"Mollllllyyyyy… Smarrrrrrt. I… smarrrrrrt."

"I know, Cedric," she replied softly. "I…"

Wait. Was he trying to tell her something? Molly collected herself before aiming the gun at his head. If he knew what she was about to do, the infected man made no move to stop her. The creature that was once Dr. Ellis, that was once a good and decent person, disappeared then as the spark left him forever, and the fiend returned.

The zombie bared its teeth, screeched, and sprang at her.

But it never made the distance between them, as the final bullet found its mark, embedding itself in a brick façade along the back wall but not before ripping completely through the undead monster's brain. Molly collapsed on the floor and wept—whether from relief, sadness, or exhaustion she could not say, although she did know one thing: the nightmare was finally over. Dr. Ellis had been put mercifully to rest.

She soon made her way upstairs back to Sean, who was still lay unconscious where Molly had left him, and allowed herself to fall into a welcome slumber by his side, hoping they would both wake up soon to better days ahead. There would be many more if she had any say in it at all.

While some three hundred feet below them a wave of first responders surrounded the Nakamura Plaza, its roof still ablaze from an apparent, massive gas explosion. Among them, Sargent Vel Howell of the Los Angeles Police Department, who was helping secure the perimeter by cordoning the area off with tape.

Howell tied one end off on a branch at the end of a thick set of bushes before pausing to look around. "Hey. Did anyone else hear that?"

"Hear what?" a nearby cop replied.

"I swear I heard… well, it sounded like a monkey," said Howell. "Aw, what the hell would a monkey be doing out here anyway?"

"Nothing good, I bet."

"You got that right," Howell agreed, as he looked up and saw the flames dance around the skyscraper's crown, a trail of acrid smoke receding off into the darkness. "This night's got nothing but bad written all over it…" ♜

HOWL

By Katya de Becerra

A LONE, DISTANT HOWL DRIFTS in from the moors, perforating the brick of the pub's walls. My hand shakes, and I drop the chalk, my work incomplete. Even with the last year's chart topper *Don't You Want Me Baby* playing on the jukebox I can still hear that blood-chilling howling in my ears... Too soon! The sun has only just begun its downward trip. It has to be an animal then, crying out, disturbed as it senses danger thickening in the crisp air.

"Hurry up, kid, will you?" The old man Randal picks up my crumbling piece of chalk and hands it over, so that I don't have to come down from the ladder. Even from my perch, I can smell the lingering perfume of dark ale on his skin. One of the oldest locals, Randal is a daily fixture here. On certain nights he doesn't go home at all, choosing to spend the long, dark hours sipping his drink, throwing darts, and dozing off at his regular table.

I nod and thank him, then resume my task, but the image is now coming out all crooked, uneven. I gather up my sleeve to fix it but only make a bigger mess. The dark wool of my oversized sweater, washed so frequently its color can no longer be determined, is now stained with white chalk. I don't care. The evening is approaching, and with it our collective fate. The candles still need to be replaced. And then there are regular pub duties to attend to. I erase my imperfect creation and start again.

This drawing task I was given is typically a responsibility of the youngest male in the community, but with my brother missing since the last full moon, today it falls on me. Jonathan and I are twins. We turned eighteen this autumn, but our worry-free adolescent lives came to an end long before that. We were twelve when Dad had drawn the slate gray marble from the lottery box. The only dark marble in the sea of yellowed white is a death sentence in our community. After Dad was gone, Mom has not been the same. She became a faded shadow of her older self before passing away in her sleep thirteen months ago. She came here from the city when she was in her twenties, but the rural change never took. Once an outsider always an outsider, especially around these parts. Of course, her weakened sense of belonging was only partly to blame for her demise. This village and its curse were the main cause. Before all that, when Mom and Dad were younger, I used to overhear them whispering about leaving, about escaping into the city. But that was idle talk, a fantasy. We could never leave; I know that now. No one can leave this place; the curse won't let it. The last person who tried had been found torn to pieces near a construction site off the partially finished stretch of A1. He'd never even made it outside the parish lines.

As I focus on finishing my drawing, I wonder for the umptieth time what became of Jonathan and the rest of the missing hunting party dispatched nearly a month ago. Their prolonged absence is an answer enough, I suppose. They aren't coming back. Unlike what they had failed to kill. The creature will want its sacrifice tonight, more than ever. It must be so angry...

In my mind I picture Jonathan's face, its resemblance to mine beginning and ending with a pair of expressive green eyes, as I finish the village's symbol of protection. As is our tradition, the sigil sits on the wall, squarely between two lamps shaped like old-fashioned lanterns.

As I go about the pub, fetching the candles and dusting the countertops, my eyes keep finding the old box used to keep the lottery marbles. This set, the same one that had sent Dad to his untimely death, has been in the community for close to a century. It is likely as old as the curse. I am tempted to grab the box and run, to throw it as far as I can, to see the damn marbles roll away into the darkening moors... I suppress the urge. That would surely get me in trouble, and it definitely wouldn't excuse me from having to participate in the lottery. I try not to think about that. As my family's last standing member, I have to represent my line. What are the chances of me drawing the gray marble tonight? That would be some terrible luck, given what had become of my brother and my parents before him.

The evening comes abruptly, bringing the deadly drop with it. The winter is still nearly a month away, but its tightening grip can already be felt. The wind that rolls in with the fog is the kind that goes right through you, as if your leathers and wools are nothing but a cotton nightie. I tug my bulky sweater tighter around my frame and I wait. The rest of the lottery participants gather in an anxious circle around the table that holds the box of marbles.

"Alright, let's do this thing," says Willa, the no-nonsense barmaid and my closest neighbor. I resist the pull to hide behind the protection of her significant frame. The mom of two rumbustious teenagers, Willa takes turns with her husband when partaking in the lottery. Given that both of them are still around, their luck is enviable. Willa must believe that too because she is the first to step up to the table and stick her left hand through the slit in the box. The opening is big enough to accommodate a hand as it grips a marble but not big enough for the lottery participant to see inside.

Willa doesn't hesitate once her hand is in the box. She retrieves her marble and shows us her fate, the reveal prompting a collective exhale. A white marble rests in the center of Willa's palm.

"And there's that," she says, placing the marble into a nearby collection jar. She makes her way through the small crowd and goes about her business, preparing the pub for the opening.

The old Randal is next. He lingers by the box, spends a small eternity riffling through its contents.

"Just pick one already, grandpa!" Someone teases from the back.

White marble in Randal's hand.

I stare at it in awe. How did Jonathan make it through this, again and again, without losing his mind? One needs to possess the nerves of steel just to stay here, to go through with this.

One by one the participants draw their lot, white marble after white marble. When it is my turn, I am a nervous wreck. I keep hearing that howl. Whether it is my imagination or the real thing, I can no longer tell. The rough sound clings to the gentle skin inside my ears, makes a permanent home in my chest. I lower my hand into the slit in the box and let my fingers feel their way around. Not a lot of marbles remain, their scarcity filling my rib cage with dread. I focus on the pentacle on the wall, the sigil I had drawn earlier today, but it offers little reassurance.

Someone's impatient sigh drives me on. I grab my marble and show it to the gathering before I see it myself. The crowd grows silent. Their eyes are heavy on me.

My marble is dark. Slate gray. The color of the beast, of our curse.

My lot is cast.

As the night falls, so begins the last evening of my life. No one protests or bemoans my fate. Perhaps, they can appreciate the dark balance of having an entire bloodline wiped out, the last in line folding. Or maybe it's just that they are grateful it is not their turn tonight.

It is hours later. The pub's evening is in full swing. Candles are lit and their burning marinates the space in aromatic smoke. We make our own candles in the village, mixing protective herbs into the recycled wax.

Some patrons are playing chess, others throwing darts at the wall with a drunken hand, and others yet sitting quietly, drinking their ale. The jukebox is quiet now, music deemed too dangerous tonight. What if it attracts the beast?

The light of the full moon finds its way in despite the heavy layers of protection placed around the building—wreaths of dried flowers and herbs covering the windows, symbols like the one on the wall marring the glass. I spend my last moments alive nursing my giant pod of beer and fiddling with the dark marble. I am meant to return it to its keeping place, but I just can't let it go.

The door opens, letting in the freezing wind and the scent of the beast. All conversations come to an abrupt stop as two strangers enter the bar. They are so obviously not from around here, in their puffer jackets and with their youthful faces. This here, with only a few exceptions, is a village of old men. I gawk at the new arrivals but avert my eyes when the one in the red puffer looks directly at me and grins.

The noises of the bar resume as the pair claim an empty table. Willa approaches them, and from the overheard bits of their conversation I learn that the strangers are Americans, tourists, determined for some mad reason to hike the moors.

The dark marble grows unpleasantly warm in my grip. I release it, watch it roll away and off the table. It slides against the floor, and I lose track of it. Damn it!

One of the Americans, the one in red, picks it up. The bar grows quiet once more, so quiet that I can hear the collective beating of our cursed hearts, the strumming of our blood.

The American lifts his find in the air, as if offering the marble up to the patrons. There are no takers. I stay at my table, my self-preservation instinct overpowering whatever sense of justice I have left. With a shrug, the American hands the marble to his companion, and I watch it disappear into his pocket. *A little souvenir*, I imagine them thinking. *Something to remember this weird place by.*

I am saved. In synchrony with my fellow cursed villagers, I watch the two Americans leave the pub and walk out into the dark. Someone tries to warn them, but the tourists are dismissive. To them we are a small-town folk, our hearts full of superstition. They can think whatever they want of us, it won't be for long. With my deadly lot transferred onto them, their hours are numbered.

After the door shuts behind them, I cave in, my guilt surging me like a punishing wave. I run after them, to herd them back into the warmth, into the illusive safety of the pub. But they are gone, swallowed by the night.

I hear a howl. The creature that plagues us is not far now, circling in for a kill, eager for its due. I turn my back on the moors and walk back inside. In the pub, all eyes are on me for a second, and then the noise resumes, the night picking up where it left off. I live. ♜

GUESTS FOR DINNER

By Henry Herz

A SOFT BREEZE STIRRED SOUR-FACED retiree Franklin's wiry brown hair. He wore a tie, sweater vest, and sport coat, the layers keeping him warm in dusk's chill. His chair creaked as he rocked on the shallow front porch of a gray two-story house with white trim, ruefully contemplating the might-have-beens of his life. When his fifty-year-old upstairs tenant, Mandy, drove up and stopped at the curb, he groused, "You can't park there."

Mandy's shoulder-length brown hair had recently begun to gray, though her blue eyes remained bright, and she retained the slender figure of her younger days. She sighed.

What a curmudgeon, she thought.

She grabbed two heavy brown paper bags filled with groceries from the back of her old open-topped blue Jeep CJ-5.

Franklin eyed Mandy closely, too closely for her comfort. He didn't offer to help her carry the heavy load to her second-floor unit. He never did.

Why so bitter, Franklin? I know you regret divorcing your wife. But life's filled with difficult decisions. Better to embrace your choices than let them suck the joy out of you.

Mandy reached the front door, awkwardly shifting both bags to one arm to open it, since the boorish man continued rocking. The house, built in 1900, had its share of charming features, including an attic with a cupola. But just like a person, it showed its age, the stairs creaking under Mandy's steps. Unlocking her second-floor unit door, she crossed the living room and set her groceries on the kitchen counter.

The sun set as Mandy prepared a simple dinner – a tube of ready-to-bake crescent rolls, spaghetti with store-bought meat sauce, and steamed broccoli. Checking the pantry, she considered making brownies. *Maybe later.*

She unscrewed the cap from a bottle of red wine to let it breathe, for all the good that would do for a bargain brand.

Marc, her long-time housemate, descended from his bedroom in the attic. The handsome twenty-something-year-old had a square chin, clear pale blue eyes, and shaggy brown hair. He wore khaki pants with suspenders and a long-sleeved cotton shirt with horizontal orange and blue stripes. "How was work?"

Mandy shook her head. "One day at the coroner's office is pretty much like any other."

Marc tilted his head toward the stove. "That smells delicious."

"Liar," she replied with a smile. She crossed the distance between them and lightly snapped Marc's suspenders. "Haven't I told you these went out of style years ago?"

Marc shrugged. "What can I say? I'm a creature of habit." He gently brushed her bangs to the side.

Her eyes twinkling, Mandy swatted away his hand. "Stop distracting me. Dinner doesn't just appear magically."

"Ha. Wouldn't that be nice? I'm famished." He kissed her cheek. "I'll be in my room watching TV. *Happy Days* starts in five minutes."

Once the pasta, sauce, and broccoli were ready, Mandy shut off the stove burners. "Marc," she called. "I'm going out now to get our dinner guest."

"Okay," echoed from the attic as Mandy locked her front door and made her way to her car.

The old fart's gone inside. Good.

She drove west on Pine toward downtown. Turning left, Mandy headed south on 14th Street.

I don't see any homeless. That new city shelter program must really be working.

She turned right on Canyon Boulevard, and right on 13th Street. Passing Pearl Street Mall on her left and the Boulder Court House on the right, she spied no homeless people. Two more lefts had Mandy driving south on Broadway.

There. Finally.

A man with an unshaved, unwashed face, dirty hair, and multiple ratty layers of clothing crossed Broadway at Walnut, heading west.

Mandy turned right and parked. Leaning against the side of her Jeep, she waited for the man. When he walked within ten feet of her, Mandy said,

"Excuse me. Would you like a hot meal?"

The man halted and considered Mandy through the narrowed eyes of a hard life. Experience had taught him how to spot danger, but the petite middle-aged woman offering him food didn't seem threatening. Nor had he eaten all day. "For free?"

Mandy shook her head. "Yes. My name's Mandy. What's yours?"

"Walt. How far?"

"I live less than half a mile from here." Mandy pointed at her car. "Come on, get in."

#   #   #

As Mandy escorted her guest from her Jeep to her front door, Franklin emerged. "Again?" His face twisted with disapproval. "Always bringing in strays and lowering the property values. No good will come of this."

Mandy kept her anger off her face. "Everyone deserves to eat, Franklin."

She whispered to Walt, "Don't pay any attention to him." She led him upstairs to her dining table. "Please, have a seat, Walt. You can take off your coat if you want."

Walt sat where Mandy indicated, but he did not remove his coat. He eyed the apartment, checking for threats.

Old habits, thought Mandy.

"I just need a minute to warm up the food. Would you like some wine?"

Walt's eyes widened at the offer. He nodded. The smell of crescent rolls and meat sauce dispelled his remaining doubts.

Figuring Walt was more interested in food than chitchat, Mandy ate with him in silence. She offered him seconds and thirds and refilled his glass.

When was the last time you drank from a glass? she wondered.

Eventually, Walt put his hands on his belly. "I'm stuffed. Thanks." His face flushed slightly.

"What is it, Walt?"

He cleared his throat. "Sorry, but could I use your bathroom?"

Mandy nodded. "Of course. Please use the one in the attic."

As Walt headed up the stairs, Mandy busied herself clearing the table. She flinched at a brief scream from Walt.

I'll never get used to that. A tear rolled down her cheek.

Three knocks echoed from Mandy's floor.

Stop banging on your ceiling to scold me, Franklin.

"It's bad enough you bring vagrants to my house," came Franklin's muffled yelling, "but at least keep the noise down."

Mandy stuck out her tongue at the floor. She put away the leftovers and loaded the dirty dishes into the dishwasher.

Fifteen minutes later, Marc came down, carrying a large steamer trunk with little effort. "Thank you for dinner, Mandy. I think it's lovely that you always give them a final meal."

She nodded. "It's the least I can do." Grabbing a kitchen cloth, she gently dabbed a drop of blood from the left side of Marc's mouth.

Marc kissed her forehead. "You're very special to me. But the landlord's becoming a problem."

"Oh, you heard Franklin's complaint?"

"Of course." Marc scratched his chin. "We may need to move again. Let's dispose of the dinner guest." He carried the steamer trunk down to the Jeep, accompanied by Mandy.

Mandy drove west on Pine St., turned right onto Broadway, and left onto Mapleton Ave, which became Sunshine Canyon Drive. The uphill drive took them toward the wooded Seven Hills area.

Marc pointed. "Pull over here." Once Mandy stopped the car, he opened the steamer trunk lid and laid Walt's limp body over a shoulder. Marc jogged easily into the woods, returning a few minutes later without the corpse.

Mandy drove them home, fighting back tears… as she had for years.

#   #   #

"I knew it!" exclaimed Ezekiel, pounding a fist into a gloved palm. The gangly middle-aged man had raven hair and an aquiline nose. He wore black clothing, binoculars, and night-vision goggles. Lurking in a hunting blind high in a mature blue spruce tree gave him a wide view of the mountain road. "No one believed me," he muttered to himself, a fanatical wildness gleaming in his hazel eyes. "But now I've seen you dump a body, you spawn of the devil. I've got your license plate, and tomorrow, my friend at the DMV will give me your address. You cannot escape the Lord's justice."

Ezekiel scrambled down a rope ladder to the ground, racing to where Mandy had parked. He clicked on his flashlight. Sweeping the beam from side to side and treading carefully, he followed Marc's tracks into the wood. Minutes later, he came upon Walt's body, the skin unusually pale.

Ezekiel checked Walt's neck, locating two puncture wounds. He nodded, mumbled a prayer, and made the sign of the cross. With a sharp pocketknife, he made a small incision in Walt's wrist. Almost no blood oozed out. "Now I have proof a vampire killed all those missing people. Who's crazy now?"

The voices in his head remained silent on the matter.

GUESTS FOR DINNER

\# \# \#

Two weeks later, Marc kept Mandy company as she ate dinner. He lit two candles. "More romantic, don't you think?" he replied when Mandy raised an eyebrow. Marc caressed her hand.

Not quite as soft as it once was, thought Marc. *The years take their inexorable toll. That's the true curse of vampirism – always outliving those you care about.*

"You'll have to try again tomorrow, I'm afraid. It's been weeks, and I can't last much longer without feeding. I feel myself weakening."

Mandy nodded. "Of course. I'll try again tomorrow. I'm having trouble finding solitary homeless people now that the city's shelters are fully funded and cold weather chases people inside at night."

The phone rang. Mandy answered it on the second ring.

"Where's your rent check?" demanded her landlord, Franklin, without preamble. "It was due today. If you're delivering it after the due date, it needs to be a cashier's check."

Mandy sighed. "Sorry, Franklin. It was a hectic day, and I forgot. I'll go to the bank and bring a check to you tomorrow."

"It's always due on the first. I shouldn't have to remind you." He hung up.

"Why does he always have to be so obnoxious?" asked Mandy rhetorically.

"It's in his nature." A grin dawned on Marc's face. "Speaking of nature… I could kill two birds with one stone."

Mandy sat up to consider the unexpected suggestion. "That would be the first time I don't feel sorry for your victim. Are you sure you want to strike so close to home?"

Marc raised his hands, palms upward. "It doesn't seem like we have much choice given how slim the pickings have become. We'll have to move to the backup residence I set up southeast of Cheyenne."

Sipping her wine and tilting her head, Mandy said, "The problem is, he never comes up here. That's been his one redeeming characteristic."

Marc's eyes twinkled. "I think you underestimate your allure."

Mandy blushed. "You always were gallant. But look at me. I'm fifty." She spread her arms. Mandy wore a long-sleeved, loose-fitting white blouse and faded jeans. "I'm not the catch I was when we met decades ago."

Marc took her hands in his and gazed into Mandy's eyes. "My sweet, you're still beautiful. You'll always be beautiful." He hugged her gently, soothed by the heat of a living body.

#   #   #

At 7 p.m. the following evening, Mandy changed into tight black leather pants and a low-cut pink cotton top.

I can't believe these pants still fit.

She fixed her hair in a ponytail, went downstairs, and knocked on the door of Franklin's unit.

He opened the door with a scowl. "Well, it's about time." His eyes roved over Mandy's figure appreciatively. "Do you have the rent?"

"Yes, it's upstairs." She leaned forward to give Franklin a fuller view of her chest. "My finances have been tight this month, Franklin." She lowered her voice. "I was wondering if you'd like to come upstairs and *discuss* if there's anything I can do to cover a portion of the rent."

Franklin's eyes widened slightly. Though considerably older than Mandy, he was not so old as to have completely lost his sex drive... or the delusion that a pretty woman could still find him attractive. "Hmmm. I suppose we could *discuss* things."

He followed Mandy upstairs, enjoying the view as her hips swayed with each step. *Things are looking up,* Franklin thought.

Mandy ushered Franklin into her apartment, locking the door behind him. "Have a seat on the couch, Franklin. Would you like some wine?"

A rare grin appeared on his face. "Sure." The grin vanished as quickly as it appeared when Marc strode into the room. "Say, what's this now, Mandy? I'm not into threesomes... unless you get rid of this guy and invite another woman to join us." He smirked at his own wit. Turning his head to Marc, he barked, "Piss off. I've got things to *discuss* with Mandy."

Marc stared across the room into the landlord's eyes with such ferocity that Franklin shut his mouth. "As if she would even consider sleeping with a human turd like you. Now, apologize to her for your years of rudeness."

Franklin stood. "Who do you think you are? Nobody talks to me like that in my place." He shifted his gaze to Mandy, standing in the kitchen. "Looks like you have a choice. You can tell this jerk to buzz off and undress, or you can expect a lease termination notice from me tomorr–"

Marc moved across the room to Franklin, a blur of supernatural speed. He delivered a right hook to the jaw that snapped the man's head viciously to the left, knocking two teeth loose.

Franklin crumpled unconscious to the carpet.

"What, no complaint about the racket?" asked Marc before ravenous hunger crept into his eyes. His canine teeth lengthened.

"Please feed upstairs, Marc. I know you have to eat, but I can't stand to watch."

Marc nodded, collected Franklin's bicuspids from the floor, and dragged him toward the stairs. "You should pack your things. We'll need to leave tonight."

#   #   #

Mandy was still filling suitcases when the satiated vampire set the loaded steamer trunk on the living room floor. "That meal was long overdue. It still amazes me that the taste of a person's blood is not influenced by what an ass they were." He dangled Franklin's keychain. "I'm going to check his apartment for valuables, then I'll help you load the car."

#   #   #

With the relentless zeal of a fanatic, or perhaps of the disturbed, Ezekiel staked out Mandy's home every night since his friend at the DMV provided her address. Parking his dark blue police surplus Chevy Suburban with blacked-out windows well back from the front of her house, he surveilled anyone coming or going. The well-lit street obviated the need for him to use his NVGs.

Ezekiel sat fully prepared to confront a vampire, spiritually, sartorially, and militarily. He remained willing to risk his life to fight any bloodsucking hell-spawn. He wore a white tabard with a large red cross sewn on the front like a Knight Templar. Around his neck hung a string of garlic cloves. Unlike a Crusader though, he had a 9mm Glock 17 pistol with a twenty-four round high-capacity magazine holstered on the right side of his brown leather belt. He ran his fingers over the top of the holster.

Thanks for the open carry law, Colorado, he thought.

The pistol could make short work of any human thralls but would be worthless against a vampire. For that, Ezekiel made a special purchase, a Cobra Rx Adder tactical repeating crossbow. The weapon featured an adjustable butt-stock similar to that of an AR-15, a vertical fore-grip, and a clip on the left side of the muzzle that held a zoomable flashlight and laser pointer. A loading bar extended from a hinge at the bottom of the fore-grip to the bottom of the pistol-grip. Levering that forward loaded the next 7.5" bolt from the six-round magazine with a 130-pound draw weight. It was no sniper weapon, but at close range and with God's blessing, it would slay a vampire.

Ezekiel glanced at the crossbow sitting on the passenger-side floor. Upon acquiring the off-the-shelf weapon, he made an important modification. Replacing the carbon fiber quarrels with hardwood turned the crossbow bolts into flying stakes. In Ezekiel's basement workshop, he further increased their lethality by hollowing out the front portion. He dripped holy water, taken surreptitiously from a church, into the small cavity, sealing the opening with wood putty.

Slouching in the car seat, he bolted upright when the vampire hauled a steamer trunk from Mandy's house to her Jeep.

The Lord rewards my patience and dedication at last. "And I shall wreak great acts of vengeance with rebukes of fury, and they will know that I am the Lord when I lay My vengeance upon them," he quoted.

#   #   #

Mandy and Marc loaded her car with as many suitcases of her belongings as would fit.

"It's about a hundred-mile drive. Shouldn't take long at night," Marc mentioned.

Mandy nodded and headed east on Pine, turning north on 28th Street. At the on-ramp to route 119, she drove northeast, turning north on Interstate 25.

The highway lights abandoned them after they passed Wellington. Fewer and fewer vehicles shared the road.

On a dark, deserted stretch of I-25 about ten miles south of the Wyoming border, Marc sat up, twisting his neck to peer behind them. "Speed up, Mandy. Someone's turned off their headlights and they're gaining on–"

Ezekiel's Suburban drew alongside the Jeep. Steel crunched as the Suburban swerved hard right, slamming its thick right-side push bumper into the Jeep's left rear quarter panel. The impact shoved the rear of the lighter vehicle to the right.

Trying to stay on the road, Mandy spun her steering wheel hard, but she overcompensated. The Jeep turned sideways before tumbling side-over-side off the pavement. Crunching metal and shattering glass drowned out Mandy's screams. The car halted upside down into an empty field, engine idling and wheels still spinning.

The Suburban skidded to a stop behind them, its headlight beams illuminating the scene.

Marc snarled but restrained his fury for a moment. *Is Mandy okay?* He tore off his seatbelt and gently lifted his unconscious thrall out the passenger side door.

Marc sniffed to check for leaking gasoline. Detecting none, he laid Mandy in the grass on the side of the Jeep opposite their assailant's vehicle. His fists clenched as he strode toward the madman who hurt his beloved.

I will end you.

Thwack. A crossbow bolt struck his left knee. Intense pain like he'd

64

never known, living or undead, radiated throughout his body. "I'm going to tear off your limbs one at a time," he growled, utterly consumed with fury.

Marc's normally cold flesh smoldered around the wound. *Holy water*! Temporarily blinded by the glare of headlights, he could not yet make out his assailant. He tried to sprint to his right to gain a clearer view, but the searing agony slowed him.

At the sound of running footsteps, Marc snapped his head in the direction of the Jeep. Pain slowed his thinking. He squinted. *A man. With a crossbow.*

Thwack. A second bolt struck his right shoulder. He gasped at the pain.

"Surrender, vampire. Or I'll put a bullet in Mandy," ordered Ezekiel, no fear in his voice.

Anger boiled within Marc at the impudent mortal's threat to Mandy. He howled like a wolf. His fangs lengthened and sharp claws erupted from his fingertips. Agony and fury raged within him like a hurricane. He charged at Ezekiel, not noticing the red dot glowing on his chest.

Thwack. A third bolt punched between the ribs to the left of his sternum. *No*! The pain forced his eyes closed, but his keen sense of smell led him unerringly to Ezekiel before the fanatic could reload. A wicked slash with his right hand tore open the man's throat as the aroma of garlic seared the vampire's nostrils. Marc collapsed atop his foe, his undead body turning to ash while Ezekiel's lifeblood soaked the earth. ♜

AUTHOR'S NOTE

This story parodies the TV series *Mork & Mindy*, with the obvious parallels: Marc (Mork), Mandy (Mindy), Franklin (Mr. Bickley), and Ezekiel (Exidor), who quotes Ezekiel 25:17 in a wink at *Pulp Fiction*. Mork and Mindy lived in the upstairs half of 1619 Pine Street in Boulder, CO, with Mork sleeping in the attic. Mindy drove a blue Jeep CJ-5. Mandy is the vampire's long-time Renfield (thrall), akin to two characters in the terrific Swedish vampire movie, Let the Right One In. This story shares the same theme as *King Kong*—"'Twas beauty killed the beast."

HELL COPTER

By Jim Towns

1.

GUSTAVO ALWAYS CALLED IT 'THE chopper'; or sometimes, in jest, 'the whirlybird'.

But the *Archimedes' Claw* was so much more than that. A one-of-a-kind, nearly unstoppable space-age helicopter: able to fly at supersonic speed, armored to withstand the pulse of an electromagnetic detonation, armed with rockets, missiles and machine guns the like of which even the military's most gunned-up warbirds couldn't match, and state-of-the-art computer tracking and navigation systems. It had been built by a super-secret government agency called "Spindrift", but Saigon John had stolen it on its first trial run.

John's own story was complex: an exceptional student, he'd been recruited right out of the Air Force Academy to fly test fighters. His nickname had come from his service in Vietnam, where John flew thirty-seven successful combat missions—shooting down more than a dozen MIGs before his F-4 was hit with flak and crashed deep behind enemy lines. The V.C. held him prisoner for thirteen weeks before he escaped from his POW camp.

It was during that escape, in the jungles west of Hanoi City, that John encountered the rare Vietnamese wolf: *Siamis Lupis*, and drank rainwater from its paw print to survive.

From that time on, he was a werewolf.

Now, he was a werewolf with a helicopter.

2.

They'd been given a mission, but Saigon John didn't want it.

Lucius, the head of Spindrift, had shown up at John's mountain retreat. John had had a girl over the night before and had to first get her dressed and into her Mercedes before they discussed work.

Lucius wore his customary all-black suit, shirt, and white tie. He had a scar that ran vertically down the side of his cheek—his own souvenir from the War. The two sat on John's boat dock, drinking coffee.

"If it was simple, I wouldn't have come to you. You're the only one who can do this, John. You and Archimedes."

"And Gustavo."

"Yes of course, and Gustavo. He's vital to your team."

"Lucius, you know what tomorrow night is."

"Yes: the Full of the Moon. Look, if this goes according to plan, you'll be back with the cargo, home and here in your Safe Room before moonrise."

"Since when has anything you or I were involved in gone according to plan?"

Saigon John stood up and walked to the edge of the pier. Far off on the lake, a bald eagle swooped down, catching a fish in its talons and flying off with it to its eyrie.

"There's no one else?"

"SAS has already tried. They lost two men trying to HALO jump in and had to abort."

John was doing the math in his head: weighing the risks, measuring the costs.

"You'll keep the government off our backs? Get them to stop trying to find where we're keeping *Archimedes' Claw*?"

"I'll do my best," Lucius rose, and the two shook hands.

"Guess that'll have to be good enough."

3.

They kept *Archimedes' Claw* in a dormant volcano sixty-six miles away from John's mountain cabin: at least they hoped it was dormant. Mt. St. Helens was only a few hundred miles south and had erupted just a year before.

Luckily, this helicopter could fly through a pyroclastic cloud.

Gustavo was already running telemetry checks on the bird's targeting and navigation software when John pulled up in his jeep.

"Good to go, old timer?"

"You talking to me, or our girl here?" Gustavo had been flying before Saigon John had been born. He knew everything there was to know about aeronautics, lift-to-weight ratios, and combat above seven thousand feet: the rack of medals in his office attested to as much.

John ran a hand along Archimedes' hull: she was jet black—larger by a third than most assault choppers. Her rotors were surrounded by a reinforced turbine housing to protect them from fire, and her windows were tinted black. Seen in silhouette, Archimedes looked like a narrow slice of darkness—until her side-mounted canons unfurled and rained down a hellish barrage of fire on their target.

The system checks were nearly complete: John pulled on his flight suit, making sure to tuck the silver medallion he always wore inside, so it was next to his heart. He could feel the familiar burn of it against his skin, and it comforted him. He would accomplish this mission, and he would do so as a man, not a beast.

"Fire on one," he told Gustavo, and with a whine and then a roar, *Archimedes' Claw* came to life. Its twin propeller blades swung slowly, then faster and faster until they were a circular whirl above the cockpit—nothing short of spinning death.

4.

"Time on target is twenty-two minutes on our present course, Sai." Gustavo's voice came over the cabin intercom. Both Saigon John and Gustavo wore magnetic helmets that hardwired into the helicopter's controls. Gustavo's gave him command and control of the armaments and weapons deploy systems, while John's showed a HUD display in the visor for navigation and targeting—even at night.

"Mission parameters:" John requested, and Gustavo ran down their objectives.

"Primary target is Maxine McMillian, daughter of the Governor. She's being held by General Umberto Riis, the leader of the *Escuchame Front* army and our secondary target, on Isla Malverdas: and island point-four-niner south southeast of Santa Catalina. It was an old Spanish outpost back in the day."

"So plenty of reinforced walls, bars, and guards between us and the girl."

"The fort is nearly a ruin, John. I'd be worried if we use any of our rockets—"

"—it could bring the whole place down on top of her. Right." John's hand gripped the throttle: "So it's the guns and flare bombs until we get her out of there—then we can rain hell."

"Moonrise is at six twenty-five, John. Just to keep in mind."

"Yeah. Not much of a window to get her and get back." Up ahead, Catalina Island came into view, and the Port of Los Angeles on their left. And then in just moments they were over and past the island, sending a herd of buffalo scurrying away as the chopper flew low under the radar.

"Ten minutes."

5.

The *Escuchame Front* was ready for them:

"Incoming!" Gustavo hollered in John's ear, but his display had already shown him several surface-to-air rockets coming at them.

"Flares," he ordered, and the ship deployed a series of incendiaries to either side, attracting two of the three heat-seekers, which exploded and shook the hull of the Archimedes.

"Those are Russian-made!"

"Guess we know where El General is getting his supplies from," Saigon John pulled the stick left and shoved it down, and the helicopter dove down past the old fort and over the cliff side to its north—the rocket following them.

"Don't push her too hard, John—remember I just got her back in shape after that New Mexico mission."

"She'll take it." But John's teeth were gritted: even the *Archimedes' Claw* couldn't withstand a direct hit by a Russian R-73.

He waited as long as he could, then yanked back on the stick and gave the throttle full thrust. "Afterburners." He called out, and Gustavo engaged the ramjet engines on either side of the fuselage. The kick pushed them both back in their seats, and the wave-crests splashed the belly of the craft as they pulled out of the dive.

The R-73 could not recover as quickly. There was a splash and a roar behind them as it hit the water and exploded.

Over the intercom, John could hear Gustavo breathe a sigh of relief: "That was too close. Can we go get this girl now?"

6.

General Riis had come into the courtyard of the fortress to make sure the aircraft had been destroyed. His men were a mixture of longtime believers in the Cause, which made them loyal, if not especially well trained; and mercenaries who excelled at their work, but only cared about being paid.

It was hard to find good soldiers these days.

"It's down? You got it?" he asked. He had spotted the gigantic helicopter approaching. In thirty years of warfare, it was like no air combat vehicle he'd ever seen.

"We think so, General. It dove down over the north cliff, and we heard an explosion."

"You *heard*? Go check for wreckage—right now!" Riis ordered.

His man only made it a few steps before they all heard it: the low *thump thump thump* of whirling rotors. In a moment the helicopter floated up over the west tower of the fortress: black as night with a glittering array of weapons deployed.

"Madre dios!" Riis heard one man say.

"Es un diablo," exclaimed another.

"It is no devil—it is the Americans. They want our hostage. Open fire!" the general screamed above the sound of the spinning blades, and a deafening roar of gunfire erupted: the clacking of AK-47s, the *pop pop* of handguns, the buzzsaw whistle of a .50 caliber.

The bullets just bounced off the hull of the ship. Even the windshield was impervious. Riis had never seen anything like it. Through the darkened plexiglass, he could just make out the helicopter's pilot staring at him through a slit in his helmet—his finger on the joystick's trigger.

"It *is* a devil," Riis whispered, and then the helicopter's guns belched flame, stitching lines of lead into the grass of the yard, sending topsoil and shrapnel everywhere. To his left and right men were cut down even as they fired—or turned to flee at the last moment. True believers and guns-for-hire: they all died the same.

He drew his own handgun—a nickel-plated M1911 automatic that the former *Presidente de los Estados Unitos* had once given him: back when the gringos considered him a revolutionary, rather than a terrorist.

His bullets did no good. He knew they wouldn't.

General Riis turned and fled into the fort.

7.

Maxine had heard the explosions and gunfire from her cell. She had no idea how long she'd been a prisoner on the island—it felt like weeks, but it was probably more like days.

She'd gone out with friends to the club on Saturday night, the same as always. And the same as always, she'd managed to ditch her security detail after about an hour.

But unlike the other times, when she and her friend Diana had darted out the club's backdoor into the alley to escape her chaperone and go hit up another, more risqué club, they'd come face to face with armed men.

They'd shot Diana right in front of her, and the next thing Maxine knew she was blindfolded in the back of a van—then carried onto a boat. When they'd finally taken it off, she'd found herself here, in this cell.

There was shouting outside, mostly in Spanish. And she'd heard cries of pain amidst the gunfire. Maxine hoped her daddy had made the President send the Army or Green Berets to rescue her. Maybe even Delta Force. After all, he was a powerful man—the leader of one of the largest states in the US. Maxine told herself she'd never disobey him again.

The bolts of her door slid free, and she stood up, expecting to see Americans in uniform here to take her home.

Instead, she saw the grinning face of General Riis.

8.

Archimedes' Claw set down in the center of the courtyard on its three retractable landing wheels. John removed his flight helmet, donned a pair of aviator sunglasses, and drew out his sidearm.

"I'm turning defensive system control over to you, Gustavo. Keep the blades spinning. Hopefully I'll be back soon."

"I won't tell you to be careful," Gustavo yelled after him as Saigon John jumped out of the helicopter and began making his way to the fortress.

The partially ruined building was not huge, but its passageways were narrow and dark, which slowed John's process. He came across several soldiers on his way to the cellblock but managed to eliminate them.

When he reached the cells, there was nobody there—but something caught his attention: the coconut scent of suntan lotion. Since John highly doubted any of Riis' hired guns cared about getting sunburnt, he was sure Maxine had been here, and recently.

He turned and followed the scent trail. This hypersensitivity to smells

71

was a wolf trait—one that stayed with him even during the thirty days of the month when he was a man. It had presented itself not long after he'd been brought back to the states and given a discharge. John didn't like using it—it felt like cheating. But now was no time for that.

He followed the suntan lotion smell back up the rough stone hallway, towards the old watchtower. He was moving faster than was probably wise, opening himself up to any snipers: but he knew every moment Gustavo and the chopper sat on the ground, they were a target.

Saigon John hurried up the circular stairs of the tower, still tracking on Maxine's scent. A dozen steps away from the top, several bullets whacked into the stone near his head, showering him with small rocky pieces. He ducked and took aim, only to spot Riis on the top landing holding Maxine in front of him.

"Don't come any closer, you son of a bitch! Take your bird and fly away, or the Governor gets his daughter back in *poquito* pieces!"

"I'm staying put—don't hurt her, General!" Saigon John called up, meanwhile tapping his com mic to whisper:

"Gustavo, I need *Archimedes' Claw* up to the tower. Weapons hot but hold fire, he's got the girl."

He heard the double click of Gustavo acknowledging.

9.

John called up: "I've been sent here to negotiate, General. What can we do to resolve this?"

"Negotiate? With that flying death machine? You must think I'm *estupido*! How about I toss the girl off the tower, and then we talk?"

John had to stall for time. He took his automatic in his opposite hand by the barrel, showing it to Riis.

"I'm putting my gun down, General. I just want to talk." He placed the weapon on the stone, and took a few steps up, hands raised.

"Slowly..." Riis commanded. Saigon John could see the girl now: blonde hair that had probably been curly, but now hung lank and straight. A sequined cocktail dress cut short to the thighs—probably designer, but now stained and torn and ruined from her days in captivity.

Most of all, John saw the fear in her eyes. Maxine McMillian was certain she wasn't going to survive this, and it was up to him to prove her wrong.

John took a few more steps, hands still raised. He was now on the top landing with Riis and the girl. It was barely ten feet across, the floor covered

72

in rough, wind weathered boards. He could see Riis was nearly vibrating with a mixture of anger and terror, which made it impossible to predict what he'd do.

"Look, General—I can't promise anything, you know that. But if you let the girl go with us, then you have options. Otherwise..."

"Options... you killed all my men! What options do I have now but to go back to the Cartels, and beg for more money and soldiers? What do you think they'll do to me, *gringo*, eh? Laugh? Maybe. Shoot me? Likely." His finger tightened on the trigger of his nickel-plated gun, shoved up under Maxine's jaw. John knew it would take only a few ounces of pressure, and the girl *and* the mission would be lost.

"You need to trust me, General: this is your only option," John said, only to have the ousted militant turn the barrel on him.

"No," the man hissed through gold teeth. "Not the only option: I kill her, take *you* hostage, and fly your gunship to the State Capitol—where I blow her *padre* the Governor to hell."

His finger tightened on the trigger, but even as it did, they all heard the low *thump thump thump* rising, coming closer. Behind Riis, past the stone pillars supporting the tower's broken roof, a dark, massive shape floated up into view.

It all happened in a flash: John saw Riis' eyes widen as he sensed the chopper right behind him. He spun around with a defiant roar, raising his gun. As he did so, he let go his grip on Maxine, and Saigon John reached out and snatched her arm, yanking her to him. Riis began firing, emptying his clip at *Archimedes' Claw*, and John caught a glimpse of the bullets sparking off the helicopter's windshield as he hurried the frightened girl down the stairs. Riis ejected the empty magazine, slapped a new one into his gun, cocked it and prepared to fire again.

They were clear, and John knew what was coming: he slammed Maxine down flat on the stone steps as the deafening roar of *Archimedes'* Gatling guns opened up above them, tearing through stone, flesh and anything else in their sights. John kept the girl's face covered, but he watched Riis' body torn into shreds by the hellfire with satisfaction.

Finally, it was over.

"Come on, we need to get out of here," he helped Maxine to her feet and led her down the spiral steps, up the narrow corridor and out into the courtyard. Glancing up, he saw the crumbling ruin of the watchtower, and from behind it *Archimedes Claw* coming in for a landing in the courtyard's center, floating above the ground like some great bird of prey, its guns still smoking.

Then a shot rang out, and Saigon John felt hot metal pierce his shoulder.

10.

Gustavo saw his partner fall to the ground, pulling the girl with him. He spotted the shooter right away—a mercenary in one of the fortress' windows, brandishing a Kalashnikov.

His finger pressed the joystick's trigger, and twin bursts of flame erupted from the ship's paired front guns, vaporizing everything in his sights.

He pulled off his helmet and jumped out of the helicopter.

Saigon John was already struggling to his feet by the time Gustavo got to him, pulling his arm over his shoulder.

"Can you walk, Sai?" he asked, and his friend nodded. The trio hurried back to the helicopter.

"Here, get in back," he told John, but John shook his head, pushing his way to the pilot seat.

"I'm fine. Get her secured," he grunted, and hauled himself painfully into the cabin. Gustavo helped the disheveled girl up into the back, got in behind her and took his seat at the rear controls. It was cramped in here with three people, but manageable.

He watched as John primed the fuel pumps, checked his gauges, and pulled back on the collective pitch control, raising them up until they were hovering twenty feet off the ground.

"Give me everything," he ordered. Gustavo had seen this side of Saigon John before and switched over targeting and weapons without a word.

A terrible barrage of missiles and rockets erupted out of the chopper's side weapons bays, streaking away to slam into the crumbling walls of the fortress, erupting in balls of fire that sent old stones hurtling into the air. John kept firing rocket after rocket until the place was fully engulfed in fire. Gustavo saw Maxine look at him in fear, and finally he said: "John..."

His friend's finger released the trigger, and his head cocked a fraction. Gustavo could clearly see the bleeding hole in his flight uniform, and the blood running down the back of his pilot's seat.

John pulled back on the stick, and the *Archimedes' Claw* banked and turned to fly away from the little island and the smoking ruin that was once a fortress.

11.

They flew low over the ocean, headed north. The sun had almost sunk to the horizon, and its rays skipped over the wave-crests less than fifty feet below them. Maxine sat staring straight ahead, still in shock from what she'd been through. They'd get her to people who could help her soon enough.

"Time to return, seventeen minutes, Sai."

"Copy," John responded. His shoulder was killing him, but he didn't want to say anything—after all, regular bullets couldn't kill him. Not anymore.

But regardless, John found himself struggling to stay focused. His vision kept going blurry, and the controls felt loose in his hands. Seventeen minutes to their volcano hiding place, and the reinforced steel room he locked himself into every full moon, until he was no longer the wolf—plenty enough time, if nothing went wrong: especially with his silver medallion holding off the change. John reached up to touch it where it rested against his chest, and found it wasn't there.

Cold fear washed across him, and he felt around the inside of his flight suit for it. Nothing. It must have come off during the firefight at the fortress.

"You okay, Sai?" Gustavo asked over the mic.

"Yeah, fine," John lied, knowing his partner didn't believe him: for one, his helmet measured all his vital signs and the readouts displayed right in front of Gustavo.

"Your heart rate just jumped, kid."

"I'm just—we need to get back fast. Can we engage the afterburner?"

"We used up most of the fuel getting there, Sai. We're getting close to bingo as it is."

John acknowledged. He'd wasted too much time shooting up the island. Useless. His vision blurred again, then cleared. And then something else washed over him: the familiar chill that preceded the change, like a momentary fever—come and gone in a moment.

"John, your vitals..." Gustavo said.

"You said moonrise was 7:25, right? It's only 6:30."

He heard Gustavo behind him flipping switches, then pause.

"Sai..."

"What? What's wrong?" He could feel the change coming over him.

"The World Clock. I left it set to Mountain—from the New Mexico mission."

Another chill went through John's body. He could feel sweat breaking out on his forehead.

"You're saying it's 7:30?"

"No, it's half-past six."

"Then—"

"Sai, moonrise is *right now*."

Even as he said it, Saigon John saw the first silver light of the moon crest over the cliffs to their right.

"No..."

"I don't understand—we got away," Maxine spoke up. "What's the big deal about the moon?"

"Quiet, hon," Gustavo told her, "We're in trouble."

12.

The change was always slow in coming—until it wasn't. It started at the base of Saigon John's skull: a feral chill that tasted like hard rain on rocks and smelled of blood-soaked earth. He could hear Gustavo talking to him over the intercom, but his friend's voice was muted and hard to understand.

"T...time?" he growled into his mic: "Time until landing?"

"Nine minutes, kid."

Too long: he needed to be in his cell in the volcano *right now*, not piloting a multimillion-dollar flying death machine. The change was growing—he could feel the telltale itch in his palms and that familiar weighty feeling, as though his body had grown heavier, or more dense.

"What's happening to him?" he could actually smell Maxine's fear, along with the reek of the chopper's fuel, the grease keeping her rotors turning; magnesium and gunpowder loaded into the rocket tubes; even the salt of the sea rushing by below them.

Gustavo was yelling at him: "Sai, you've got to put down!" even as John saw the hair growing on the back of his hand that held the throttle, and his fingernails turning into claws.

"I—can't!" he managed to get out—talking was getting difficult. "No place to land... water and rocks..." he was losing his fight against the wolf: soon it would be free, and they would all die.

But Gustavo's voice kept coming to him through the haze: *Sai, you have to fight it! Sai, hold on, kid!* Nobody else called John "Sai", that was just Gustavo—like his "whirlybird" nickname for *Archimedes*. John didn't have any other family, and very few friends left—most had died in the jungle. He had to hold on.

Somewhere from far away, Maxine was screaming, and he knew the change was fully on him now. He tore his helmet off with a clawed hand and dropped it to the floor by the pedals, where he could see his feet had burst out of his combat boots. His ears were growing, his facial features pushed forward into a snout with the sound of bones stretching, snapping, and reforming. It was agony.

He looked up and could see their volcano coming up in the distance, even as his vision went red.

13.

They were only three minutes out.

Gustavo had switched the *Archimedes Claw*'s systems to autopilot as soon as he'd seen Sai begin the change: now he stared in horror as his friend thrashed in the pilot seat, kicking on the rudder pedals and slashing the stick— if he'd still been piloting, they'd be in an uncontrolled nosedive headed straight into the Pacific. Their volcano landing pad was pre-programmed into the computer in case one or either of them was injured during a mission and couldn't fly home, so the ship would land okay—but that didn't change the fact that they now had a wild beast trapped with them.

"What is that?" Maxine screamed over the com, even as Saigon John thrashed in the pilot seat—barely held in place by his safety harness.

"He's a werewolf! It happened in Vietnam!" Gustavo yelled.

"Why would you let him fly a helicopter?"

"Because he's the best," he replied, even as his hand reached down under his own console for the nine millimeter he kept strapped to its underside— the one loaded with silver slugs for a worst-case-scenario.

One exactly like this.

Two minutes out. Sai was roaring—unrecognizable under a mane of fur and claws. His fangs gnawed at the straps holding him to the seat, even as his fist banged on the bulletproof glass of the side window, cracking it.

The girl saw the gun in his hand: "What are you gonna do?"

"I'm gonna protect us—no matter what. It's what he would want," Gustavo fought back the tears that threatened to blind him and make it impossible to take aim when he needed to.

The helicopter had begun to gain altitude, rising up the side of the dormant volcano towards the central vent.

14.

Maxine had never been so terrified, not even in the darkest moments of her recent captivity. The thing up in the front seat was like some kind of demon—covered in hair, shrieking and straining against its seatbelt. Its eyes were red and bulging with rage and bloodlust. She didn't know who was piloting the helicopter, but they were flying up the side of what looked like a volcano and nothing made any sense to her anymore.

Then a glint of something metal caught her eye—on the floor under the pilot seat—a silver medallion on a thin chain.

"What's that?" she asked the older man, who held his gun ready.

"What's what?" he asked, and she pointed. His eyes widened, and he jabbed a finger at it.

"Get it! Put it around his neck!"

"What?" she screamed at him. "Not a chance in hell!"

"You want to live, little girl?" he hollered. "We came a long way to get you, you know!"

Maxine debated only a moment, and then undid the buckle of her own seatbelt. The shaking of the chopper made it impossible to stand, even if she hadn't been weak from days of being held captive, so she got on her hands and knees and crawled up the narrow passage towards the howling creature up front. Two feet away, she hesitated: its claws swung wildly, and she could see the needle-like nails at the tips of its elongated fingers.

"Hurry!" she heard the old man yell from behind her, and in a sudden rush, she lunged forward and snatched the necklace, backing up out of reach of the monster.

She still had no idea why it was so important.

She heard from behind her: "Put it around his neck!" and turned to stare at the man.

"No. There's no way I'm doing that!"

"Then I have to shoot him!" the old man held his gun ready. "You want that? He rescued you, remember!?"

He had. She remembered when the young pilot's handsome face had appeared on the steps when the general was holding her. She'd been sure then that she was about to die—but she hadn't. Her hand gripped the necklace.

If she could survive that, she could survive this.

The helicopter came to hover over a vast crater, which fell away below them into darkness.

"Hurry!" the man in the rear yelled: "We're almost out of fuel!"

"Why can't you just land?"

"He's jamming the pedals with his back paws! Autopilot should be in control, but he's too strong!"

Maxine crawled forward another foot. The thing had almost managed to chew through the webbed belt across its chest now. Once free of that, it could climb out from the lap belt, and kill them both—or the old man would shoot it. Either way, they'd probably crash.

Her hands moved forward as if of their own volition—closer to where the wolf-like head strained with the belt in its jaws. Closer.

Closer.

"C'mon!" she heard from behind her.

Another inch, and her hands were over its head. But just as she was going to put the chain around the thing's hairy neck, it sensed her, and lunged.

Maxine let out an involuntary scream, letting go of the necklace and falling back as the beast's teeth snapped at her. But she'd been close enough that as she dropped the necklace, it fell around the creature's head, the pendant coming to rest on its neck.

The change was rapid: within seconds, the eyes staring at her were no longer red and wild, but soft and blue once more. The handsome pilot was himself again, gasping for breath.

"Sai! Sai, let go of the pedals!" the old man yelled, and her rescuer seemed to come back to himself, like a man waking from a dream—or rather, a nightmare.

The helicopter began to lower down into the darkness of the magma chamber.

15.

The *Archimedes' Claw* sat dormant on its landing pad. The wolf had been quelled for the moment by the power of the amulet, so Gustavo and Maxine had been able to help Saigon John to his cell, closing and locking the time-locked door behind him. It would release at six o'clock AM, well after moonset. Before it closed, Sai had looked up at Gustavo, and nodded. Just a simple nod between friends, but Gustavo had understood the depth of what he was saying.

He now stood waiting for Lucius to arrive in his white Jeep. Maxine stood nearby, wrapped in a silver survival blanket and drinking coffee.

"So what now?" She asked him.

"What now what?"

"You're gonna fly with him again, after that?" she glanced back at the chopper.

"He's only a wolf once a month. The other days—"

"I know: he's the best."

Gustavo nodded.

"He is. He really is."

Down the mountain, he could see Lucius' vehicle approaching. ♜

NOVELTY

By Will McDermott

BRAD PICKED AT THE EGGS with his fork. Mom placed the two sunny-side-up eggs and strips of bacon to form a little smiley face on his plate, just like she had when he was a kid. But Brad didn't feel like smiling. Not today. Maybe not ever again.

The eggs mocked him with their bright, yellow orbs, a stark contrast to the red, bleary eyes he had seen in the mirror before coming down to breakfast. He stabbed them with his fork and smeared the runny yolk into the smiling bacon, forcing the ends of the strips down into a yolk-tear-stained frown.

"That's better," Brad mumbled before pushing the plate away.

"What's wrong, sweetie?" Mom asked.

Brad wanted to scream, but then he glanced at Mom and saw the same reddened, tear-soaked eyes on her face that had stared at him in the bathroom mirror. Brad might have lost his father, but Mom lost the love of her life. How could he scream at her for trying to make him feel better?

But how could he not scream at all? How could *she* not scream—at the world, at the injustice of it all, at just everything and everyone forever?

Brad thought about how he and his college friends had talked about how you could get a 4.0 for a semester if your roommate committed suicide. It was a bad joke spouted during the stress of midterms and finals weeks.

"Ha ha. I wish Frank would kill himself so I can pass Aero 202." Brad said during study group last semester. Not funny now.

Brad wouldn't be going back to school this semester. He couldn't concentrate on thrust percentages, lift ratios, and drag coefficients now. He would have to start sophomore year over if he ever felt ready to return to a normal life. And if he and Mom could afford it without Dad.

"Is there anything I can do to help you today, Mom?" Brad asked, realizing he had stared at her for more than minute since she asked if he was okay. "I need something to do. Something to keep my mind off Dad for a while."

"This isn't what I had in mind, Mom!" Brad complained as he looked at the wall of boxes in the garage. "I want to forget about Dad, just for a while. Not go through his old crap!"

"You asked what you could do to help," Mom replied, resolute. "This is what I need. Your dad kept everything he ever bought. Would never get rid of anything. I can't keep this house now, but I can't sell it until we clear out all this stuff."

Mom stared at Brad in the middle of the garage, arms crossed over her bathrobe in her best *do this now, mister* pose. She might have looked more commanding without the pale-pink bathrobe and matching slippers she'd worn all day, every day for the last week. Or if her hair didn't look like squirrels had nested there for a month.

After a moment, Mom relaxed a bit. She uncrossed her arms and held them out and open to Brad, although it seemed the weight of them would drag her already drooping shoulders down to the floor. Mom even tried to smile, but the sadness in her eyes seemed to push down on the corners of her mouth.

Brad relented and melted into the hug. It felt good, despite the weariness in their arms and their bodies.

"Don't ever forget your Dad," Mom said in Brad's ear. "Sift through his 'treasures' and try to remember the good times. You never know what you might find, what happy memory some piece of his junk might spark."

"You really want to get rid of all this stuff?" Brad asked after the hug ended and he faced the wall of boxes again.

"Most of it, yeah," Mom said. "But you can keep anything you want. Anything that reminds you what a wonderful father your dad was."

Brad smiled at his mom. She returned the smile, and this time it almost looked normal, as if some of the sadness had lifted.

Brad dug into his task with a zeal he hadn't felt since choosing a college. As with that task, he divided everything into three piles: keep, toss, and check with Mom. Most of this stuff was going in the toss pile, though. Dad had been a pack rat. There was no doubt about that. Not only did he have everything he had ever bought. He had the receipts for all of it, too.

Luckily, his dad was a meticulous hoarder. Every box was clearly labeled with year, place, and category. There were boxes Mom and Dad moved halfway across the country and back several times as they followed jobs from one city to another.

Brad found some treasures along the way, too. He found one box filled with clippings, ribbons, and team photos from when Brad played ball during summers.

Another box had photos of hunting trips and even a mounted set of antlers from the first – and only—deer Brad ever shot, which had all of four, six-inch-long points. Dad had loved hunting with Grandpa, so Brad indulged him that one time. It obviously had meant more to Dad than to Brad. He put the hunting trophy in the keep pile.

By midafternoon, Brad had dug down to the last few boxes, which contained stuff from when Dad had been a kid. He opened one box labeled 'toys' and found a cornucopia of vintage items from the 1980s.

Brad pulled the box into the only clear space in the garage between the enormous pitch pile and the much smaller keep and check piles. He sat down cross-legged and began pulling out toys his dad had played with when he was younger than Brad was now.

Every toy was a treasured memory. Some Dad had given Brad to play with before returning them to the box when Brad outgrew them. He remembered Dad on the floor of his room helping him set up the little green army men for pretend battles.

A tear welled up in Brad's eye as he held the bag aloft and turned it around and around. He placed the bag of army men atop the keep pile and reached back into the box, where he felt something round and squishy. It felt like a ball of worms.

"What the hell is this?" Brad wondered aloud as he pulled out a multi-colored ball of plastic strings that looked like one of those trippy afro wigs people wore to '70s-themed costume parties.

Brad dropped the hippy ball on the garage floor to see how high it would bounce, but it thudded with a dull clank, making the red, yellow, purple, and teal plastic strings shudder in a weird wave, like the three-dimensional ripples a large mass creates in space-time models.

"Huh," Brad muttered as he stared at the inert bounce-less ball. "Where is the fun in that? Maybe you need more force to get it to bounce."

Brad grabbed the hairy ball and stood. He took aim at a spot on the overhead garage door and went into a wind-up, pretending he was back on the mound again. Brad reared his arm back, twisting his torso around to put his weight behind the pitch, and flung the ball forward.

The weight, size, and drag of the ball threw his aim way off and the ball thudded against the concrete floor before ricocheting into the garage door where it clanged so loudly the ringing in Brad's ears lasted for a minute.

"What the hell?" Brad asked again as he rubbed his ears. He sat down and began rummaging through the folder of receipts tucked into the box with the toys.

Oddly, there was no receipt. Even the bag of army men had a receipt; it was old and faded and dated from 1972 from a store Brad had never heard of called Mr. Wiggs. But there was no receipt for the hairy, hippy ball.

Brad decided to put the ball in the 'ask mom' pile and move on, but he couldn't find it when he went to retrieve it. The ball must have rolled into the pitch pile. He looked around for a minute, poking his foot into the pile here and there where it might have rolled, but Brad couldn't find the ball.

Brad was just about to give up and let it go with the rest of the trash, when he heard a faint beep coming from the far side of the pile. Brad sidled around the pile, his butt up against the wooden shelves on the side of the garage, but he still didn't see the ball. It beeped again. He was closer but couldn't pinpoint it.

"This is like trying to find which smoke detector has a failing battery," Brad muttered, exasperated after several unsuccessful minutes tracking the intermittent beeping.

The next beep, though, pulled his attention to a faint red, blinking light tucked under the edge of the pile, right up against the leg of the wooden shelves.

Brad bent down as best he could in the cramped space and reached into the pile. Expecting to find the soft, plastic tendrils of the weird ball, Brad yelped when he sliced open the tip of his finger on raw metal.

"Ow! Damn! Mmmm!" Brad grimaced. A bright-red line of blood welled up atop his middle finger. He stuck the finger in his mouth to suck the blood off as he prodded at the pile with his shoe to dislodge whatever was stuck down there.

A moment later, he kicked the ball loose. it skittered across the concrete, spinning like a top, turning its blotches of colors into a weird, four-colored rainbow. When it came to a stop, Brad noticed the ball had cracked open, exposing two halves of a metal sphere at the core of the toy.

As he stared at the broken ball, his finger still stuck in his mouth, the red light flashed from inside the metal core at the same time Brad heard the faint beep again.

When he walked over to investigate, Brad opened his mouth in awe, releasing his still bleeding finger as his arm dropped to his side.

The one-inch diameter metal sphere held what Brad could only describe as a miniature cockpit. Several rows of tiny dials, knobs, and levers were arrayed in a semi-circle above two needle-sized flight sticks that jutted up in front of what looked like steel, Matchbox car seats.

What made Brad gasp, though, were the two delicate skeletons strapped into the tiny metal pilot chairs. The miniature pilots couldn't have been more than a half-inch tall, but their whitened bones stuck out from the tattered remains of intricate, little flight suits.

Decaying straps around the pilots' bulbous skulls held some sort of gas masks to their faces with hoses that connected to the console in front of them. One mask had rotted through, causing the hose to drop to the cockpit floor, exposing jutting bony features around the tiny alien's nose, chin, and ear holes.

And that's what they were, Brad realized: Aliens. Wasp-sized aliens who had once piloted a miniature spaceship disguised as a furry, children's toy ball.

"This is crazy," Brad said. "It must be a joke. The company that made these toys must have put these inside the balls to terrorize little kids who broke them open."

Of course, that didn't explain the red light blinking in the middle of the panel opposite the 'dead' pilots. That light had caught Brad's attention from across the garage. It was just a pinprick of a light but shone so brightly he couldn't look at it straight on.

Maybe it was an LED light. They were that small. But no, this ball had come from the 1980s box. They didn't have LED lights back then.

"I need to show this to Mom," Brad said. "At least that will tell me if I'm crazy or hallucinating."

Brad reached for the ball and cupped his hands around the two halves. The blinking light began to burn bright and steady as his fingers encircled the broken toy.

Brad ignored the light and picked up the ball, being careful not to dislodge the tiny pilots from their seats.

The light burned brighter and brighter, making Brad wince and squint as the laser-like ray almost blinded him as it flashed between his thumb and fingers. The light intensified suddenly, and Brad turned his head to move his eyes away from the intense beam.

"Ow! Wow!" Brad screamed.

A pinprick of red light burned through Brad's thumb, pierced his nail, and shot past his face. He blinked away the afterimage of the streaking light from his eyes as a lance of pain seared across his cheek.

Brad dropped the ball-ship and stared at the tiny hole in his thumbnail. Beads of blood welled up on the nail and more dripped onto his palm from his thumb tip. The light had burned straight through the thick digit. It really was a laser!

Worse still, an acrid aroma wafted through the air around Brad's face that smelled a like the charred skin on the chicken Mom had burned the night before while she cried in the bathroom.

Brad rubbed his sore cheek with his palm and felt something wet and sticky. When he pulled it away, his hand was covered with blood and pus and tiny flecks of blackened skin.

"What. The. Hell?" Brad yelled, followed quickly by "OW! Dammit!" He shuddered to think what would have happened if he hadn't flinched a moment before the laser fired.

Brad scrambled away from where he dropped the ball-ship, hoping to put some distance between himself and the alien's laser defense system. But as he backpedaled, Brad realized the broken ball no longer lay on the concrete.

"Oh, shit!" Brad hissed.

He continued backing away as he scanned the garage for the ball-ship. He couldn't see it anywhere, but the piles he had made while sorting made it impossible to see very far.

This could be a blessing Brad realized. If he could just keep the stacks of boxes between him and the deadly ball, maybe he could get to safety in the house and warn Mom.

Brad sidled around the three piles, constantly twisting his head around to catch a glimpse of the split-open, multicolored ball.

After making it to the other side of the garage, around two of the three piles, Brad had a clear shot to the kitchen door and still hadn't seen the broken ball anywhere.

Maybe that single laser beam shot had just been an automated defense system, Brad thought. The toy had been in that box for years, maybe decades. Any power the ship had left must have been minimal.

Brad was just about to make a mad dash for the door when he heard a whining hum above him. He ducked down into cover and looked up to catch a glimpse of the toy, fully reformed into a seamless sphere. It hovered in the air above the tall pitch pile, twisting and turning and darting about, as if searching for him.

The multicolored tendrils fluttered in a rhythmic dance as the ship darted around above the pile, almost as if they were part of the guidance system—like dozens of tiny ailerons providing lift, drag, and lateral force to maneuver the ball through space.

As the ball searched, Brad made a decision. The next time the ball darted away from the house, he ran for the door. Hearing the whirring behind him, Brad zig zagged as he ran. The laser cut into the concrete, burning long cracks into the cement to one side of his legs and then the other as he weaved.

He reached the door and pushed it open. Luckily it never latched completely unless you slammed it hard, which Brad did after sliding through into the kitchen.

"Bradley!" yelled Mom. "What have I told you about slamming doors?"

"Not now, Mom," Brad called back. "We're under attack."

"What happened to your face?" Mom screamed, finally looking up from her afternoon tea.

Brad didn't answer. He could hear the whirring sound of the ball-ship through the door. It was just on the other side. He snaked his hand toward the deadbolt.

"What's going on?" Mom demanded as Brad twisted the knob on the lock. "Brad? What's happen–"

A red beam sliced through the door just below the deadbolt and began arcing a path around the lock. The smell of burning wood filled the air as the laser cut a perfect half-circle through the door.

"Mom!" Brad yelled. "Run!"

He thrust his mother out of the kitchen into the family room. Behind him, Jack heard the deadbolt fall and clatter on the linoleum as he pushed his mother toward the hallway to the bedrooms.

"Into your room, Mom," Jack yelled, practically shoving her through the doorway. Close the door!"

Jack glanced back as he continued down the hallway. The ball flew out of the kitchen behind him, its tendrils undulating like octopus tentacles around the core.

Jack stopped outside his bedroom door and waited. He needed the ball to follow him, not Mom.

When the ball reached the middle of the family room, it hovered a moment before green beams spread out from its core. The beams scanned every corner of the room in a 360-degree arc, finding the TV, couches, photos on the walls, the front door—everything.

Several beams reached down the hallway, eventually lighting on Brad. As soon as the green beam, touched him, the rest of the beams coalesced into that one, which changed color, working through the spectrum from green to yellow to orange to…

Before the beam reached red, Brad dove into his room. Above him the red laser lanced through the door. It cut a swath through the wooden frame, the open door, and into the plaster wall before it stopped. As Brad scrambled across the floor toward his closet, the top of his door tumbled to the floor behind him, sliced clean through.

Brad glanced back to see a long gash scorched through his wall on either side of the severed door, right where his head had been a moment earlier.

"Holy crap!" Brad muttered as he pulled junk from the floor of his closet. "This better work!"

Brad tossed old toys, rumpled clothes, shoes, and literal trash behind him as he dug through the pile of stuff he'd left in his closet when he went off to college.

Sweat beaded on Brad's temple and slid into his eyes as the seconds ticked by. He glanced at the hallway—expecting the ball-ship to fly into his room at any moment—before returning to his frantic search for the only weapon he could think of.

Finally, his hand landed on something soft and firm in the back corner of his closet—his old ball glove. Brad pulled it into the light, dragging the aluminum bat shoved through the wrist strap along with it.

As Brad yanked the bat free of the glove, he heard his mom scream!

Brad ran from his room just in time to see the undulating fur on the ball slip through a hole in the door to his mom's bedroom.

"No, you don't!" It was supposed to follow *him,* not go after Mom.

He burst through the door into the darkened room. Mom hadn't opened the black-out drapes since Dad's death. The only light in the room came from the family room down the hall and Brad blocked most of that.

The ball-ship fixed that problem for Brad, though, as it began scanning the room with its 360-degree green beams. Brad ducked and rolled, tucking the baseball bat into his gut, as the beams lanced toward him.

The beams continued searching, turning to yellow and then orange as they narrowed down to a 90-degree arc focused on where Brad had been, but his roll had taken him beside the bed, shielding him from the ship's scans.

Well, he had its attention now, Brad realized. But it would cut him down before he even got close if he got caught in those orange beams. He glanced under the bed to see if he could crawl through, but the frame was too low. He was trapped.

He did see Mom crouched on the other side, though. She curled her lips into a weak, almost straight, and sad smile. At least she was okay, but Brad had run out of ideas. They were both going to die.

Brad heard the whirring of the ball-ship moving above the bed and realized it was moving toward his side. As soon as those orange beams touched him, they would turn red. He gave Mom a thumbs-up and gripped the bat as he prepared to spring to his feet.

As the orange beams crested the mattress, Brad heard Mom scramble to her feet on the other side of the bed.

"Hey, Ass-Ball!" she yelled. "Over here!"

The tendrils undulated around the ball above Brad as the orange beams narrowed, reddened, and revolved around the room. The red beam cut a gash through the bedroom walls, door, and frame. The laser sliced right through Dad's dresser as it arced around the room toward Mom.

Mom screamed and Brad heard her feet pound the carpet as she bolted for the master bath. But Brad didn't think she would make it, and he knew the walls wouldn't be any protection even if she did.

He sprang to his feet behind the beam, cocked the bat behind his shoulder and swung as hard as he could.

Brad had solely been a pitcher by the time he reached high school, so hadn't really practiced batting since little league. He'd had dreams of being another Babe Ruth – both a pitcher and a slugger—but he'd never been that great a hitter.

Still, a floating ball at shoulder height was pretty hard to miss.

Brad's bat sliced through the rippling tendrils and hit a glancing blow against the metal core, sending the ball-ship spinning to the floor in the back of the room, behind the bed.

Brad ran to the bathroom to check on Mom. She stood at the counter, rummaging through a drawer. She looked up when Brad reached the door.

"Is it over?" she asked.

"I don't know," Brad replied. "Maybe? I think so. I'd better bash it a few more times to be sure."

As Brad turned to search for the furry ball, the orange beams arced up from the floor beside the bed. The beams scanned his body from feet to head before settling between his eyes.

The orange beams narrowed and darkened again, but Brad was transfixed. The shock of the morning's events had finally overwhelmed him. He was rooted to the spot, unable to move.

"Brad!" screamed Mom.

The prismatic rays merged into a single, bright red laser beam.

A blur of motion from the side caught Brad's attention as Mom jumped in front of him.

"Mom! No!"

The laser shot forth, striking Mom.

Or so it seemed.

Mom stood her ground, unharmed by the lethal laser. A moment later, the room erupted in a blinding flash of light that turned everything white.

When Brad could see again, his mom turned to give him a hug. In her hands, he saw what she had been searching for in the bathroom: Her hand mirror.

He looked at the ball on the floor, which sizzled as electricity crackled along the severed edges of its two halves. The reflected beam had cut through the ship, slicing it—and its skeletal pilots—in half.

"What the hell?" Mom said after their hug. She bent down to look at the long dead remains of the tiny alien pilots.

"Automated defense system?" Brad asked, shrugging. "The thing broke open in the garage and then came to life, beeping and blinking before it attacked."

"We better call the cops," Mom said as they left the bedroom.

"Or maybe MIB?" Brad offered. He had no idea what authority would even believe them.

"And a contractor," Mom added as she surveyed the damage in the hallway.

Mom stopped to run her hands along the cracked plaster where the laser had gone through her bedroom wall as Brad headed toward the family room to grab the phone.

"What worries me," Mom said behind him, "is that thousands—or tens of thousands of these cushy ball toys were sold back in the '80s. Were they all tiny alien spaceships?"

"Maybe," Brad whispered as he stopped dead in the middle of the family room. Outside the picture window he saw dozens of floating balls, their multicolor tendrils all undulating in unison as they hovered in the front yard.

Mom handed Brad the hand mirror and turned to head back down the hallway.

"Where are you going, Mom?" Brad asked.

"To the den to get your dad's hunting rifle." ♛

LATE NIGHT RERUNS

By Bryan Young

Content Warning: This story contains depictions and hints of child abuse, scary settings, the supernatural, and murder.

MICHAEL LAY AWAKE IN BED, covered in a blanket adorned with characters from his favorite Saturday morning cartoon. They could save the sewers and the streets of New York, but they weren't real and couldn't save him.

He had hoped that when his family moved, things would change. Maybe a new house and more room would help calm his dad down, but there was something wrong with his father. And there was something wrong with the house, too. He couldn't quite tell what it was, but he felt something there. He knew things moved inside it at night. He heard them. Creaks in the walls. Cold spots when he crept to the bathroom in the middle of the night. The hairs on his neck would stand on end.

The skittering that kept him awake that night echoed from beneath his bed.

He assumed this was common to children since he'd seen it in so many movies. They were always afraid of something under the bed, but the movies and the shows never understood how much scarier his parents' room was.

That's where the real danger was.

Even if there were ghosts under the bed, they couldn't hurt him more than his father.

When the shuffle of something—or someone—walking beneath his bed sounded, displacing toys and crinkling papers, he couldn't help but yelp. A deep and desperate cry for help he knew would never come.

The help was always worse than the thing he was scared of.

Michael covered his mouth, hoping he'd suppressed enough of the noise so that no one, not the thing under his bed, nor his parents, might have heard him.

But when he saw the crack of yellow light brighten beneath his closed door and the heavy footsteps, he knew that the worst had happened.

The door swung open, and he flinched, pulling his head beneath the covers and doing his best to lay perfectly still, pretending to sleep.

"What's wrong, baby?" came the soothing voice of his mother. Relief washed over him.

Things would get a lot worse for everyone if he'd woken his father.

"I heard a noise," he said, slowly lowering the blanket to uncover his eyes. "Like it was under my bed."

"It's okay, baby, there aren't any monsters in your room." Michael's mother was little more than a black silhouette in the bright corona of the hall light. He couldn't make out any of her kindly details and assumed that she could have been as annoyed as much as concerned.

"I know," Michael said softly. "I'm sorry."

Fear gripped the little boy once more when he heard another voice. Distant and angry, calling from the next room. "What the hell does he want?"

His father.

"It's okay, baby," his mother whispered, caressing the hair from Michael's eyes. He flinched at her touch. "There's no one here to hurt you."

"He needs to just be a man and suck it up!" came the distant voice again. "Now get back to bed before I get upset!"

Michael didn't know if his father was yelling at him or his mother. There was never a way to tell. Everything was a shout, and every move could have been Michael's last.

"Can you leave the door open and the light on?"

He still couldn't quite see her face through the glare, just a black void, but he saw her look back and consider it. Maybe she bit her lip, unable to decide. "You know how that upsets your father…"

"Just for the night? Please?"

"All right. I'll try to make sure I'm up before him and get the light turned off and your door closed."

She leaned in to hug Michael awkwardly, but the affection was better than the alternatives that kept running through Michael's mind, so he accepted it gratefully, hoping there were no more accidental outbursts of his own.

91

When his mother left, she left the door open as promised, but he heard some heated exchange and then the light shut off.

Laying in the dark, Michael hoped that would be the end of it.

He tried to get to sleep. He really did. He closed his eyes. He tossed and turned. But with the light off and the door open, it only made things worse. He thought about getting up and closing the door himself, but then he'd make enough noise to wake his father and that would have been bad for everyone.

After what felt like an eternity, he heard the high-pitched whine of the television turning on in the next room. The blue glow lit up the darkened hallway, just enough for him to see the details of the hall and make sure his father wasn't coming for him.

With that little extra bit of help and the hint of blue light from the television, Michael was finally able to drift to sleep despite the creeping sounds from inside his closet, beneath his bed.

And he could quiet the voice of his father in his mind enough to get some rest.

#   #   #

Breakfast came early in the Freeling household. Michael's mother worked quick to make sure the bacon was crisp and the pancakes sizzled. It didn't do anyone any good if Michael's father was grumpy in the morning. A grumpy dad turned into an angry dad mighty quick, and everyone was already on thin ice with him in the mornings as it was.

He arrived, dressed in jeans and a t-shirt, wearing his construction company's ballcap. His eyes were narrowed, already upset and suspicious about something.

"Why are you sneaking out at night, Michael?" he said, his tone grave.

Michael's stomach tightened and his breath suddenly felt as if it were being sucked through a straw. Michael put his fork down, even though it was loaded with a chunk of syrup-dripped pancake. He lowered his head and avoided eye contact; his father took direct eye contact as something of a challenge. Even from a seven year old. Michael tried to suck down another deep breath and calm himself before tears started leaking from his eyes. Crying set his father off as well. All he had to do was tell the truth and he'd be okay. The truth would always win. That's what they said, right? "I wasn't, sir," he said softly.

"If it wasn't you, then who was it?"

"I was in bed all night, promise. I didn't even get up to pee until the sun came up." Michael realized his tone became more pleading. But he was telling the truth, and that should have been enough.

"Then why was the TV on this morning? You think we have money to waste on all that extra power? Who is going to pay for it? Are you, Michael? Are you going to pay for it when we can't afford our power bill anymore? Are you going to go out and get a job when we're out on the street?"

Michael froze.

That was a lot, and he didn't know how to respond. He was too young for a job and surely his father must have known that. But he didn't know anything about how the TV turned on. He didn't do it himself. "It wasn't me, sir," Michael said, meek as a church mouse.

"Carol," Michael's father said, looking up to his wife. She stood dutifully behind the counter, putting the finishing touches on his elaborate breakfast. "You didn't turn the television on last night, did you?"

"No," she said, delivering the plate of breakfast and a steaming hot cup of coffee in front of her husband.

Maybe she thought the food would mollify him, like music for savage beasts.

But he didn't even notice.

"There are only three of us here in this house. And I know I didn't do it. And your mom said she didn't do it. And I know it wasn't the dog. Are you calling her a liar?"

Michael assumed it had been his mother who turned the television set on to help with the light since she'd been forced to turn off the hall light. But he trusted her well enough to know she was telling the truth. He also knew that if he called his mother a liar, his father would turn into King Kong, beating his chest and then beating Michael's.

"No, sir."

"Why were you watching the television?"

Instead of accepting the blame directly and lying to his father, which he had been told would result in worse things than telling the truth, no matter how incriminating it might be, he shrugged his shoulders. Maybe that would be taken as somewhere between the two.

Michael's father folded his hands together with his elbows up on the table. His anger rose as his knuckles turned white and his jaw tightened. "I need you to listen to me and I need you to listen well, Michael, that if you do that one more time, if you sneak out and turn on the television in the middle of the night to watch it just once more, you will not like the consequences. Do you understand me?"

Michael nodded.

Of course, he understood him.

It meant getting yanked by the ears. Or slapped. Or spanked with a switch. Or held down and screamed at. Held down by the neck. The last time it had happened, his father left a purple bruise on Michael's neck. His mother kept him wearing high collared shirts and turtlenecks until it faded.

"Say it," Michael's father said.

"Yes, I understand you, sir."

"Good." Michael's father clenched his jaw and picked his piece of bacon. "I'd hate to have to discipline you again, but you never really leave me a choice."

"Yes, sir."

Just as he took the first bite of his bacon, a quiet beep emanated from Michael's father's watch. "Damn it," he said through a mouthful of crispy bacon.

"Time to get to work, honey?" Michael's mother said in as cheerful a voice as she could.

"Yes," he growled, rising from his chair.

With one hand, he rolled up his pancake and took it with him. With the other hand, he pointed a threatening finger at Michael. "You don't make me late again. You understand me?"

Then, Michael's father snatched Michael's plate of food and took it into the kitchen. Dumping the food in the garbage, he looked back to Michael with a stone face. "If I miss breakfast, so do you."

Then he was gone.

Michael had to leave for school then, too, and he hoped the school would be a respite, despite his rumbling stomach.

But it wasn't the first time he'd gone to school hungry before, and for similar reasons.

Michael's mother just sighed and told him not to be late as he walked out the door.

The last thing either of them needed was Michael's father getting a call from the school that afternoon to let him know Michael had been tardy.

Pulling his backpack's straps tight over his shoulders, Michael headed out, hoping the day would get better.

#   #   #

Michael finished his homework and ate dinner without incident, but something in the house—some presence—made him feel uneasy about going to bed. Like he was going to get in trouble.

It didn't come from anywhere in particular. It just sat there, across everything, weighing down on his chest like an elephant. He was grateful he could just go to bed without an argument from his father, who was too busy

94

drinking beer and watching television.

And then Michael lay there again.

In the dark.

Alone with the sounds. The shuffling skitter of big feet, too big for under his bed or in his closet. Something was there. He knew it.

Faintly, through his closed door, he heard a television program of some sort. It was Thursday night, so it was probably one of his dad's favorite shows, which explained why Michael had been dismissed for bed so early. Every few moments, he could hear the television audience laugh, and then his father would punctuate that with raucous laughter of his own.

But above that, the room had its own sounds.

Yes, there were the sounds of the house settling and creaking. From the corner of Michael's eyes, he thought he saw the flicker of candlelight, but when he moved his head in the direction to see, the flash of light had vanished.

"What's wrong with me?" Michael asked when he thought he saw a face in the closet, peering out at him with bright yellow eyes and even brighter sharp teeth.

"Nothing," the monster answered in a matter-of-fact voice.

Michael flinched and buried his head beneath his pillow.

"It's not real," he whispered into the bed.

It was just the shapes of his clothes and the light from outside playing tricks.

He'd just imagined the voice speaking to him.

Laying there in the dark beneath the blanket, Michael tried to blank his mind and the pictures of horror playing inside it. He wanted so badly for all of it to go away. He plugged his ears and knew that none of it was real.

But, over the din of his father's obscene laughter, he heard one of his windup toys activate, crawling across the floor with a spark of light.

Michael covered his mouth in the hopes of not screaming.

If he interrupted his father's show, that would be the end of the night, and no one would get any sleep. It would be a family fight until sunrise. His father would wrestle him to the ground and shout like a monster, his mother would cry and cower in the corner, unable or unwilling to do anything to help him, and they would carry on like that until Michael had apologized at least a thousand times from the perceived slight.

No.

Michael had to remain silent.

Turning over to cover his stomach and the softest parts of his body, Michael wondered what it was that had spoken to him.

But he got distracted.

95

The tell-tale whine of the television tube winked off and the angry footsteps of his father marched through the hallway on his way to bed.

His parents shouted at each other in the distance.

He couldn't even make out the words, just their angry, combative tone. He wished the pillow could have filtered all of the sound and he could float like a spaceman in a void of peaceful silence.

But that was not the case.

He had to listen to every agonizing shout between them.

Finally, the light in the hallway winked off and his room darkened even further. Tentatively, Michael peeked his head out from beneath the pillow and looked around. First to the door to make sure the lights in the rest of the house were off and his parents were likely asleep. Then to the phantom in the closet. Michael could make out their bright eyes and face again, but they must have closed their mouth, because he could no longer see the glimmering zipper of teeth. Finally, he looked down to his toys on the floor. The one toy that had crawled across the room seemed to have changed direction and it was aimed right at the door.

Michael shivered when he looked over.

The faint blue light shone in the hallway beneath the crack of his door.

Someone had turned the television on again.

But Michael knew his parents were asleep.

He could feel it.

"Did you do that?" he asked the closet monster.

And for just a moment, he saw the flash of light that made it look as though the creature were smiling.

Michael sighed.

He was going to have to turn the television off if he wanted to make it to school the next day. And school was the only place he felt at least a little safe. Lonely, but safe.

But he would have to be so quiet.

Carefully, Michael kicked the blanket from his body and took an uneasy step onto the carpet. Every ounce of weight he put on his feet felt like more danger weighing him down. But he was on a mission, and he couldn't fail.

He heard the faint jingle of the television station.

The oldies one that played old black and white TV shows.

Michael took a step toward the door...

...and so did the toy, the little robot on two mechanical feet. It activated with the sound of a beep and a laser, and Michael thought his heart might stop.

He pounced on the robot immediately, keeping it from making it any closer to the door.

Michael ripped the batteries out of the robot.

Silence came back to the room, aside from the hum of the television outside.

He waited, listening hard for any signs of his father.

After another eternity, Michael felt like the coast was clear. He left the robot on the floor and approached the door, slowly twisting the knob and pulling the door open quietly, doing his best to keep the hinges from squeaking. If there was anything his father could pick out, it was the sound of a door opening when it wasn't supposed to. That was why Michael figured his father insisted that he keep his door closed, so that if it were to open, he'd be alerted quickly.

With his door open, the sound of the television grew louder, but still not terribly recognizable. The voices on the show were a dull roar, indistinct like his parents had been. Michael looked back and forth in the hallway. The faint glow of the television beat against the door to his parent's room at the end of the hall. It flashed as the scene changed and got bright and he knew the light spilled into their room at the bottom of the door. He had to hurry.

Michael tiptoed into the living room, which was already a forbidden jungle to him. He was not allowed in the room without the express permission and supervision of his father, so being in there without his watchful gaze somehow made him feel more uncomfortable than if his father had been there.

Looking up to the TV, Michael saw a man in black and white, staring at him from inside a muted gray room.

"Good evening," the man said.

"Shhh." Michael raised a finger to his lips.

"Oh, yes," the man said in a quieter voice. "Of course. We wouldn't want to disturb anyone, though that seems to be the order of the day for every story we tell here."

Like a cat, Michael padded closer to the television, reaching out toward the dial.

But he was cut off by the man inside. "Do not adjust your television set," he said. "Everything is exactly as we have set it for our own nefarious purposes."

Concern grew on Michael's face, tightening it at the brows. Without waiting for the man to say another word in his British accent, Michael touched the button to turn the television off, but nothing happened. The light remained and so did the man.

"It won't work," the man said. "Everything is just so."

Michael reached up, covering over the man's face with his own hand against the screen.

"That won't work either," the man said. "And would you please be so kind as to remove your hand from my face?"

Michael pulled his hand back, an electrical shock arced from the TV to his tiny fingers. He looked at his hand, then back to the TV, and then he didn't remember anything else.

Darkness took him.

#   #   #

"What the hell is this?" Michael's father said.

Michael awoke with a start, yanked by his arms off the ground.

He'd almost forgotten where he was, but found himself in the morning, curled up in front of the living room television, fast asleep. The TV played nothing but snowy static.

"I don't..." Michael said, but a slap across the face stopped him.

"I thought I told you what the consequences would be if you pulled this shit one more time. Just once. You think I'm playing? You think this is a game?"

Tears dripped from Michael's eyes and breathing got hard again. Michael's chest tightened in a vise, and he didn't know what to do. His arm, hyperextended above his head, hurt almost as bad as the sting across his cheek.

Michael tried not to think too hard about what happened next. He didn't know how to tell his father that it wasn't what it looked like. He didn't know how to tell his father that the TV had done it itself and he'd tried to turn it off.

Before he could say a word through sobbing tears, Michael's father growled, "Why are you crying? I'm the one who is wronged here. If you want something to cry about, I'll give you something to cry about."

#   #   #

Michael didn't go to school that day.

He found himself locked in his room without meals.

As penance for the crime he committed.

He didn't think he'd be able to go to school as it was. He couldn't think about much without crying. And he was scared, too. For a time, in the hours of the afternoon, he inspected his closet, trying to find the buttons and zippers and folds of clothes that made it seem as though that face had been present, but try as he might, he couldn't figure out the puzzle. He put the batteries back in the robot and tried to coax it to move by itself again, but, for the life of him, he couldn't. For a long time, he tried to hide under the blankets. He fell asleep a few times. He tried to read a book, but that put him to sleep even more fitfully throughout the day.

It was difficult to keep track of time locked inside his haunted room. The only thing could tell was when it had gotten dark.

His father had unlocked the door long enough to march him to the bathroom to pee and brush his teeth, then march him back and lock the door behind him.

Michael made sure not to say anything, but that didn't stop the occasional flinch and whimper when his father raised his hands too quickly. That always elicited a growl from his father.

"Get to sleep," his father said, depositing him back inside of his room. "And if this shit happens again, it's going to be a lot worse than a day in your room. You understand me?"

Michael nodded. Then, before he could be reminded, he eked out a small, "Yes, sir. I understand."

"Good. Now get to sleep."

The door closed. A key hit the lock and trapped Michael inside the room. He couldn't figure out why it was so easy to fall asleep in the room during the day, but now that night had fallen, it felt so much more frightening.

Looking up to the closet, Michael found the face so much more pronounced. He'd even rearranged all the clothes in the closet just so this wouldn't happen with the tricks of the light, but the face was still there, grinning its toothy grin.

"What do you want?" Michael asked, hoping he'd receive no answer.

But a low, grumbling voice that could have been his father's from the next room said a word that Michael could have sworn was, "Blood."

Michael buried his head in the covers and pillows again, wondering when a good spirit would haunt him. Why did they all have to be bloodthirsty monsters?

He couldn't tell if their new house was really haunted or if it was just his eyes playing tricks on him. His head was stuffed, and his eyes were itchy from crying all day and he knew that could have caused some sort of hallucinations, right? Maybe he was dreaming. That could have been it. There was no way the man in the television was talking to him because he had been dreaming. It was a dream. But if it were a dream, why did he wake up in the living room in front of the television again?

He couldn't understand.

"Because you're not dreaming," another voice said.

Michael looked around for it until he decided it was a voice in his own head telling him that. Surely. There was no one there.

The house was deathly silent.

He must have fallen asleep for at least some time because it suddenly felt like the middle of the night. The noises of the house settling were more pronounced. Hinges squeaked from outside the window. And suddenly he became very cold.

Michael pulled the blanket tighter, hoping it would all go away if his eyes were shut tight enough.

But he couldn't keep them closed when he heard the faint sound of a key scraping into the lock of his bedroom door. Michael looked over and saw the knob twist ever so slowly. His mother didn't have a key to his room, so unless she suddenly got braver than she'd ever been, it wasn't her.

That left his father.

But as the door crept open, there stood no one.

The key was in the lock without a hand to turn it.

And then the blue glimmer of the television snapped on.

Michael's eyes widened.

The robot started again, noiselessly this time, but with its flashing lights and whirring motor, carrying itself toward the door, as if it were a fairy beckoning Michael to follow.

Feeling like he didn't have a choice, Michael got out of bed and slowly moved toward the hallway, half-convinced it was a trap.

He could imagine his father hiding on the other side of his wall, waiting for Michael to foolishly leave the room and then get himself into even more trouble.

"You should have stayed in bed!" he could practically hear his father shouting inside his head.

But the hallway was clear.

The glow of the television called him closer.

And the same old man waited for him with a grayscale smile. "Good evening."

Michael said nothing as he approached.

"There comes a time in the life of every person where murder seems to become a viable option," the man said. "Sometimes, these are crimes of passion, other times they are of opportunity. Sometimes, they are meant to right a wrong."

Those last three words sort of echoed in Michael's head as he got closer and closer.

"Sometimes, though not often, they can be all three," the man said in his proper accent. He kept his hands behind his back to show off his perfectly tailored suit and black tie.

"But what if an opportunity presented itself to you? Would you take it?"

Michael looked down to see a broad kitchen knife glistening in the light of the television.

"That's what our story is about this evening, and I do hope you enjoy it. It's about a young boy who finds that he's been asked to deal with far too much and finds a mysterious way out. And with that, I leave you..."

The screen faded to black and then to the snow of a dead station.

The reflection of the snow danced across the knife's blade.

Michael stared at it, wide-eyed, mesmerized, hypnotized.

He didn't know what to do.

But when he blinked, the knife was in his hands.

Behind him, he heard a creak of hinges and the unmistakable swish of his parents' bedroom door. But there was no sign of them. As far as he could tell, they were both fast asleep without a care in the world.

And suddenly, he knew exactly what to do.

Standing over his sleeping father, knife in hand, Michael felt like a vengeful spirit.

"Be careful," a grim voice said, "the knife is sharp."

Michael gripped it tighter.

"Just drag across the throat and it's over."

Michael loved his father.

And he didn't know if he could do it.

But sometimes love hurt.

And if there was anything his father could understand, it would be that.

"Now, before he wakes up," came another voice.

"We'll take care of him," a third voice hissed.

A light breeze picked up through the room, a vortex of evil energy. And Michael couldn't make a choice.

But when his father's eyes opened and took in the scene, a snarl appeared on his lips. Before his father had a chance to speak, the knife practically moved itself, cutting the life from his father's throat.

Blood spurted in a fountain in time with the beat of his father's wrathful, loving heart.

Michael paused, ready to cry.

His father was dying.

Bad as he was, Michael loved him. He was his father. Wasn't everyone's father like this? Michael had believed that everyone lived like this. It wasn't any better or worse for him. And now he'd killed his father. But, strangely, for the first time in a long time, Michael felt like he was going to be okay.

He looked over to his mother, sleeping peacefully. She wouldn't have a care in the world any longer either.

"And there you have it, friends," came the stuffy voice from the

101

television as Michael's father clutched his throat, gurgling. "The opportunity to strike at evil presented itself, and the young boy made his bloody choice."

"But what happens next?" another voice asked.

"We turn off the television," the British man said.

The faint blue light winked off against the blood.

Darkness returned.

And Michael smiled. ♜

THE DONJON

By John Pritchard

SOMEONE IN THE LAST VILLAGE had told him that he'd know which way the Hell-column had passed as much by the trail of bodies they left behind them as by the light of the things they'd set on fire.

He knew he was getting close when he heard the shooting: a crackle of muskets in the wintry dusk. He could smell burnt wood and the sulfur-stench of powder. The body of some passer-by lay face-down in the ditch.

He gave the corpse a glance as he rode past it, then peered ahead along the muddy road. His horse was plodding slowly but he sensed its wariness as the smell of fire got in its nostrils. He tightened his gloved hands around the reins. He wore a cocked hat and a caped black greatcoat. The hat sported a tricolor cockade, the insignia of the revolutionary vanguard.

It was a mark of blood and terror now.

The previous year, the west of France had risen in rebellion. The Royalists had been defeated. Now the Blues were taking their revenge, burning and slaughtering their way across the Vendée region in formations called Infernal Columns. The villages in their path had been laid waste.

A little further on, an unlit building loomed up against the ashen evening sky. It looked to be an inn. The door stood open, but no traveler would feel welcome here. The place had a gloomy, desolated air as if the winter wind had blown right through it and stripped away all trace of warmth and life. The rider stopped outside and stared towards it.

Then someone barked an order and a ragged crash of muskets split the dusk.

The horse gave a start, and the rider drew the reins taut while he murmured to it soothingly. The volley had come from the far side of the house. He heeled his mount around the corner to the stable yard, and a bank of fog rolled out to greet him, stinking of bad eggs. Ragged figures showed through it like scarecrows round a bonfire. The dense smoke dissipated slowly, and he saw the soldiers in the yard.

They turned towards him, bringing up their muskets. The barrels might be empty, but the bayonets were fixed. The man glanced at the bodies lying crumpled by the wall.

"Citizen!" a rough voice called. "What is your business here?"

"I'm looking for the general," the man said. There was silence for a moment. Then the soldier who had spoken came across, suspicion written on his face. "What kind of accent's that? You speak French like a foreigner. Get off that horse and let me see your pass."

The man dismounted easily and reached into his greatcoat, aware of the soldiers closing in. The last light glinted on their bayonets. They looked like vagabonds conscripted to a poor man's army. The one who'd spoken was a sergeant, shabby like the rest, but self-assured.

He took the folded paper he was offered and squinted at it fiercely. The rider wondered if the man could read. One of the others moved in close and lifted a dark lantern. The sergeant looked up from the paper, studying the man in front of him.

The lantern's glow showed a set face with a wry twist to the mouth, a sardonic challenge in the cool blue eyes. The horseman had fair hair which brushed his collar.

"What are you – an Austrian?"

"American," the man said evenly.

"And what would an American be doing in our country?"

"You helped us with our Revolution. Maybe I can do the same for yours."

The sergeant didn't seem impressed. "This paper tells me nothing. Perhaps you robbed a patriot's body for that decoration on your hat. How do I know that you're not with the brigands?"

"I have another pass," the horseman said.

He reached into his coat again as the sergeant's bleak face twisted, defying the stranger to offer him a bribe. Next moment he was staring at a double-barreled weapon which the other man had jabbed into his gut. The sergeant froze and felt his stomach cringe against his backbone as the right-hand cock was thumbed back with a click. He looked up at the other's face with its hint of grim amusement.

"This is good for clearing obstacles," said the American.

The gun was a fine fowling piece, its steel inlaid with silver – the sporting weapon of an *aristo*. But no *aristo* would countenance the way it had been treated. The barrels had been sawed down to half their length, so the gun could be readily concealed, and when fired at close range its shot would scatter murderously wide.

"So," the sergeant said after a moment. "No servant of the Royalists would do *that* to so elegant a piece." The ring of bayonets had tightened round them, like the jaws of a giant trap about to spring. He waved them back with a show of irritation. The pressure of the twin barrels relented graciously.

"I've a feeling the general might like to meet you," the sergeant went on, veiling his relief. "Come on, then... Citizen. He's at the chateau. If you're lucky, you'll get a bowl of soup while he hears your traveler's tales."

#   #   #

Elise had been praying for hours now. What else could a girl do when she'd been captured by a band of devils who might have their way with her at any time?

The soldiers who had marched into the district had shot almost every man who crossed their path, but they'd rounded the younger women up and put them in this house – "for your own protection," so they'd been assured. Elise had not believed that for a moment, not even when they'd been invited to have coffee with the officers. It had been a scene of skin-crawling politeness: those rough men who had risen from the ranks feeling a curious need to mimic the old order, having scarcely washed the fresh blood off their hands.

The women had been too afraid to say much, resisting the crude blandishments and cringing in the chilly candlelight. But then Catherine, the miller's headstrong daughter, had slapped away a lieutenant's groping hand. He'd simply dragged her from her chair and out into the passage. Elise had listened to her screams as she stared into her coffee's bitter dregs. When the women were taken back upstairs, they had passed her crumpled body. Her dress had mostly been torn off, and he'd used a bayonet to finish her.

The sight seemed fixed behind Elise's eyelids, so she tried to focus on the cross instead. It was on the wall of the house's private chapel, and she knelt before it on the cold stone floor. The little room was full of drafts and shadows which threatened to overwhelm her candle's flame. The plain metal cross barely showed up in the dimness. She gazed up at it through a veil of tears.

One of the soldiers had let her use the chapel. She could smell his pipe tobacco. He was waiting just beyond the open door. Was he kinder-hearted

105

than the rest, she wondered? Or would he expect some payment in return?

Her clasped hands tightened in her lap. Her lips moved silently as she begged for help from her fellow-virgin. *Pray for us now and at the hour of our death, amen.*

Catherine's body floated like a drowned swan in the darkness. Elise blinked the image from her streaming eyes and concentrated on the cross. Her vision was distorted, her tears tinged with the candle's trembling light. But when she blinked again, she saw it wasn't an illusion. Her prayer stopped and her eyes grew wide.

The cross above her had begun to glow.

#   #   #

"Well then, Citizen Berger," said the general at length. "What brings you all the way from Paris, never mind from your United States?"

Berger was just finishing a bowl of greasy stew, while the officers round the table were already on their brandy and cigars. He kept chewing for a moment, as if considering the question, then raised his eyes.

"A mission to retrieve some valuables."

The room was cold and dim, despite the light of sundry lanterns and the candelabra on the table. Berger hadn't taken off his coat, and the sawed-off fowling piece still nestled under his left armpit. He wore his shabby gloves and scarf as well.

"You'll be lucky," said the general. He was a grizzled man, his face gnarled by weather and experience. "Our orders are clear: to wipe out this whole region. To put even the woodland to the torch. Any valuables my men don't get their hands on are well hidden."

"And yet," said Berger lightly, "there are priceless items in this very house."

The officers stared at him. "What information do you have?" the general asked, his gaze intense. "Some treasure hidden here? By a supporter of that brigand rabble?"

Berger smiled fleetingly. "It wouldn't be much help to them, I guess." He reached for his glass of wine. "This house has quite a reputation – not least for its extensive library. Some of the books are very old and contain a deal of knowledge. The Committee of Public Safety would prefer to have them under its control."

The general gave a snort. "They sent you all this way for *paper*? My men can line their clogs with it and wipe their arses too. The other pages will feed the flames when we burn this place behind us. The Royalists won't read a word of them."

106

"Well, General, I can see you're a no-nonsense kind of man. I like that. But I have my orders too. There are one or two rare volumes that they want to see in Paris. If you'd kindly let me spend a few hours in the library, I'll take what I need and be on my way by sunrise."

"And they ask this in the middle of a war!" The general shook his head and swirled his brandy round the glass.

"Goldilocks!" shouted an aide, "come clear the meal away."

After a pause, a young blonde woman came into the room, looking as nervous as a deer walking into a wolf's lair. Giving the officers a wide berth, she picked up Berger's bowl. He glanced at her. Her eyes were green. They watched him warily. The corners of her mouth seemed to quirk naturally upward, as if she had an easy smile. But he guessed she hadn't smiled in quite some time.

"More wine, sir – I mean, Citizen?" Her voice was low and husky.

He shook his head and watched her all the way back to the door.

"She's pretty, that one," said the general. "I think we'll keep her."

"What knowledge do these books hold, then?" one of the others asked.

"Secret writings. Rituals," said Berger.

"So. A conspiracy of the Church?"

"The opposite, I'd say. Maybe you've heard about the lord who once lived in these parts. Gilles de Rais. A child-murderer. A black magician. Hanged in the fifteenth century. But some of the books he used have been preserved."

He took a sip of wine. The soldiers watched him, as if not certain that they'd heard him right. One gave a shrug. "A dead man's books. What of them?"

"Could be your Committee's wondering what power they really have. De Rais claimed he had summoned up a demon. Imagine if the Royalists could strike a deal with one."

"Pah!" The general leaned forward and stubbed his cigar out on the tabletop. "What are they thinking of, to believe such peasant superstitions?"

"Do the peasants believe them?" Berger asked. "Perhaps that's all that counts."

"Perhaps." The general sat back and eyed him balefully. "Listen to me, Citizen. You fancy that you come from the New World – but over there it's still the year seventeen-hundred and ninety-four. Over here, it's Year Two. *Our* world is new as well."

Berger inclined his head, allowing that.

"And the things we've done to make that world... The work we're doing now.... Whatever these books of yours contain, they're children's bedtime tales compared to that."

The American nodded and wiped his mouth. It occurred to him to wonder who the blonde girl was, and if she'd cross his path again tonight.

"Well, Citizens," he said, "if you'll excuse me, I think I should find out for myself. If you'd direct me to the library...?"

"It's upstairs," said an officer, "on the first floor of the annex between the main house and the dungeon."

Berger frowned, momentarily confused. Surely the dungeon was underground. But then it dawned on him that he'd misunderstood the other's French. The word the officer had used was *donjon*.

The annex between the main house and *the keep*.

#   #   #

Danielle went slowly up the stairs, still nauseous with fear. The drafty house was cold enough, but her skin felt colder still. The soldiers let her move around the place like a tame servant, but she knew she was a prisoner and – like Catherine – could be snuffed out on a whim.

Though she'd grown up locally, she'd never been inside this house, and not just because it was too grand a place for a modest country girl like her. It had a somber reputation, though nobody could quite remember why. The people who lived there were seldom seen, the windows mostly shuttered. Whenever she passed, it seemed deserted, except for the crows which seemed to flock to it.

Originally, there had only been the tower – a round stone keep on a commanding crag. Raised in the twelfth century, so somebody had told her. The chateau was from the 1600s, built when the land was thought more civilized. A bridge now linked the rear of the building to the keep, spanning the ravine which served the latter as a natural defense. The bridge supported a three-story building, with the library on the middle floor giving onto the disused entrance of the tower.

So the keep, which was once an isolated fortress, was impregnable no longer, though that hardly mattered now. Faced with the onslaught of modern-day barbarians, the owners of the house had fled, not taken refuge there. Danielle knew a boy who'd climbed the rough wall to an arrow-slit and reported that the tower was hollow. All its wooden levels had collapsed.

She imagined it was a ghostly ruin, even in the daylight. But the house had a creepiness of its own, and she couldn't help wonder what might lurk in it. Scared of the soldiers though she was, she at least knew they were human. What if the house were haunted by much older, colder things?

As she came to the top of the stairs, she heard a commotion on the landing – the sound of running feet and then a shout. It came from the chapel between the stairhead and the library. She knew Elise had been praying there and her heart leaped with a sudden pang of dread.

She started forward and then stopped short as she saw one of the soldiers emerging from the chapel, dragging Elise by the hair. "You murderous bitch!" he yelled and threw her down, then raised his musket, aiming the butt to stave her head in.

Danielle lunged and grabbed hold of his coat.

She was slightly built but took him by surprise and dragged him clear. Elise lay rigid on the floor, her pale face like a doll's. The man tried to shake Danielle off, but she clung on like a lover till he jabbed the musket's butt against her ribs. Winded, she released him with a groan and staggered backwards. The soldier rounded on her, bringing up the gun to fire at point-blank range.

"Stop there!" someone shouted from behind her. His voice had an authority that made the soldier flinch. Danielle cowered with one hand raised as if to fend the ball off, but the man stepped back and lowered the musket, looking resentfully towards the stairs.

Breathless from the blow and with the shock of what had happened, she turned and saw the foreigner – the fair-haired man in black. The officers were coming up behind him. He met her eye and then made way for them.

"What the devil's going on?" the general demanded.

The soldier gestured at Elise. "Michel's dead. Look at what she did to him!"

"Dead, you say?" The general went over to the chapel and stepped into the doorway – then recoiled. "My God," he said, and turned towards the soldier. "What happened?"

"It was witchcraft," said the man.

An instinct made Berger's fingers twitch towards his holstered shotgun, but he kept his hand outside his coat. The general gave him an appraising look. "Well, my friend from the New World – what do you make of this? Something a sorcerer would write about?"

Berger came to join him in the doorway. The chapel was lit by a single candle flame. The body of the soldier lay before them. Its upper half was a charred and shapeless mass, as if he'd been thrust head-first into a furnace. But his white breeches weren't even singed. A clay pipe lay beside him on the tiles.

An acrid haze hung in the air. It caught in Berger's throat. He turned to the girl still lying on the floor. Her face was blank and white with shock, no trace of malice there. He crouched in front of her. "What did you see?" he asked her quietly. She gazed back at him with wide eyes. "A light," she said. "A light came from the cross."

Frowning, he straightened up again and went into the chapel, stepping around the body to approach the metal cross. No light came from it, just the candle's faint reflection. He touched the dull, smooth surface. It was cool.

"He's been *incinerated*," said the general behind him.

Berger turned. "There's a phenomenon I read about somewhere. People can catch on fire for no good reason. It's like the flames come from within. The body's consumed, but the surroundings are untouched."

The general grunted. "You read too much – just like your friends in Paris." He stared down at the body. "No, a reasonable man can answer this. The man had his pipe, and a spark from it set off his cartridges. The powder ignited in one great blaze."

Berger didn't think that would burn down to the bone, but clearly the other man wanted to believe it. He gave the cross another glance.

"Go find your books, then," said the general.

He seemed impatient now with the whole business and strode back out into the corridor. "Bachelet! Put these women with the others, and then get some men to clear this mess away..."

#   #   #

Danielle put her arm round Elise and felt her trembling as the officer took them to the bedroom where they and the others had been put. She embraced the girl as the door was shut behind them. Elise started sobbing against her shoulder. Danielle held her close and stroked her hair.

The bedroom was dimly lit. The men had made a fire for them, but the logs in the grate had mostly been consumed. The red glow made the room seem like a vestibule of Hell. There were three other women sharing it with them.

Nicole and Henriette lay on the bedspread, gazing into each other's eyes as if they could forget the outside world. Anne was sitting at the dressing table, inspecting her reflection by a stumpy candle's glow. One of the soldiers had struck her face and left it bruised and swollen. Anne was proud of her good looks and had been studying the marks obsessively.

Glancing at her, Danielle thought of something that a childhood friend had told her once with solemn seriousness. *If you look into a mirror with a candle and say the Lord's Prayer backwards, you can summon up the Devil.* Danielle wasn't sure if she believed that, but she'd never dared to try it for herself.

She raised Elise's face and stared into her tearful eyes. "What happened back there?" she asked in a low voice.

"Like I said, the cross began to glow. Its light filled the whole

110

chapel. The soldier came in and went towards it. Then his body just burst into flames!"

"My God... Did the candle touch his cartridge pouch or something?"

Elise shook her head. "It was holy fire. It devoured him, and an angel spoke to me."

Danielle held her gaze. The younger girl was blinking back her tears, but a gleam of fervor filled her eyes. "His voice was beautiful."

Anne turned in her chair, her bruised face scornful. "The voice of an angel? Who do think you are – Joan the Maid?"

Ignoring her, Elise gripped Danielle's arms, her gaze imploring. "He said there's treasure hidden in this house. A horde of silver to help the Royal Army fight the Bluecoats, if we can just escape from here with it."

"Lise, we can't escape from here. They'd kill us."

"They're going to kill us anyway!"

Danielle's eyes flicked to Anne. It didn't need an angel to predict that. She looked at Nicole and Henriette, but the two girls were still lost in their own world.

"Did he say where this silver was?" she asked, not sure if she was humoring Elise.

"In the cellar of the keep. It's been there since the Middle Ages."

"And how could we get into the keep?"

"There's a door at the far end of the library."

"Which has probably been locked for years."

"But he's told me where the key is."

Danielle shook her head. "Lise, this is madness."

"No – it's God's will. How can you say no?"

Danielle was silent for a moment, chewing on her lip. Anne had lost interest in the argument and was peering glumly back into the mirror.

"Where's the key, then?" Danielle asked. It felt like stepping backwards down a slope.

"It's in the library."

"We'd never get there."

"They let you come and go, don't they? Just say you need some help. An extra pair of hands down in the kitchen."

That might get them past the guard outside. "But if they catch us in the library..."

"They won't," said Elise with unshakeable conviction. "Remember – an angel's watching over us."

#   #   #

The library stretched the whole length of the annex between the chateau and the keep. There were three tall windows on each side of it. Between them, the walls were lined with books in floor-to-ceiling cases. Berger moved along the shelves, his shuttered lantern lighting up the spines.

Some of the books that he had found had shocked him. There were dusty volumes here which were just rumors up till now. Forbidden works which he thought had been destroyed to the last copy. Here was the *Endemoniada*, a black magic text from Spain. *Le Veilleur Silencieux*, banned since the fifteenth century. And Book III of the *Psychonautica*, with its rituals from ancient Babylon...

He put them in his saddlebags with a kind of reverence – not for their obvious content but for the arcane knowledge they preserved, hidden within. He was leafing through an unfamiliar text printed in Hebrew – *The Book of the Watchers*, it was called – when he heard a sound in the passageway outside.

A footfall from beyond the door; a muffled whispering. For a moment he stood motionless, then laid the book aside and closed the lantern's shutter, stepping back into the darkness. The library felt like a long, deep grave. He drew his fowling piece and thumbed the cock back.

The door was opened cautiously, and a candle was brought in.

Its light didn't reach to the corner where he waited. His eyes narrowed as he saw it was the fair-haired girl again, with a smaller brunette at her heels. They crept between the bookshelves to the reading desk halfway along, where a medieval Bible was displayed. As he watched, the dark girl started turning pages while the blonde set down the candle next to her. Towards the back of the great book, a hollow was uncovered, cut deep into the layers of vellum.

Elise gave a gasp. "You see? He spoke the truth."

The space contained a long, gaunt key. She took it and hurried on to the far end of the room. There was a green baize panel there. She folded it aside to reveal a door which looked like solid iron.

"In the name of God," murmured Danielle. "How long since that was opened?"

Elise pushed the key into the lock and tried to turn it, but it scarcely budged.

Then Berger slid the lantern's shutter open, and the two girls swung around to stare at him.

He moved towards them with his shotgun levelled. Danielle recognized him with a glimmer of relief. At least it wasn't a bloodthirsty Bluecoat. But she'd felt the coldness of his gaze, and the gun he held looked murderous enough.

She moistened her lips. "Oh, sir, have pity! We're trying to escape."

Berger kept his finger on the trigger as he put his lantern on the reading desk. "It's not *your* escape I'm fearful of," he said after a moment. "Who told you that the key was there?"

Elise stared back at him defiantly.

"You wouldn't believe us," Danielle said, almost apologetic.

"Wouldn't I? In a room like this, full of books so evil they could send you mad?"

"There's no evil here," Elise said. She was trembling, her passion vying with her fear. "It's *you* who serve the Devil, after all! An angel told me where to look..."

"There's silver in the tower," Danielle broke in. "We'll take you to it, if you let us go." She sensed the scalding glance that Elise gave her, but her eyes stayed locked with Berger's.

"So there is," said the American at length. "But it won't set you free, nor help your cause. It's a ransom that keeps him trapped within these walls."

Danielle frowned at him. "Keeps who?"

"You really don't know, do you?"

She gave her head the smallest shake. And then they heard a stealthy scraping noise.

Elise turned first. Her eyes grew wide. The key had started moving, turning this way and then that, as if someone was trying to work the rusty lock. She took a step away from it, her hand going to her mouth.

"Take it from the lock!" snapped Berger. Danielle wavered, as startled as her friend, then reached out for the key – and snatched her hand back. The metal had begun to glow dull red.

As they looked on, mesmerized, the key kept twisting, moving a little further round as the mechanism began to come unstuck. The glow was brighter now, reminding Danielle of a horseshoe being hammered in her father's forge. The key was rattling insistently. Then somebody or something started pounding on the door. The girls flinched back, and Berger raised his gun. Together they retreated as the noise grew thunderous, as if Satan himself was demanding to be let out.

The infernal racket brought several soldiers running. One was the bookish officer who'd directed Berger to the library. Berger led the girls past them and out into the passage as the men deployed, their muskets levelled at the iron door. "Brigands hiding in the keep!" the officer called out. "Get ready to repulse them, men!"

Berger put his back to the wall beside the door, the shotgun gripped in one hand and Danielle's arm in the other, while Danielle clutched Elise's hand. He glanced at them. The blonde looked petrified, but the brunette's staring eyes still gleamed with fervor.

Then they heard the iron door burst open with a clang.

A brilliant light was cast upon the wall across the passage, as if every book in the library had suddenly caught fire, the flames intense and blue as burning brandy. They heard the screaming of the soldiers – not like sounds that came from human throats. The cries were quickly choked, as if their breath had been consumed, along with the lungs expelling it. The searing glare went out and a cloud of thick, cold smoke came through the doorway, heavy with dust and bits of ash.

Berger's free hand was now clamped to Danielle's mouth. Her eyes stared like a frightened mare's. Elise cowered behind her friend.

The fog was congealing in the passageway.

Its stench was foul, and Berger scarcely dared to look at it, but he thought he could make out a hulking shape, like a shadow cast on the swirling pall of dust motes, its contours outlined by suspended ash. Like a human figure sketched in smoke. It almost touched the ceiling. As Berger watched it, frozen still, he heard the thud of footfalls on the stairs. More soldiers appeared at the far end of the passage. The first one yelped a challenge at the shape, then let fly with his musket and retreated. The filthy smoke flowed after him, absorbing the dense cloud left by his shot. Through the gloom, Berger glimpsed a flicker of blue fire in the stairwell and heard the screams begin again.

Elise ran past him to the library.

She halted on the threshold and stood staring for a moment, then darted in. Berger released Danielle and stumbled in pursuit. The blonde girl followed. When they saw into the library, they both stopped short as well.

The books hadn't burned. They seemed untouched. The lantern on the reading desk still glowed. By its light, wreathed in an eerie mist, they could just make out the bodies, as black and gnarled as bits of bog oak, fused in rigid postures by the blaze.

Elise had already reached the open doorway to the keep, which gaped like a mouth about to swallow her. She looked back at Danielle, ignoring Berger. "It's all right now. He's cleared the way for us!"

Beyond the iron door there was a stone cell of a landing which gave onto two spiral staircases. One led down, the other up – both twisting into darkness. Elise went groping down towards the bottom of the tower.

Berger crossed the library, not glancing at the bodies. Danielle stayed on the threshold, horrified. Then she heard more shots downstairs – another strangled scream. She started, glanced behind herself, and scuttled after him.

He had paused at the reading desk to get his lantern. She picked her way between the blackened shapes. Some of the limbs were still intact, their

114

clothing barely scorched, on bodies which were otherwise destroyed. Her gaze briefly locked with a pair of blind, boiled eyeballs in a charred face that still smoldered. She fled past it with a whimper of disgust.

Berger was delving in his greatcoat pockets. He produced a pair of snub-nosed pistols, thrusting one of them into her hands.

She stared at it, then raised her eyes. "For God's sake, what was that?"

"A demon, girl, and your friend let it out. And there'll be worse to come unless we stop her." He gestured at the lantern. "I'll go first – you bring the light."

It didn't even cross her mind to argue. She picked the lantern up with her free hand. He went to the doorway and listened for a moment, then started slowly down the steps, his shotgun and pistol pointed at the dark. She followed two steps behind, holding up the lantern so its glow crept round the flight ahead of them. Her right hand grasped the unfamiliar pistol. The bore of it was very large, and she drew a desperate comfort from its weight.

"Do you know this place?" she whispered as she aimed over his shoulder. She had to talk, or else her heart might burst.

"My family used to own it once," he told her. "Then they left for the New World. They thought that they could leave the past behind. But the curse of our duty was handed down..." He paused as something rustled, perhaps a rat further down in the pitch dark. "When I heard there was a civil war being fought here, I knew I had to come back to this house, make sure that certain books didn't fall into the wrong hands... and that the oubliette stays undisturbed."

"So... you're not with the Blues?"

"Of course I'm not. This war's irrelevant."

She felt her anger spark, despite herself. "It's not irrelevant to us. I watched them shoot my father!" They descended for a few more steps. "What oubliette?" she asked belatedly.

"The pit beneath the dungeon. There's an evil man down there. My ancestors imprisoned him three hundred years ago."

"And he's not dead?" she asked in disbelief.

"He's dead," said Berger. "But that won't be enough to keep him down."

They reached the bottom of the steps and stepped out through an archway onto the ground floor of the tower, the darkness giving way to cold blue light. Danielle looked up and realized it was moonlight. The floors above her had fallen in, just like that boy had said, and she could see the sky, as from the bottom of a chimney.

Another door stood open on the far side of the wreckage-littered space.

Berger went towards it, and she followed. A narrow corkscrew of stone steps led down into the depths. She hugged herself. The air down here was chilly, much colder than the library. The shaft in front of them felt colder still. When Berger spoke, she saw his breath spread palely in the moonlight.

"Don't follow if your faith is weak."

She wavered, then descended after him.

Berger went down very slowly, both his flintlocks levelled, and she raised the lamp behind his shoulder, craning to illuminate his path. The stairwell opened on a vaulted space beneath the tower. A faint glow seemed to cling to the damp wall, like the phosphorescence of rotting fish. Danielle saw a black hole at the center of the dungeon's floor. Elise was flitting round it frantically.

There were niches set into the wall at chest height and she moved from one dark socket to the next. Hearing their footfalls, she swung around. "It's kept in one of these!"

Berger went forward warily, while Danielle peered around her. "What's that light?"

"All things decay," he told her, "even magic. The power that seals this place is breaking down."

She turned to the nearest niche and raised the lantern. It put her in mind of a church crypt, with openings for relics in the walls. A bundle wrapped in sackcloth lay in this one. She moved in closer, wondering if it was full of coins. Raising the pistol, she poked the bundle with it. The contents shifted with a brittle sound.

"Don't touch anything," said Berger sharply.

Danielle flinched back, realizing the bag was full of bones. She could see the like stuffed into other niches. "What is this – a catacomb?" she asked.

"Those are guardians," Berger said. "The bones of murderers and suicides, condemned to keep eternal watch. But the silver is what binds him to this place."

She glanced towards the pit and felt a curious pull towards it, as if the level floor on which they stood was actually a slope, distorted downward. The sense was so compelling that she had to brace herself.

"How much silver is there?"

"Thirty pieces."

She turned and looked at him in disbelief. He was watching Elise go from one niche to another, recoiling from each bony sack she found. "Relics brought back from the Holy Land," he went on softly. "The coins He was betrayed for? Who can say?"

"Here!" Elise called suddenly. She'd found a smaller bundle and was lifting it out of its niche. He brought his guns up, pointing them at her.

"No," blurted Danielle. She darted forward, around the hole that seemed to suck at her and over to Elise, who turned to face her. "It's here, just as he promised." She held out the bag she'd found. By the light of the lantern, Danielle saw a lump of blackened leather. It made her think of a rotted piece of meat.

"Lise, we have to leave it here," she whispered.

"What do you mean? The war's not done. Our fathers and our brothers need it now."

Danielle was conscious of the guns behind her. She didn't know how patient the man was. Elise's face looked ashen in the lamplight. There was accusation in her eyes. "You've sold yourself to him!"

She made to push past; the purse clasped to her bosom. Danielle had the pistol in her other hand, but the thought of threatening Elise did not occur to her. Instead, she let the firearm go and tried to grab the purse. The texture of the leather made her skin crawl, but she dug her fingers into it and felt the tight-packed contours of the coins. Elise tried to wrest it free, and they swung around each other. The leather split and the coins spilled out, cascading to the floor.

Elise reeled backwards, staring at her wildly. Too late she sensed the void behind her. Danielle lunged forward, reaching out her hand, but Elise fell back into the hole with a wail of helpless protest. Danielle cried her name, collapsing to her knees. She peered over the edge and raised the lantern, but the darkness of the pit was total.

Somewhere below, Elise began to scream.

She sounded agonized, like someone being torn to pieces. Danielle almost dropped the lantern. She recoiled and scrambled back on her behind. Berger had come round the pit and was on his hands and knees, scrabbling for the scattered coins. His face was anxious now.

The screams stopped abruptly. Danielle sat and trembled, watching as he picked the rough-edged silver pieces up. Then she heard a furtive sound behind her and looked around, her fine hairs prickling. There was nothing to see in the sickly light, but she heard the sound again. It was coming from the nearest niche. She told herself that it was just a rat.

As she stared, eyes narrowing, the bag stuffed in the niche began to stir.

For a moment she thought the dimness had deceived her. But then the bag seemed to squeeze out of its hole and dropped to the floor with a dull thud, its bones crunching together.

Berger had stopped moving. He was staring at it too.

Slowly the bag began to crawl across the floor towards them, contracting like a maggot. Danielle watched it, open-mouthed. The scraping slither of its movement seemed to fill the silence. Berger had laid his guns down; now he picked the shotgun up and sighted on the thing. He pulled the trigger. The hiss-*bang* of the discharge made her flinch, reverberating off the walls around them as a burst of thick white smoke spread through the vault. The buckshot ripped the bag apart and scattered its dry contents. She glimpsed a jawbone skittering away.

The pungent smoke was difficult to see through, but she heard more noises in the shadows. Other bundles had begun to move.

Impulsively she crawled to her dropped pistol and snatched it up as she looked from niche to niche. The trigger was slack, and she realized that she hadn't even cocked it. Sobbing, she levered back the flint. Her heartbeat seemed about to burst her chest.

Berger rose and approached one of the niches. He came up short, then fired the second barrel into it. The twitching bag exploded in a spray of bony fragments. Berger backed away, knelt down, and started to reload.

She watched him take each cartridge from his pocket, biting them open to pour the powder in, then ramming the shot still wrapped in paper down on top of it. She willed him to go faster, but he worked with stony calm. Another of the bags was creeping closer, but he focused on the job in hand – then turned and blasted it at point blank range. Danielle was so absorbed, she almost missed the noise behind her. She twisted round and cowered back from the shapeless sackcloth lump. Bringing her pistol up, she fired. The ball tore the bag open, and the muzzle flash set it afire. A splintered eye socket glared out at her.

"Get the coins," snapped Berger. She sat rigid for a moment, still holding the loose trigger down. Then she let the pistol fall and looked around for the muted gleam of silver. The fog of powder smoke hung in the air, muffling the lantern's glow and the dungeon's phosphorescence. She picked a coin up, and another one, crawling on hands and knees towards the opening in the floor. And then she froze.

An arm had emerged from the hole in front of her.

It wasn't Elise's, she could tell. The arm was bare, and male, and muscular. The forearm was braced against the floor, the hand pressed to the flagstones, the fingers seeking purchase in a crack. As she gawped at it, another arm slid up over the rim. The skin of both was the color of rusty iron. The muscles bulged with the effort of trying to lever up a body.

"Sir!" she cried, but it came out as a squeak.

Berger had been taking aim at an approaching guardian. He turned his head, and even through the smoke she saw his eyes grow wide. He swung the gun round. "Get back!" he called, but Danielle had seen another of the coins, just out of the newcomer's reach. She knew he mustn't have it. She craned forward to clutch at it, and his monstrous head rose up in front of her.

He was human – or he had been, once. Half his face was burned away, revealing a cheekbone and bared teeth. The eye sockets seemed deeper than the pit. No sign of eyes, but she felt his stare transfix her as he struggled up over the rim.

Berger stepped up close behind her and fired down.

At that range, a charge of buck and ball should have shattered the man's head and cast him back into the oubliette. But when the smoke dispersed, he was still leering like a death's head, with more of his blackened face stripped off but the bone beneath intact. A drifting smut stung Danielle's cheek but she didn't even feel it. Then Berger grasped the collar of her dress and yanked her back.

The fabric ripped, which she didn't notice either. Her eyes stayed fixed on the figure from the pit. His shoulders were clear of it, and she could see his upper chest, which like the face was partly burned. "Has he come from Hell?" she asked in a small voice.

Berger let her go to start reloading. "He never got as far as that," he said. "He was hanged and burned, but the fire wouldn't consume him. There was too much sorcery in his bones. So they bound him here instead."

The man's black sockets stared at them. She sensed that he could see them with older things than mere eyes. Berger dropped the ramrod and thumbed back the cocks. "De Rais!" he called, rising up and stepping forward. "Your demon missed us, and we're going to seal your tomb again!"

He triggered the right-hand barrel, then the left one, engulfing the figure in churning smoke. The clumps of hot lead gouged away more flesh. But the man shrugged the impacts off and kept on coming, heaving himself onto the flagstones. Berger cursed and fumbled for fresh loads.

Danielle made to cross herself and realized she was still holding the coins in her clenched fist. A desperate thought occurred to her. "Shoot the coins at him!" she blurted. "Silver can hurt the creatures of the night."

Or so her grandmother had said. Berger turned and met her gaze, weighing her words up for a moment. Then he poured a charge of powder in and dug out the clutch of coins which he had gathered, working them into a roll which he fed into one barrel of the gun. Danielle scrambled over to him with her contribution, and he loaded the second barrel as the half-charred sorcerer began to rise. He was indistinct in the hellish smoke, but his form loomed like a monster's. She thought of the burned men upstairs and wondered if his touch could do the same.

She clung to Berger as he raised the shotgun and felt the jolt go through him as he fired. The blast was shot through with an eerie jingling and she saw the coins go spinning through the smoke, catching the light of the muzzle flash like stars glimpsed through a storm cloud. They tore into the man's broad chest, some edgeways, some full-on.

This time the impact threw him back, and he went down on one knee.

119

Danielle heard a piercing cry that filled her head, though she didn't think his mangled mouth had voiced it. The cry of an enraged beast – but there was pain in it as well.

Berger stepped forward, his face set. "Take this to pay the ferryman," he said, and fired the second barrel. More coins carved into the monster, shredding the black meat from its bones and blasting it back down into the pit.

The cry came again, and Danielle pressed her hands against her ears, but the baleful screech was in her brain. The American grimaced as he heard it too. But gradually it faded, as if over a vast distance, till there was silence. Only then did Berger lower his gun.

Danielle, still not sure she could believe it, felt a sudden change of pressure in the air, as if a heavy door had opened somewhere. She realized then that the clouds of powder smoke had begun to churn as if collapsing inward. They were being drawn into the oubliette.

Berger took her arm and pulled her over to the wall, then knelt and drew her down beside him. "Brace yourself," he said, "and don't look round."

She glanced at the nearest niche, but the bundle in it wasn't moving. There was a sense of suction in the vault, like the air being drawn into a forge. The murky air was clearing as the smoke withdrew towards the oubliette. Then more smoke came pouring through the doorway to the tower, filthy with soot and bits of ash. It mingled with the pallid powder smoke and began to swirl round the opening like a whirlpool. Danielle pressed her cheek against the stonework, feeling the pull of some colossal gulf.

The stygian smoke which had spread throughout the chateau came streaming back into the dungeon, sucked down by an elemental force. She risked a fleeting glance over her shoulder and thought she glimpsed a hulking shape in it, elongated by the flow, as insubstantial as a shadow. She quickly turned her face away as the demon disappeared into the void.

Eventually the air grew calm. They looked at one another, then clambered to their feet again. The dungeon was still tinged with ghostly light, strewn with shattered bones and pieces of torn sackcloth. One of the rags was flickering with flame, fanned by the wind which had just blown through the chamber. Berger went over and picked it up, then took it to the opening in the floor. The oubliette was completely black. He dropped the burning rag in. It didn't land on the floor of a stone cell but fell away and dwindled to a faint spark in the darkness, before it vanished in undreamed-of depths.

#   #   #

By the time they got outside, the day was breaking. The sun wasn't up but the sky was pale, the darkness leached away. Berger's mount was tethered by the dovecote. He lugged over his book-filled saddlebags and slung them across the horse's neck, then looked back at the women. They stood huddled close together, watching him.

None of the soldiers in the chateau had escaped the demon. The building was littered with carbonized remains. A charred shape in the dining room might have been the general, still sitting bolt upright in his chair, an unfired pistol in his blackened hand.

Henriette, Nicole, and Anne had heard the screaming as they clung to each other on the bed. Then the smoke began to creep under their door – only to be sucked back out again. They'd listened to the silence, till they heard Danielle outside, calling their names.

"You ladies better lie low with your families," said Berger. "This column found out what Hell means, but another one might follow soon enough." He caught Danielle's eye. "Thanks for your help – and I'm sorry about your father. I know this war is your whole world right now. But like you saw, there are other worlds... and other wars to fight." He gestured, almost helplessly, and turned back to his horse.

The animal was nervous, having scented the night's terrors. He soothed it, then swung up onto its back. When he gathered the reins and turned its head, three of the women were gone, but Danielle was still standing in the yard.

He heeled his mount across to her and looked down quizzically. Her dress was torn, her face begrimed with smoke, but her upturned gaze was steady and appealing.

"I want to join this war of yours," she said.

He looked away. "You've seen what it's like. No place to take a lady."

"I'm not a lady, sir. And I can shoot."

He stared at her, considering, then reached down from his saddle. She clambered up and sat behind him, wrapping her arms tight around his waist. As he nudged the horse into a walk, she looked over her shoulder, the dawn breeze stirring her pale hair as she cast a final glance towards the keep. ♜

JUMP

By Dennis K. Crosby

OFFICER JULIE HUFFMAN ENTERED THE Murder Chapel, as it was affectionately known, with an apprehension that she desperately tried to put aside because of the opportunity ahead of her. She'd heard rumors of an elite undercover unit but dismissed it as hearsay. Others dismissed it as legend. Now, she had an opportunity to not only find out if it was real, but to possibly join them, too.

Here…in an old, beat up, weathered tomb, called St. Lazarus, on Spring Street.

She'd driven past the church a few times over the years, but it was in an area of town that was quite foreign to her. She'd neither grown up, nor patrolled near there. That was perfect though. If she got this assignment she could come and go easily without people in the neighborhood knowing she was a police officer. She'd just be another curious looky-loo trying to figure out if the church was haunted—like everyone else.

She'd arrived early, as she was prone to do. With any investigation she'd ever been a part of Huffman liked to arrive early and get her bearings, so she'd have a leg up on her fellow officers. It was hard being a woman in law enforcement. Harder still for a black woman. Huffman took every opportunity to gain the advantage. She had to be better, smarter, and faster, at every turn.

The church had been abandoned for years. Seemed both a strange and perfect place to house a mysterious unit that may or may not exist. Strange, perfect, and terribly cliché. When she'd first arrived, she took in the sight of the structure. The building was solid brick and stood two stories from step to steeple. It was adorned with beautiful, now dulled and cracked, stained glass. The large wooden double door in front was very ornate with intricate, hand-carved biblical images, most of which had been chipped away by weather and vandals. Some gang signs were spray painted and chiseled into the wood. Huffman imagined how beautiful this thing had once been long ago.

Before the murders.

First a priest, then four officers who'd tried to solve the murder.

Once inside she tried to envision how lovely it may have been. Now though, it was clear that St. Lazarus, the Murder Chapel, was indeed a tomb. The rafters above had seen better days. The upper level had a balcony and when Huffman looked up, she imagined seeing the faces of people staring down at her…in a grave. The lower level was very much like that—a grave. A giant open coffin filled with dust, dirt, mold, spiders, roaches, and mice—alive and dead. She moved down the center aisle toward the pulpit, the sound of scurrying feet echoing in the cavernous expanse serving as a soundtrack. The streetlights outside did little to illuminate the space through the high stained-glass windows. Every step she took ended with her kicking up dust or crushing the skeleton or exoskeleton of something that may have once led a thriving existence.

Crash!

Huffman turned and reached for her service weapon in one fluid motion only to remember that she'd put it in her purse. She was reluctant to wear a holstered weapon in public when off duty because she didn't want to deal with stares and backlash. In her mind, non-blacks saw her as a token, and blacks thought she was now too *blue* for their community. She didn't fit and hadn't settled into a state of comfort yet to the point where she didn't care.

Slowly, she retrieved her service weapon from her purse and moved toward the source of the crash. It came from a backroom to the right of the pulpit. Stealth was not her ally as each step was louder than its predecessor with all the dead and decayed insects on the floor. As she inched closer, she heard more movement, and a whisper.

Huffman.

Her name was carried lightly on the air, and she froze, turning only when she felt the light tap on her shoulder. Her movement was swift, fluid, and Officer Julie Huffman was ready to fight off anything that came her way.

But there was nothing.

No one.

Only empty space and faint light from outside.

Huffman was trying desperately to control her breathing, which she'd only then recognized as swift and erratic. She took a deep breath, then turned, preparing to follow the original sound from the backroom. When she reached it, she pushed the door open slowly, brought her service weapon up and—

"Ahhh!"

"Police! Don't move!"

The short middle-aged man in overalls complied, the broom he held fell to the floor, kicking up more dust.

"I'm just the janitor," he pleaded. "I'm just here to take care of the place."

Behind her, Hoffman heard voices and footsteps and saw a dim light come on in the main hall. She recognized one voice. It was the captain that had called her to this meeting. Turning her head slightly she shouted to them.

"Captain! It's Huffman! I'm back here."

After a few beats she heard multiple footsteps approach, then stop behind her.

"Officer Huffman? What are you doing?" asked Captain Fulton.

"I caught this guy sneaking around back here. Not sure what's going on. He claims to be the janitor, but I highly doubt that. Have you seen this place? It's a tomb. Seems he's sleeping on the job," said Huffman.

The collective silence seemed as loud as the insect carcasses she'd stepped on to get to the back to the back room.

"Officer Huffman? Julie. You wanna put the weapon down," said Captain Fulton. It was certainly more of a command than a question. A light command, but a command, nonetheless.

"Sir, I haven't had a chance to search him yet. I—"

"Officer Huffman, there's no one there," said Fulton.

She heard the words, but it took an eternity for them to settle in. When she finally did comprehend, she looked back at the captain and, for the first time, saw the three men he'd arrived with. All of them gave looks of confusion to her and one another. Turning back to her suspect, Huffman saw exactly what they all seemed to.

Nothing.

The janitor was gone. The broom was gone. Everything…gone. But not just gone. It was as if none of it had ever existed. It was as if the entire incident couldn't possibly have taken place. The backroom was as much a tomb as the rest of the church.

Huffman holstered her weapon, and sheepishly pushed past the captain and the three officers.

#　　#　　#

124

"Is this some kind of hazing ritual, Captain?"

"Hazing is for kids, Officer Huffman. Are you a kid?"

"No, sir," said Huffman.

"Then hold the smartass remarks to yourself and pay attention to the task at hand."

Huffman took in the scene and scoffed, internally. She'd heard about Captain Fulton. Word on the street was he walked in between the black and white of the badge. He was certainly concerned about policy and procedure, but he wasn't afraid to dispense justice—legal or the poetic, karmic type. She wasn't sure how to take that exactly. She wasn't sure she could work with someone who walked the line between right and wrong like a tightrope. For her, everything was about the law, the job, and doing the right thing for the community. She wanted this assignment. At least, she thought she did. But she wanted to be able to do the job the right way. It was important to her. It was the best way to honor her father.

Fulton reminded her a bit of him. Like her father, Fulton was tall, somewhat muscular, but not overly. Saying he was fit, seemed to be accurate. He was older, the salt and pepper beard the only thing betraying his true age. If not for that, she might think him younger. His skin was smooth. No wrinkles, no crow's feet, no scars. Fulton looked distinguished. Perhaps that's what helped him rise through the ranks to his current position. Not an easy feat for a black man in the city they lived in. But he'd done it, and she'd admired that, which is why she took his call and agreed to come to St. Lazarus.

"Huffman, meet Officers Todd Hanlan, Daniel Pembrooke, and F.R. Trang," said Fulton.

"F.R.?" Huffman questioned as she extended her hand to shake his.

"Stands for Franklin Roosevelt. Want to take a guess as to when my family immigrated to the states?"

Huffman simply nodded and smiled, then shook the hands of the other officers. At least two of their names sounded familiar. More rumors among the precincts. Something that was fairly frequent in her short time on the job.

"It's nice to meet you all. And sir, thank you for the opportunity here."

"Well, don't thank me yet, Huffman. We've got a long night ahead."

"Sir?"

"You've heard rumors of an elite undercover unit?" asked Fulton.

"Yes, sir," said Huffman.

"Well, this is it," said Fulton. "These three officers, formerly four, have been responsible for closing some of the most notorious cases in the city. Cases that most people will never know about."

Huffman felt a warmth inside that seemed to fill her very spirit. The thought of being so deep undercover, so hidden, able to do the job she'd wanted to do since she was a little girl, was intoxicating.

"We're kind of a big deal," said Pembrooke.

Huffman regarded him. He was somewhat tall, stocky, seemed more like the class clown. But if he was in this unit, he must be something special.

"With respect, sir, why am I here?" asked Huffman.

"Oh didn't he tell you?" asked Hanlan.

"Tell me what?"

"The Murder Chapel is haunted," began Trang, "and you're here to help a ghost cross over to the other side."

"Wait. What?" asked Julie.

"You're here, because we think you may be right for this team, Huffman," said Fulton as he gave a look to both Hanlan and Trang. The look a father normally gives when he wants his kids to stop acting up. "But to be sure, you're going to need to prove that."

"Sir?"

"It's simple. Tonight, you and the boys will attempt to solve a cold case. Or, at least, try and figure out more pieces to the puzzle," said Fulton.

"Which cold case, sir?" asked Huffman.

"The only one that matters," said Hanlan.

"Yeah," began Pembrooke, "the death of Father Thomas Casey. The former pastor here, at the Murder Chapel."

Huffman's eyes widened. She'd heard of that case. Everyone had. Father Casey was brutally murdered in this church almost twenty years ago. He been attacked, tortured, and killed, and there'd been no sign or evidence left behind by the killer. Not one fingerprint. No sign of break in. In fact, when they finally found Father Casey in the basement, he'd been decapitated and left in a room that was locked from the inside. No sign of how he'd gotten in, or how anyone could have possibly gotten out. The rumor had always been that it was the church that killed him. Or whatever spirit dwelled within its walls.

"So, we solve the case, and I'm in?" asked Huffman.

"Potentially," said Fulton.

"Sir?"

"Look Huffman, you're good police. I've read your file and I've talked to your CO's."

"But?"

"But…you have a tendency to only think in black and white. You need to think outside the box in this unit. Not everything is straightforward. And… you can't do everything alone. You need to trust your instincts, you need to trust your training, and you need to trust your team. Mistrust in any of those will get you, and those around you, dead...really quick."

Huffman didn't appreciate the evaluation happening in front of her fellow officers. She didn't like the thought of others thinking of her as weak or incapable of doing the job. She felt like she was being dressed down, and that put her on the defensive. She'd show them though. She'd show them that she was not only worthy, but the best recruit they could hope for.

And she'd do it her way.

The right way.

Huffman.

She turned at the sound of her name. It had come from behind, but again, there was no one. Just like last time. Were these guys toying with her?

"You all right, Huffman?" asked Fulton.

"Um, yeah. Yeah, Captain. I'm good."

"So? Are you interested in this assignment?"

Huffman.

There it was again. Her name floating through the air of this old, dilapidated, church of death and horror. The voice sounded male, but old, tortured, and angry. In the air of this church her name sounded like a plea.

For mercy.

For absolution.

For death.

Was this really what she wanted? Could she do it at all? Was this really the best way, the only way, to move up in the ranks and achieve her goals?

"Let's do this, sir. Where do we begin?" she said.

Huffman.

#   #   #

"I've heard of you," said Huffman.

"I won't even ask if it was good or not. I know how this story goes," said Hanlan.

"For what it's worth, I think you did the right thing."

"Yeah, well, you'd be in the minority on that."

As they descended the stairs to the basement of the church, Officers Huffman and Hanlan made their way toward a room at the end of the hallway. The basement smelled of mildew and something else Huffman couldn't quite place. Whatever it was, it attacked her senses relentlessly. She wanted to stop and vomit. But she was determined to see this through and not seem weak. It was difficult enough being a female in a male dominated industry. She was a black female to boot, so there was zero room for error or weakness.

"It's okay, I'm used to that," she replied. "Seriously though, you did what needed to be done."

"I left my wounded partner alone to chase a suspect who turned out to be just some scared kid trying to get away from gunshots," began Hanlan. "Because I was so gung-ho and desperate to be a hero and catch the bad guy at any cost. When I realized what I had done, that I'd chased the wrong guy, that's when I heard them."

"Heard what?" asked Huffman.

"Two shots. When I'd doubled back, I found my partner dead. One bullet went into his heart. The other, his head," said Hanlan.

"But you didn't—"

"Think. I didn't think. I didn't think about anything or anyone. I was focused on showing people that despite my baby face and young age, that I could do this job. That I was...better than my old man," said Hanlan. "My ego and pride got in the way."

"Didn't stop you from getting into Fulton's unit, though."

"Sure. But getting here cost me everything," said Hanlan. "Don't you get it, Huffman. This unit is elite. But it's also a unit for lost causes and second chances. Just like this old church."

Huffman wasn't sure what to say to that. She was saddened that the officer she'd revered for his dedication to the work, turned out to be jaded and likely influenced by the thoughts of others. There was a right way and a wrong to do this job. Serving and protecting was the mission, end of story. How could he not see that?

"And you probably believe in the ghost stories of this place, too, right?" asked Huffman.

"All I know is, ten years ago, four officers came into this place to investigate, and none of them came out alive."

"So they're obviously still here, scaring people, huh?"

"At least one of them, probably," said Hanlan. "That's what ghosts are, right? They're spirits that are either stuck here and trying to cross over, or spirits trying to help others cross over."

"And you believe that nonsense?"

"Until I have a reason not to...yes," said Hanlan.

"Can I ask you something?"

Hanlan nodded.

"What happened to the officer I'm replacing?"

Huffman noticed hesitation, as if the subject were still painful. Hanlan looked at her at first, then looked away. Finally, he seemed to gather himself.

"She died. Chasing a suspect without backup. She was good, thought she could do everything on her own. In the end, it cost her."

"How'd she die?"

"She slipped at the top of some stairs, fell back, and tumbled. Broke her neck about halfway through the fall."

Huffman felt a tingle as he told the story. But she let the conversation go as they reached the locked door down the hall. Instinctively, she reached for her service weapon.

"What are you doing?" asked Hanlan.

"*We* are going to breach this door," replied Huffman.

"*We* are in a church that's been abandoned for over two decades. This is not an active crime scene. I think we'll be okay."

Huffman curled her lip in a sneer. She hated being shut down. After what she saw earlier with the disappearing handyman, or janitor, or whatever the hell he was, she was not about to take any chances. Cold case or not, she pulled her service weapon and reached for the handle. She looked at Hanlan and mouthed a countdown from three, then turned the knob and breached, entering first.

Right into a community of cobwebs.

"Dammit!" she screamed, arms flailing about trying to free herself from the wispy cocoon.

"Just shoot it," said Hanlan.

"To hell with you."

As Hanlan's chuckles subsided, so too did Huffman's struggle with the cobwebs. She holstered her weapon, blowing bits of organic string from her mouth and stared at Hanlan.

"Thanks for your help."

"You seemed to have everything in hand."

"Okay then genius, what do we do now?" asked Huffman.

"Well, this is the room where some dark things happened. This is where they found Father Casey's head. Problem is that the room was locked...from the inside."

"So there had to be a way out. We need to find the secret pathway."

"Yeah, but there isn't a secret pathway. The room was torn apart. The floor is solid concrete, the walls straight brick and mortar."

"There's got to be something," said Huffman.

Surveying the room, Huffman saw just what Hanlan described. There were four solid brick walls, all adorned with cobwebs, spiders, and other swift multi-legged insects. In the corner was a cot. Next to it, a desk with an overturned chair underneath. Huffman scanned the walls looking for anything that seemed out of place. A sconce, a portrait, something, anything that could be used as a trigger for a secret room.

Huffman.

"What?" she asked.

"What?" asked Hanlan.

"You just called my name," said Huffman.

"I didn't."

Huffman.

"You don't hear that?" she asked.

"All I hear is you and a little wind from some draft in the hallway," said Hanlan.

Beyond him, Huffman saw a dark figure emerge from the shadows in the hallway. It seemed to be there, then, not. Was it a trick of the dim light? She stepped closer to Hanlan who was near the doorway. She saw the shadow again, only to see it fade away...again. Huffman drew her weapon, pointing it toward Hanlan.

"What the hell are you doing?"

"Shh," said Hoffman, gesturing with her finger to her lips. "There's someone out there."

"Put that damned thing away. I told you, there's no one here but you, me, and—"

Hanlan's face contorted, his back arched, and Huffman was frozen for a moment, unsure of what was happening. When the shadow appeared behind Hanlan, Julie's eyes widened. The shadow's hand reached around Hanlan, with a crimson smeared dagger in hand, and Julie's mouth went wide. The shadowy hand plunged the dagger into Hanlan's stomach, and Huffman screamed. Hanlan fell to the ground, revealing the shadowed figure standing in the doorway. Huffman could barely make out the facial features, but she could see bright green eyes with a fiery, ethereal glow.

"Come and get me," said the figure, before it turned and ran down the hallway.

Julie moved swiftly, leaping over Hanlan ready to head full speed down the hallway when she heard Hanlan's voice.

"Don't...leave...me."

Julie stopped, looked back, then forward. A quiet voice inside urged her to stay with her partner. To help him in his time of need. It was overshadowed by a voice carried on the musky winds of the basement air.

Huffman. Come and get me.

"I'll be back for you," said Huffman as she turned and ran down the hall and up the stairs.

When she reached the top, she heard two gunshots ring out.

#   #   #

Huffman did her best to stifle the anxiety within. She'd left an officer to die to chase a suspect. She left…a wounded…officer. That was the right thing to do though, right? Her job was to solve this cold case. Her job was to bring justice to the streets. They all knew the risks when they put on the badge, so why did she have this knot growing in her stomach?

Once she'd reached the top of the stairs, she walked slowly, checked corners, and listened for sounds, anything that might lead her toward her shadowy suspect. Everything in the church was so dark, dank, and musty. The little light that crept through to help the ultra-dim and outdated bulbs only caused more anxiety. Shadows seemed to come off the walls and move to the floor. They danced there before flying to the ceiling. It was as if the church itself was alive.

Maybe the church killed him.

That's what they said about Father Casey.

With her weapon down, her finger on the side of the trigger guard, Huffman stepped closer and closer to the center of the Murder Chapel. The light wind outside snuck in through cracks in the walls and the stained glass creating another eerie soundtrack to the action within.

Thud!

From another back room, this time to the left of the pulpit, a sound caught Huffman's attention. She tip toed swiftly to the door. As she reached for the handle, a hand came from nowhere and grabbed her. Startled, she stepped back and pushed away from the figure now standing near here.

"Easy Huffman, it's me," whispered Trang.

"Dammit," she said. "Where the hell did you come from?"

"I heard a noise, wanted to check it out. Figured it might be your missing handyman."

He said it with a sheepish grin. Huffman wanted to punch him. In that moment she wondered just how badly she wanted to be on this unit. After all, if her own team didn't trust or believe her, how could they possibly work cases together?

"Your concern is touching," she said.

"Seriously, I didn't want you going in there alone. This place might have squatters, and who knows what could happen."

"Pretty sure I can handle a few drunks," said Huffman.

"I'm sure you can, but—"

"But nothing. Look, I'm a police officer, just like you. I got the same training you did, and I was at the top of my class. If I say I can handle it, I can handle it."

"Look, I get it. But it's not about you not being able to handle it," said Trang.

"Then what is it?"

"It's about recognizing that you don't have to do it alone."

"You mean like your old partner?" asked Huffman.

She saw Trang's face go slack. She'd hit a nerve. Some part of what she said boomeranged back and hit her in the gut. Huffman tried hard to demonstrate empathy, she truly did. It wasn't that she didn't have a heart. She simply kept it guarded so she could do the work she needed to without the emotional investment. Emotions caused mistakes and mistakes got people killed. It was just that simple for her. Huffman was on the rise because she kept her head down and did the things she needed to do to get the job done. She couldn't allow feelings to get in the way.

"I begged him not to go through that door first without checking for traps, sounds, even other areas of ingress. He wouldn't listen. He kicked the door and...and..."

"And what?" asked Huffman.

Huffman watched Trang's face as he was catapulted back to that time. It looked as if he were reliving every moment. His eyes watered, his face contorted, giving a look a sadness, fear, and anger. It seemed Trang lost more than a partner that day.

"He didn't even have time to react to the gunshot blast. It just, took him out. Like that," said Trang, emphasizing his words with a finger snap.

"Look, I get it," began Huffman, "but this is a completely different scenario. This place had been abandoned for decades. I don't even know why the damned building is still standing, quite frankly. There's nothing here but bugs, insects, rats, and right now, a murder suspect."

"Murder suspect? That's a big leap," said Trang.

"Not so big, considering..."

Huffman's words trailed off as she thought about Hanlan. She'd just... left him there. What the hell had she been thinking?

"Considering what?" asked Trang.

"Hanlan's...dead."

"Wait. What?"

"Someone came at us in the basement. He had a knife and he attacked. He got Hanlan. Then, somehow, took him out with two shots. I don't know how he could have doubled back, but he did. Now, I think the suspect is in that room."

Both officers looked to the door which rattled lightly from gusts of wind inside. Beyond the door they heard a muffled voice. Huffman put her finger to her lips and gripped her weapon tighter. Trang followed as she stepped toward the door. Feet shuffled on the other side. The scrape of a chair sliding across the floor reminded Huffman of nails on a chalkboard. She felt a cold gust of wind escape from the bottom of the door. The room seemed dark. No light escaped, but something was happening.

Huffman.

Julie looked to Trang and silenced him. The look on his face was one of confusion.

Huffman.

This time, she heard her name with her eyes trained on Trang. His lips had not moved. It was just like the basement incident with Hanlan. It had to be the guy that killed him. It had to be him inside. Huffman reached out, checked the handle, and found the door was locked. She moved, squared up, and prepared to breach.

"Huffman. No. Wait."

Trang's words were drowned out by a scream in the room behind the locked door. Julie lifted her leg and with all the force she could muster, kicked the door in. It swung wide into the darkened room. With Trang's story fresh in her mind, Huffman quickly shifted to the side to shield herself from anyone inside who may have a firearm.

Trang though, was still in position behind her.

When the shotgun blast rang out, Huffman's eyes closed. She kept them closed. Squeezed them shut. She knew what had happened. She knew what was on the other side of her eyelids and there was nothing in the world she wanted to see less...than another dead officer.

The rattling inside the room forced a different narrative though.

The screaming inside continued. Added to the cacophony of noise though was constant banging on the walls and what sounded like...chains. With great reluctance, Huffman opened her eyes. Her heartbeat added to the percussive rhythm inside the room. Her breathing was labored, and she felt something on her neck. Something crawled across it. Then she felt something drop down into her hair.

Huffman.

She moved now, preparing to go into the dark room, and as she did, she was bowled over by someone, or some...thing. Her weapon flew out of her hand and standing over her was a dark figure. She couldn't tell if it was the same person from the basement, but when its eyes flashed green, there was no mistake.

Car lights from outside briefly illuminated the church through the stained glass and Huffman caught a glimpse of the shadow's face. Only... there wasn't much to see. The man had eyes, but no nose, and his mouth was sewn shut. *"How could he be the one speaking?"* she asked herself. His face was smeared with dirt and ash, as were his clothes. He wore all black. Pants, shirt, sport coat...all black. All caked in dirt and ash.

As if prompted by the light from the outside, the man shielded his face, and ran off to the other side of the church. Huffman heard him bound up some stairs. Taking time to gather her wits, and after taking one last look at Trang, she gathered her weapon and trailed after her killer.

#   #   #

Huffman moved up the stairs, taking in as much as her senses could handle to be prepared for…whatever she'd just encountered. The silence was interrupted by the loud, painful beating of her heart.

THUMP-THUMP! THUMP-THUMP!

She couldn't control her breathing. In many ways she felt like she was drowning. Her body required frequent intakes, but Huffman was determined to control them, to control the noise she'd make with speedy, heavy breathing. That stubbornness left her feeling like there wasn't enough oxygen in the world. Tension was building within. Her legs felt rubbery. She braced herself against the wall as she ascended the stairs, but even in that, she felt little strength and gained little leverage to push off and continue her ascension. Her service weapon weighed a ton and even with a two-handed grip, she felt it slipping.

Once at the top, a trip that seemed to take longer than it should have, Huffman gave herself a brief moment to recover. She found a light switch on the wall opposite her. She assumed it was for the hallway. Flipping it, she found it did little to illuminate the narrow corridor.

Snap!

Huffman whirled, her weapon ready, pointed at whatever just snapped a floorboard. She found nothing. Saw…nothing. Peering at the steps she'd just ascended she found all of them in perfect condition. At least, as perfect as decades old, poorly maintained wooden steps could be. She turned to resume—

"Huffman."

Her heart stopped and she jumped back, braced by the wall, weapon pointed straight ahead.

"Whoa, whoa, it's me," said Pembrooke.

"Dammit, Pembrooke. What the hell?"

Huffman tried not to scream. She didn't want to alert the suspect. But every part of her wanted to launch into a maddened tirade. Everything about the night was just so…wrong. She questioned everything she knew. Everything she thought she knew. About the job, her life…the very fabric of reality. Nothing seemed as it should.

"What do you think about lowering that thing?" asked Pembrooke.

Huffman followed his eyes to her weapon, still trained on him.

Embarrassed, she quickly lowered it, pointing it down and to her right, away from him.

"I'm sorry. I'm just…wait a minute…have you been up here the whole time?" she asked.

"Yeah, I came up here when you and Hanlan went to the basement. Trang was with me, but he heard something downstairs and went to check it out. Why? Did you guys find anything?"

"All we found was confusion and…and…"

Huffman was afraid to say the next word. Death. It was death. That's what she found. Or at least, it's what found her. First Hanlan, then Trang. Was she next? Maybe Pembrooke? She didn't want to tell him, but she knew he needed to be briefed. He needed to know that they were up against something sinister, deadly, perhaps even, otherworldly. But how exactly could she say that? Especially after the fool she'd made of herself earlier when they'd all arrived.

"And what?" asked Pembrooke.

"And," she began, "Hanlan and Trang are down."

"Down? What? Like injured? Did you call and ambulance? Where are—"

"They're dead, Pembrooke. They're both dead. Killed, by whoever or whatever I chased up here."

Huffman watched Pembrooke's face as the news settled in. She didn't have the words to console him. What could she possibly say? He'd known them. Worked with them. Fought with them. He'd probably blame her and then her career would blow up in a cloud of smoke. Maybe it should, though. She definitely wasn't going to make it on this unit. Given her performance tonight, turning in her badge seemed like the best, most logical step to take.

Huffman gave Pembrooke the details and prepared herself to receive his angry retort to her debrief. But there was none. He simply looked at her, nodded, and took a deep breath.

"And you're sure the guy came up here? Because nothing has come my way," said Pembrooke.

"I'm positive. Unless there's some hidden staircase around here somewhere, this is where the guy ran."

"All right then. Let's follow the hallway and see if we can pick him up. But let's be smart."

"Meaning what?" asked Huffman, trying not to sound offended.

"Meaning, let's not let our emotions take over. I know the first reaction, after taking out two of our own, would be to take him out. We don't want to walk down that path. There's just…no returning from that."

"You say that like you've got experience," said Huffman.

An uncomfortable silence passed between them. Huffman saw strain in Pembrooke's face. Whatever he'd planned to share was painful. She hadn't heard about him. Hanlan's story had made the rounds. Even Trang's story had been shared in the grapevine, though she'd not known full details till tonight. Pembrooke though, he was pretty anonymous to her.

"A few years back, my old partner and I rolled up on a hostage situation. Suspect was using a guy as a human shield. My partner was pretty good on the range. Rarely missed a shot. Turned down a spot with SWAT because he just wanted to be a beat cop. So when we roll up, he tells me he's gonna take the guy out first chance he gets. The suspect kept moving his gun from the hostage's temple to us and back. My partner was certain he could take the guy out with a clean headshot."

"And? What happened?" asked Huffman.

"He missed. Gunman got pissed and took my partner out instead."

Huffman.

There it was again. Her name on the wind. She looked around, prepared to square up against whatever was coming.

"What is it?" asked Pembrooke.

"He's near."

"How do you know?"

"I can hear him."

"You can—"

Pembrooke stopped as both he and Huffman saw movement at the end of the hall. The dark figure was back, and he had a hostage. The entire scenario was impossible. The hostage, a priest, looked just like the former pastor of the abandoned church. But it couldn't be. He'd been dead for over two decades. Yet, there stood Father Casey, with a gun pressed against his temple.

There was no regret when Officer Julie Huffman fired the shot. As she gently squeezed the trigger of her Sig Sauer P226, life suddenly came at her in slow motion. The backward motion of the slide, the muzzle flash, the cartridge ejection, all of it, fluid. No hesitation. Just like training. Only this time she was firing into a target. A living being.

At least that's what she thought.

Because when the bullet passed through her target, he blinked in and out of existence. Like a television trying to find it's signal for a stable feed.

"You saw that, right?" she asked.

"I don't know what the hell I just saw," said Pembrooke.

They looked at each other, then stared back at the man in black down the hall. Huffman still had her weapon trained on him. The man in black still held onto Father Casey, using the good priest as a human shield. He'd moved his weapon from Father Casey's temple and pointed it directly at Huffman and Pembrooke for the briefest of moments when Julie took the shot. But it went straight through the gunman as he blinked in and out of existence.

Father Casey did, too.

The two men seemed to reset. Once again, the gun was at Father Casey's temple. Once again, the man in black snickered at Huffman and Pembrooke. Once again, he moved to fire on them. Julie fired once more. She aimed for the head, a kill shot, one that, from her current distance, was certain to end this standoff. Only it didn't. The man in black remained, in the same position, with Father Casey. Gunman and hostage, blinking in and out of existence like a show on a thirteen-inch television with rabbit ears and a tinfoil connector.

After several beats, they were simply…gone.

"Okay, you definitely saw that, right?" asked Huffman.

The silence did nothing to calm Huffman's nerves. She was at a loss for words. Pembrooke didn't seem to be the type that was typically quiet, though. They'd only met tonight for the first time, but she could tell that Dan Pembrooke was a bit of a smartass. He seemed the type to be full of ridiculous one-liners, and she was desperate for one just to put her at ease.

"Pem—"

Turning as she spoke, Huffman froze mid-sentence. Mouth agape, she stared in disbelief at the sight of Pembrooke on the ground, dead, from a bullet to the head. At the last second, Huffman heard footsteps coming toward her, a walk that rapidly morphed into a run. By the time she turned to track the source, the man in black was bearing down on her. The black mass with bright, glowing green eyes came at her, faster, faster, and then gave a shriek as it launched itself at her. She backed up, allowing her body to go a little slack, preparing to take the hit. Somehow, inexplicably, the man in black flew through her. It was too late for her though. In preparation for the hit, she'd allowed her own momentum to carry her back. Julie Huffman fell, toppling over Pembrooke, and down the stairs. It was a fall that seemed to take forever.

#   #   #

A bruised Julie Huffman lifted herself up from the bottom of the stairs and made her way to a pew in the front of the Murder Chapel. She sat, breathing heavy, her face caked with blood and dirt, streaked with tears. She didn't know what to make of the night. There was nothing in her recent or distant memory that remotely helped her put the night's events into perspective. She was supposed to be here to solve a case. She did not do that, and it cost her the lives of the very men she was to work with.

"Rough night?"

Julie jumped at the voice and hit the floor. Her weapon was gone, and when it came right down to it, she no longer had the energy to fight, much less defend herself.

"Easy, Huffman, it's just me," said Captain Fulton.

It took a few moments for the voice to register. When it did, Huffman raised her head slowly. When she saw the figure of her Captain, it took all the restraint she could muster not to run to him. She was a strong, capable officer who didn't need to run to someone for comfort. And it was terribly cliché, too. So she stood, she wiped her face to clear the dirt, grit, and dried blood away—tears, too, and she prepared to give her report to Captain Fulton. But the words wouldn't flow. The only thing that would were the tears.

So, she let them.

And then she ran to Fulton.

It was in that moment that Julie Huffman realized that she was no island. She was strong. She was capable. She was brilliant. Most importantly though, she was human. She needed others for support at times, for counsel, and in this moment, for comfort. And that was okay. Had she heeded the cautionary tales of the other officers tonight, perhaps she would have made better decisions and kept them alive. In the end, even she took a fall. It was a wonder she had not—

"It's all right, Huffman. It's over. You made it through."

"Captain…it was…awful," she said through labored breath.

"I know. But you made it through," said Fulton.

"Yeah but—"

Huffman stopped mid-sentence as she took in Fulton's words. *She'd made it through?* What did that mean? What did he know? More importantly, what didn't he share when this whole night began? Huffman pulled back from the embrace and sought answers in the eyes of her Captain.

"How did you—"

"You wouldn't be here now if you hadn't made it through, Julie," said Fulton.

Huffman sat with that statement for a moment, still searching for answers in his stare. She looked down, realizing for the first time that he'd been holding something. A…bottle. A bottle of single malt scotch whiskey.

"What the hell is going on here, Captain?"

"Just what he said. You made it through," said a voice from behind.

Julie turned to find Pembrooke walking toward them from the back room on the left of the pulpit. He seemed…very much alive. Her locked gaze was broken at the sight of Hanlan and Trang walking toward her from the back room on the right side of the pulpit. They, too, seemed…very much alive.

"I…I…don't understand," she said.

"It's simple, really," began Fulton. "Actually, you know what, it's not. It's downright insane, and there's not a person alive who would believe this. Fortunately, for this group, we don't have to worry about that."

Fulton pulled the top off his whiskey and took a healthy drink, his face acknowledging the burn he felt as the liquid slid down his throat. Huffman very much wanted to feel that burn. She eyed the bottle and reached for it. She felt some resistance at first, but eventually Fulton let her have it. She pulled off the top and put the bottle to her lips. The smell hit her first. It was strong and assaulted her nostrils, but Huffman quickly moved past that and drank.

Then she coughed.

A lot.

She handed the bottle back to a grinning Fulton and the others laughed.

"Gentleman," began Fulton, "Officer Julie Huffman has finally made it. Thanks for your help."

As he spoke, he inclined his head to acknowledge them. Huffman then looked at each member of her team. Each of them nodded to Fulton in response, then each of them, in turn, gave a makeshift two fingered salute to Huffman—before they dissipated into grey clouds of smoke, and vanished.

"What the…"

"Yeah, gets me every time, too," said Fulton.

"Captain?"

"Come on Huffman, it's time for you to move on."

"I…don't understand," said Huffman.

"You will. Once you step through those doors," said Fulton.

As Huffman walked with Captain Fulton, the lights of the murder chapel flickered. A cool breeze rushed through, picking up dirt and dust and relocating it to other parts of the dark and gloomy tomb. The doors of the church opened by themselves as Huffman and Fulton neared them—a bright white light on the other side. A hesitant Julie Huffman flickered, just like a television show on an old black and white box with rabbit ears and tinfoil. Once solid again, she took a deep breath, and stepped through.

Behind her, a short middle-aged man in overalls, with bright glowing green eyes, pushed a broom across the floor, taking care of the church, and all those within its walls. ♜

NOTES FROM PROJECT CYBERPOLICE

By Jeremiah Dylan Cook

IMPORTANT NOTICE – All following materials are confidential trade secrets. Anyone found disseminating these materials will face termination and immediate legal action.

All Purchaser Commodities (APC) Notes for Initial Pitch of Project
CyberPolice – July 17, 1987
Compiled by Senior Secretary Murphy

Meeting assembled in Executive Room A of Floor 87 of Two World Trade Center. Presentation conducted by Vice President (VP) of Technology, Ms. Paul, with assistance from Technology's Head of Operations (HO), Mr. Edward, and the Head of Research and Development (R&D), Mr. Michael. Other Executives in attendance were President and Chief Executive Officer (CEO), Mr. Boddicker; VP of Special Projects, Mr. Jones; VP of Finance, Mr. Snyder; and VP of Public Relations, Mr. Wong. Business dress code was in effect and conference table was laid out with pastries, orange juice, and water.

VP of Technology, Ms. Paul opened presentation by shutting the room's blinds and cutting off the view of lower Manhattan. Mr. Edward and Mr. Michael prepared slides and projector. Slide show started.

Slide 1: Times Square filled with theaters advertising pornography, peep show booths, prostitutes, and adult-oriented stores. Trash litters the streets. People give each other wide berths on the sidewalks.

Slide 2: Tents dominate an overgrown lawn in Central Park. A man, wearing plastic bags for shoes and newspapers for pants, pushes his black and white border collie in a shopping cart. Discarded needles litter the foreground while the city's skyline looms hazily in the background.

Slide 3: The chalk outlines of three bodies lay between seats on a subway car. Graffiti covers every inch of the ceiling, walls, and doors. Due to the images being spray painted over each other repeatedly, it is hard to identify any distinct pictures, but two stick out. One image is of a cartoonish pig wearing a police hat with blood dripping from his severed neck, and the other is of an intricately detailed phallus.

VP of Technology, Ms. Paul: "As demonstrated by these slides, our city is on the wrong path. These are just three tiny examples of the ocean of crime running rampant in Manhattan. Homicide has spiked for the fifth year in a row, drugs are openly traded on almost every street corner, and hookers outnumber our city's tourists. We at APC have already invested in one attempted solution."

Slide 4: A razor-wire-lined concrete wall divides a city street. Two police officers wearing tactical gear aim pistols at the top of the structure. A sign for Wall Street stands prominently in the picture's center.

VP of Technology, Ms. Paul: "Building the Great Wall of New York has sequestered problematic boroughs such as the Bowery and Hell's Kitchen from us in the financial district, but has that solved anything? Crime in the walled off parts of the city continues to skyrocket, and people manage to cross the barricade daily. The police are understaffed and outgunned in most neighborhoods. Worse, they outright ignore crimes they don't deem as dangerous, choosing to turn a blind eye to prostitution nine times out of ten. What we really need is a police force that doesn't rest, doesn't ignore laws, doesn't think for themselves. Members of the Executive, it is my distinct pleasure to introduce you to Project CyberPolice."

Slide 5: A spotlight illuminates an armored, metallic robot in human shape. No wiring is visible, but large pistons protrude near the elbows and knees of the armor plating. The robot has a gold badge stamped on its right breast, and a speaker where a human would have a mouth. The machine's eye-like lenses glow blue. Instead of a right hand, it has an assortment of gun barrels.

VP of Technology, Ms. Paul: "This is only concept art, but my associates in the Technology Department have created a schematic to bring this machine to life. Imagine a police force of these patrolling the streets of Manhattan. Crime will be murdered in a matter of days. We'll all sleep safer knowing our CyberPolice are always out there protecting us. The days of fragile and corrupt cops are over."

VP of Finance, Mr. Snyder: "I'd buy your concept art for a dollar, but how much will this endeavor actually cost?"

VP of Technology, Ms. Paul: "Well, the prototype will be a pretty penny, but once we've figured out mass production, the costs will go down significantly."

VP of Special Projects, Mr. Jones: "Stop stalling. How much?"

VP of Technology, Ms. Paul: "Just under a million dollars."

Senior Secretary Note: The Executive Team, with the exception of the President, broke into laughter.

President and CEO, Mr. Boddicker: "Sweetie, don't take the laughter personally. They will jump at any opportunity to belittle anyone who presents a fresh idea. I, for one, think you have a tremendous vision, and I would be extremely happy if someone else in this room could find a way to contribute to your idea instead of chortling it off. We're about teamwork at APC, not jockeying for standing and power. Does anyone besides Ms. Paul have something useful to add to today's proceedings?"

Senior Secretary Note: The blinds rose, restoring light to the room. Silence filled the air as members of the Executive Team looked back and forth at each other. President and CEO, Mr. Boddicker sat forward, drumming on the table with his fingers.

VP of Special Projects, Mr. Jones: "I actually might have a way to make this idea cost effective."

President and CEO, Mr. Boddicker: "By all means, take the floor."

Senior Secretary Note: VP of Technology, Ms. Paul, Mr. Edward, and Mr. Michael retook their open seats at the table.

VP of Special Projects, Mr. Jones: "We recently acquired the patent for a curious liquid from the financial executor of a deceased doctor West out of New England. When injected into dead flesh, the substance reanimates necrotic tissue. Unfortunately, all our experiments have resulted in overly aggressive and dangerous resurrections. The most noteworthy of these was a well-trained and sweet Saint Bernard, who came back as a vicious mauler."

VP of Public Relations, Mr. Wong: "Ah, I remember that one. My team had to spin its rampage and convince locals that rabies was to blame."

VP of Special Projects, Mr. Jones: "Mistakes were made. But, if our friends in the Technology Department can provide us with the schematics for Project CyberPolice, I'm wondering if we can marry these two ventures?"

Senior Secretary Note: VP of Technology, Ms. Paul, Mr. Edward, and Mr. Michael whisper amongst themselves.

VP of Technology, Ms. Paul: "We have done extensive work on building a central control unit to issue commands for Project CyberPolice. In theory, it should be possible to graft this unit into a living organism's brain."

President and CEO, Mr. Boddicker: "It must be humans. No one will trust animal cyborgs to police their streets."

VP of Special Projects, Mr. Jones: "I agree completely."

VP of Public Relations, Mr. Wong: "Securing subjects could be problematic from a PR perspective."

VP of Special Projects, Mr. Jones: "Isn't that why you're paid? Besides, the substance can only be used on the deceased. This is no different than what medical colleges do when they train on cadavers."

VP of Public Relations, Mr. Wong: "Cadavers used for medical training don't return to life as police officers."

President and CEO, Mr. Boddicker: "Enough bickering. This is a great idea. I want a progress report by the end of next month. Is that clear?"

Senior Secretary Note: Meeting concluded.

Confidential APC Notes for first Progress Report on Project CyberPolice – August 28, 1987
Compiled by Junior Secretary Lewis

Junior Secretary Note: The previous secretary assigned to Project CyberPolice, A. Murphy, expressed reservations over the project's direction and abruptly quit APC. Prior to departure, previous secretary signed non-disclosure agreement (NDA) related to Project CyberPolice.

Meeting assembled in Executive Room C of Floor 87 of Two World Trade Center. Presentation conducted by VP of Technology, Ms. Paul and VP of Special Projects, Mr. Jones. Technology's HO, Mr. Edward, and the Head of R&D, Mr. Michael in attendance along with President and CEO, Mr. Boddicker, VP of Finance, Mr. Snyder, and VP of Public Relations, Mr. Wong. Hawaiian Shirt Friday dress code was in effect, and conference table was laid out with Chinese food ordered for lunch. A wall of televisions, set to a default APC screen, are imbedded into the wall, opposite the table.

VP of Special Projects, Mr. Jones: "For the last month, Ms. Paul and I have worked with our teams to combine our two ideas. The results have been promising."

Junior Secretary Note: At a gesture from the VP of Special Projects, Mr. Jones, the VP of Technology, Ms. Paul, aims a remote at the wall of televisions and hits a button. On screen, a Doberman sits patiently in a large, eggshell-colored room with an animal obstacle course of hoops, tunnels, and a human-shaped dummy. The dog does not pant, and no signs of breathing are visible. Dried blood is crusted around the animal's eyes, mouth, and ears. A technician in hockey-pad-like protective gear walks into the frame with a controller and hits a button. The Doberman charges off. The camera follows the Doberman as he jumps through three consecutive hoops, stops, turns, and dives through a tunnel. The Doberman ends the display by attacking the rubber dummy stood up at the end of the course. The Doberman tears off the dummy's head and returns to a peaceful sitting position.

VP of Special Projects, Mr. Jones: "As you can see, we've perfected the reanimation and control of dogs. I have videos of dozens of other types of animals being similarly controlled. This was the first step to human trials. Unfortunately, we've run into a slight snag while transitioning to people. Animals restore quickly using our patented formula, but humans need to be freshly deceased. The quicker we inject the fluid, the better the return of muscular and bodily function."

President and CEO, Mr. Boddicker: "What about mental activity?"

VP of Technology, Ms. Paul: "Our insertion of the central control unit into the grey matter should eliminate any protocol conflicts, but Mr. Jones assured me the corpses will remain brain dead."

VP of Special Projects, Mr. Jones: "Correct. Little chance for neural activity, but we need a fresh corpse. So, I'd like to initiate an operation to obtain a perfect specimen for our prototype. I'd prefer to keep the specifics off the record, but my team has identified a candidate."

President and CEO, Mr. Boddicker: "Do what you need to."

VP of Special Projects, Mr. Jones: "Perfect. I'll get another meeting on the books as soon as we have an update."

Junior Secretary Note: Meeting concluded.

Confidential APC Notes for second Progress Report on Project CyberPolice – September 30, 1987
Compiled by New Hire Secretary Reed

New Hire Secretary Note: The previous secretary assigned to Project CyberPolice, A. Lewis, expressed reservations over the project's direction and abruptly quit APC. Prior to departure, previous secretary signed NDA related to Project CyberPolice.

Meeting assembled in Executive Room D of Floor 87 of Two World Trade Center. An unknown man sits in a metal chair opposite the table. Wires are connected to his head and neck. A large scar circumvents his skull. He appears to be in his mid-to-late forties or early fifties with a black mustache and white hair. Despite age, he appears physically fit and muscularly toned. The unknown man wears only white boxers. The presentation is conducted by VP of Technology, Ms. Paul and VP of Special Projects, Mr. Jones. Technology's HO, Mr. Edward, and the Head of R&D, Mr. Michael in attendance along with President and CEO, Mr. Boddicker, VP of Finance, Mr. Snyder, and VP of Public Relations, Mr. Wong. Business dress code is in effect, and conference table is laid out with subs ordered for lunch.

VP of Special Projects, Mr. Jones: "Gentlemen, it is my pleasure to introduce you to our first candidate in Project CyberPolice. Formerly Detective Ketch of the New York Police Department (NYPD), the man before you is being given a new purpose as our first automated cop."

President and CEO, Mr. Boddicker: "Where did we find him?"

VP of Public Relations, Mr. Wong: "I located Detective Ketch after an exhaustive search. He met all the right criteria. Formerly a great cop, but he'd recently become disgraced and forgotten. No one will miss him."

President and CEO, Mr. Boddicker: "What disgraced him?"

VP of Public Relations, Mr. Wong: "He'd become convinced Astonishing Comics was responsible for the rise in New York crime. Something about blood-ink from the band Smooch in books causing evil in kids. Tried to kill an editor at the company, but his police connections kept the incident hushed up."

President and CEO, Mr. Boddicker: "Sounds like his brain was already dead. Fortuitous that he passed when he could be of use to us. Did we get his consent for this procedure prior?"

VP of Public Relations, Mr. Wong: "When he died, all his identification was taken. He ended up as a John Doe, and we were able to claim him through various legal loopholes."

President and CEO, Mr. Boddicker: "How did we identify him if he had no identification?"

VP of Special Projects, Mr. Jones: "The less said, the better, sir. Let's just say we'd had him on our radar for some time before his demise."

President and CEO, Mr. Boddicker: "And how did he pass?"

VP of Special Projects, Mr. Jones: "I can provide more details off the record."

President and CEO, Mr. Boddicker: "Fine, fine. Let's get the presentation moving."

VP of Special Projects, Mr. Jones: "We've successfully integrated our technology into the resurrected officer's brain. He's already filled up with laws we'd like him to enforce. We plan to present him to the city within a week to start duty. Here's a demonstration."

New Hire Secretary Note: VP of Special Projects, Mr. Jones pulls a small controller from his jacket and flicks a switch. The CyberPolice Officer, formerly Detective Ketch, stands in response.

VP of Special Projects, Mr. Jones: "Officer. Please state your prime command."

CyberPolice Officer: "Protect the interests of APC."

New Hire Secretary Note: CyberPolice Officer appeared to have minor hand tremor while espousing his prime command.

President and CEO, Mr. Boddicker: "I like it, but he's not very imposing, is he? Especially with so little clothing."

VP of Technology, Ms. Paul: "I lobbied hard to provide our asset with a metal armor similar to the exterior of the robot I originally presented."

VP of Finance, Mr. Snyder: "And I shot that down due to cost, but we do have a great uniform in mind. You know how racecar drivers sell add space on their vehicles? Well, we thought we could do the same with our CyberPolice uniforms."

New Hire Secretary Note: VP of Finance, Mr. Snyder gets up and heads to the door and ushers in a team of people, two men and a woman in business clothes, carrying bags brimming with supplies. They head to the CyberPolice Officer, dress him, and leave. His uniform is a navy-blue jumpsuit with black boots and gloves. A badge is stitched over his left peck. An NYPD patch appears over both his shoulders and on his back. The rest of the empty space is filled by adds and logos for restaurants, bars, and stores. A riot helmet with a black plastic shield protects the officer's face.

VP of Finance, Mr. Snyder: "And here is the result."

President and CEO, Mr. Boddicker: "Doubling our monetary stream. I love it."

VP of Technology, Ms. Paul: "But there's no armor. The officer will be a walking bullet sponge."

VP of Special Projects, Mr. Jones: "He won't have armor, but he'll have a pistol for protection. Project CyberPolice has created a means to produce emotionless automatons who act just like robots without any of the cost. Once this guy gets us some good press, we'll be able to leverage that into a steady stream of cannon fodder."

VP of Public Relations, Mr. Wong: "People may be unnerved knowing reanimated corpses are patrolling their streets. We should leverage our media contacts to spread a story that we're studying human remains for medical improvements. We'll offer a small sum for those who donate their deceased. Then, we'll turn the process into an assembly line for CyberPolice."

President and CEO, Mr. Boddicker: "Waste not, want not. Dying will no longer be a valid excuse for ceasing work. So, what will we tell people these officers are?"

VP of Public Relations, Mr. Wong: "I say we advise they're volunteers we've put through a specialized training program. We'll look like we're doing charity service for the city while we're raking in ad revenue and putting the dead to use. Once the CyberPolice have proven effective, we can leverage the success into a lucrative government contract with the city."

President and CEO, Mr. Boddicker: "Perfect. Is that all for today?"

New Hire Secretary Note: Meeting concluded.

Confidential APC Notes for final Progress Report on Project CyberPolice – December 17, 1987
Compiled by New Hire Secretary
New Hire Secretary Note: The previous secretary assigned to Project CyberPolice, S. Reed, expressed reservations over the project's direction and abruptly quit APC. Prior to departure, previous secretary signed NDA related to Project CyberPolice. Current New Hire Secretary does not wish name to appear in record.

Meeting assembled in Executive Room A of Floor 87 of Two World Trade Center. Presentation conducted by VP of Special Projects, Mr. Jones. Technology's HO, Mr. Edward, and the Head of R&D, Mr. Michael, in attendance along with President and CEO, Mr. Boddicker, VP of Finance, Mr. Snyder, and VP of Public Relations, Mr. Wong. Business dress code was in effect, and conference table was laid out with Mexican food ordered for lunch.

VP of Special Projects, Mr. Jones: "Apologies for making the group wait a bit longer than usual for an update, but we have a lot of good news. Our CyberPolice prototype got tons of great press as he spent his first weeks chasing down muggers and sex offenders. He made over a hundred arrests, but his real test came when we sent him over the Great Wall of New York. He took out an entire drug operation. Sixty criminals were killed, twenty in a coke warehouse he raided. The mayor is already offering us a contract for our specialized police services and wants to know when we can have more officers on the streets."

President and CEO, Mr. Boddicker: "Yes, I'm aware of all that. The press has been excellent. But what about the rumors I've heard about the officer's outbursts?"

VP of Special Projects, Mr. Jones: "Nothing to be worried about. My late associate, Ms. Paul, blew that entire situation out of proportion when she visited your office."

Technology HO, Mr. Edward: "You're lying. I can't take this madness any longer. Whatever serum they gave Detective Ketch didn't just bring back his motor functions. For the last few weeks his original personality has been reasserting itself. He's taken to patrolling near the apartment of the comic editor he was obsessed with. But that's not the worst of it. He feels pain. There have been a few times when he's managed to override the central control unit. He cries and asks us to let him die."

VP of Special Projects, Mr. Jones: "Soft hearts don't belong in our company. You're going to end up just like Ms. Paul."

President and CEO, Mr. Boddicker: "Jones, I'm shocked you'd speak of a former coworker so. We all mourn the loss of Ms. Paul. It's a tragedy she decided to jump from her roof."

Technology HO, Mr. Edward: "She never seemed suicidal to me."

VP of Special Projects, Mr. Jones: "I'm sorry, but this is a minor bug. Nothing to be worried about. Since Ms. Paul's departure, I've worked directly with the technicians on Project CyberPolice, and they've assured me they can improve the central control unit so there's no more human bleed through."

Technology HO, Mr. Edward: "But Detective Ketch will still be suffering. We've gone too far here. He's a human being, not a robot. He's not our goddamn property."

VP of Special Projects, Mr. Jones: "Mr. Boddicker, if you'd allow me, I want to illustrate my point."

President and CEO, Mr. Boddicker: "Proceed."

New Hire Secretary Note: VP of Special Projects, Mr. Jones moves toward the doors and opens them. The CyberPolice officer enters the room. He is dressed in his blue uniform, filled with ads, and he wears a holstered pistol on his left hip.

VP of Special Projects, Mr. Jones: "Officer, do you recognize the name Ketch?"

CyberPolice Officer: "No."

VP of Special Projects, Mr. Jones: "Do you suffer pain?"

CyberPolice Officer: "No."

VP of Special Projects, Mr. Jones: "What do you want to do?"

CyberPolice Officer: "Protect the interests of APC."

Technology HO, Mr. Edward: "Your little demonstration is bullshit. Let me turn off the central control unit and then we'll see what happens."

President and CEO, Mr. Boddicker: "I won't have it said that I don't allow friendly competition. Mr. Edward, turn it off."

VP of Special Projects, Mr. Jones: "This is preposterous. Without the central control unit, he'll be an unhinged monster, just like the dog that got loose."

President and CEO, Mr. Boddicker: "Mr. Edward will reactivate the unit the moment the officer does anything we don't like, correct?"

Technology HO, Mr. Edward: "Yes, sir."

New Hire Secretary Note: HO, Mr. Edward and Head of R&D, Mr. Michael, from the Technology Department, leave the room and return with a remote control. Technology HO, Mr. Edward hits a button. The CyberPolice Officer screams as he falls to his knees. He tosses his helmet off and rips open his uniform revealing multiple wounds that haven't healed properly. The dozens of bullet holes and knife gashes ooze a greenish ichor.

CyberPolice Officer: "Why did you do this to me? Why can't I die?

Just kill me."

President and CEO, Mr. Boddicker: "Officer, this is most unbecoming of you. Get off the floor. Mr. Edward turn the central command unit back on."

Technology HO, Mr. Edward: "I won't do it. It's too horrible. He's a free man, not our property."

New Hire Secretary Note: The CyberPolice Officer removes his gun and shoots out the closest window. Wind gusts into the room and sends papers flying. The CyberPolice Officer gets to his feet and looks ready to leap out when he suddenly goes passive again. VP of Special Projects, Mr. Jones stands up holding a remote in his hand.

VP of Special Projects, Mr. Jones: "I had this made as a safety precaution. My own personal controller for the officer."

President and CEO, Mr. Boddicker: "Mr. Edward, I'm very disappointed you didn't follow my command. You're fired and so is your little friend, Mr. Michael. You put everyone in this room at risk. Jones, I believe you've earned a promotion today. How does VP of Special Projects and Technology sound to you?"

Mr. Edward: "What is wrong with all of you? You can't let this program continue, it's unconscionable."

VP of Finance, Mr. Snyder: "I must disagree. Project CyberPolice is showing tremendous potential for revenue growth. We'd be insane to shut it down."

VP of Public Relations, Mr. Wong: "I concur. The public loves our approach to cleaning up the streets. If we make sure there are no more outbursts, it should be fine. I recommend ramping up the program and adding new subjects immediately."

Mr. Edward: "I'm going to the press."

New Hire Secretary Note: Mr. Edward heads for the room's exit.

President and CEO, Mr. Boddicker: "That doesn't serve our interests. Officer, would you handle this?"

New Hire Secretary Note: The CyberPolice Officer sprints around the table and grabs Mr. Edward by the throat before he can make it to the room's door.

VP of Special Projects, Mr. Jones: "Looks like we found our next candidate for Project CyberPolice."

President and CEO, Mr. Boddicker: "Perfect. What about you, Mr. Michael?"

New Hire Secretary Note: Mr. Michael looks at the CyberPolice officer holding his former business associate by the neck and begins to sweat and breathe heavily.

Mr. Michael: "I won't say a word to anyone."

President and CEO, Mr. Boddicker: "Good. You're dismissed."

New Hire Secretary Note: Mr. Michael races to the door, hesitating as he passes the CyberPolice officer choking the last life from Mr. Edward. Mr. Michael exits.

VP of Special Projects, Mr. Jones: "Group, I hope we're all thinking the same thing here."

VP of Public Relations, Mr. Wong: "I believe we are. Security should make sure Mr. Michael does not leave the building."

VP of Special Projects, Mr. Jones: "I'll arrange for him to be our third CyberPolice officer."

President and CEO, Mr. Boddicker: "Perfect. You did say fresh dead were best. Here's to the continued success of Project CyberPolice. God willing, we'll expand the program nationwide in no time."

New Hire Secretary Note: Meeting Concluded. ♜

DO ANDROIDS DREAM?

By Rob Nisbet

DECKER TOOK A LONG, LAST look around apartment 9732. Behind him, Rachel waited nervously in the shadow of the doorway. There was nothing here he needed. He had his gun, and whatever money and credit he could lay his hands on. Stripes of light, from an advertising blimp outside, managed to penetrate the rain then the grime on the windows. Decker watched the lights sweep across the gloom of his meagre, and mostly useless, possessions. It was time to let go; leave it all behind. The ancient piano, for example. He had memories of playing it as a boy, but it had remained untouched for years, merely a surface to cover with even older, mottled photographs: ancestors apparently that he could barely remember. The vid-phone flashed in a corner with the call he had ignored from Byron. Decker knew exactly what the police captain would say. With the renegade skin-jobs eliminated, the only known nexus-8 left on Earth was Rachel. And now that she was 'missing', apparently on the run from the police and the Tanhauser Corporation, Byron wanted the bounty. And there was no way Decker would allow that to happen.

It was like turning his back on his old life as he faced the door. Rachel was framed in the doorway, ready to leave. Her hair hung in loose curls beneath the hood of a full-length ersatz-fur coat – just about the most impractical clothing for the persistent rain. It made her seem naive and aloof, but then it was the only clothing she had. Decker couldn't help but admire her. Her world, or what she had *assumed* to be her world, had come crashing down around her. She was a nexus-8, a replican, a skin-job. Imbued with other people's memories, she'd had no idea until a few days ago that she wasn't a natural human. And that now made her a target for every mercenary Blade Runner in L.A.

Something caught Decker's eye. He stooped and picked up the folded silver paper. His right hand was freshly bandaged, splints supporting his two broken fingers. He turned the silver paper in his left hand. A small origami figure – Graff's calling card. So, he had been here; broken into the apartment. Decker wasn't surprised. Graff, in his rain-drenched coat and brimmed hat, seemed to know more than anyone about the nexus-8s. He appeared to work for the police, but Decker was beginning to wonder if it were the other way round.

The little origami figure caught the light. A horse – no, a *unicorn*.

Decker stared at it as, around him, his world flipped. His life kaleidoscoped to settle into a dizzying new pattern.

He could hardly breathe as he rushed to join Rachel in the hallway. He *was* leaving his life behind – *his whole life* – as he slammed the door closed behind them.

# # #

They took the elevator. Decker's mind seemed displaced, somehow numb, as they ascended the further thirty floors to emerge into the drizzle and black puddles of the roof. It was dark outside. It was always dark; night and day were simply different shades. WWT had left a poisonous atmosphere of dust which choked the sunlight, forming false clouds, but the persistent rain they produced was real enough.

False clouds, thought Decker, grimly. Was nothing real, not even the sky? Suddenly he saw deception everywhere. He grabbed at Rachel's hand and led her towards his hover-car. Bad move. He looked out at the black city-scape horizon. Pinpricks of light outlined the shapes of towers and pyramids, an industrial mast erupted with a fiery gas plume, and gliding somewhere below, in the canyon of buildings, the advertising blimp enticed with utopian images of the Off-World settlements. *Off-World*, thought Decker. A fresh start. An escape.

He realized, too late, that he wasn't thinking straight - his car would be watched. And with its police tracker, Byron would have no trouble locating it.

There was a shadow of movement off to his right. One of his few neighbors had an electric sheep up here that pretended to graze on a sodden patch of ersatz grass. But this movement was not the sheep. Decker fumbled for his gun with his left hand. There was a flash to the right as a weapon discharged. Decker felt his gun blasted away from his hand along with several fingers.

Rachel screeched as Decker fell. His eyes filled with a resigned surprise more than with pain. He saw the second flash as if in slow motion. The bullet filled his vision as it took out his eye. He collapsed into a puddle, turning it red with blood.

He heard a third shot from nearby, and his world went black.

#   #   #

Decker was emerging from sleep, he stirred sluggishly in the bed, stretching life back into his arms and legs. He was still dreaming:

He was a replican. How could he not have known? Graff's little calling-card unicorn had made everything horrifically clear. The memories he had of learning to play that ancient piano were of creatures he imagined brought to a semblance of life by the music. One particular exercise required his fingers to prance across the keyboard. It had sparked an impression of a unicorn emerging white and proud from a forest glade. He'd never told anyone about this image. That exercise had become his favorite tune as a boy – or so he had thought.

Just like Rachel, his memories were false. And Graff had twisted and folded a scrap of silver paper to indicate this. Intentionally? Decker didn't know. But he knew now, for certain, that he and Rachel were both replicans, formed of bone, skin, and blood, but man-made.

He stretched again and let his eyes flicker open. His mind adjusted to the day. He knew he'd been dreaming but, as usual, these impressions were swept aside by harsh reality.

An alarm blared from the ceiling of his enclosed box bedroom, then a male voice barked instructions. "All troupers report to hanger three in thirty minutes." The command was repeated, along with the raucous alarm to ensure that all troupers were awake.

Decker swung himself from the bed. A nutrition bar, not even pretending to be food, had been dispensed onto a tray and a flagon frothed with a dark liquid steaming from a nozzle. This at least smelled and tasted of coffee.

Decker ran water into a small sink. It was mandatory for troupers to be clean-shaven. He regarded himself sleepily in the mirror. Dark close-cropped hair, a reasonable jaw, and that lazy, lop-sided grin the ladies seemed to like. His eyes – well, they were improving. Both blue, his left one was still paler than the right, but it was adjusting over time, just as the medics said it would. He switched on the razor and held it to his face letting it soap and cut.

"Enhance grid 34 to 45," he said to the mirror. He liked to get the edges around his ears perfectly straight. The reflection zoomed into close up. He shaved down from his ears, pulling his face taught with one hand while guiding the razor with the other. His hands, like his eyes, were mismatched. From his left elbow down, his arm was pale compared to the rest of his body. That was an advantage of being a replican. It wasn't unusual to be injured in battle. But it was relatively simple surgery to have nexus-8 body parts grafted together. After all, that's how he had been assembled in the first place.

"Pull back," he told the mirror. The reflection returned to normal. But he noticed something over his shoulder. He swung around to face the doorway behind him. There was nothing there. Facing the mirror again, he squinted his mismatched eyes. "Enhance grid 19 to 23." The mirror zoomed over his shoulder. And there she was. A blurred shape, a woman in his doorway. Almost a silhouette, hunched into the huge collar of a fake-fur coat.

Something stirred at the bottom of his mind and Decker tried to grasp it. But it was as elusive as his forgotten dreams. *Rachel*, he thought – though the name carried no meaning or memory for him. He turned again to the empty doorway, then back again to the mirror. He shuddered. The ghostly image of the woman had gone.

#   #   #

Rachel heard the first shot. Decker's gun was blasted from his hand in a spray of blood and fingers. He spun away from her, falling, as a second shot was fired from across the rooftop. The shadowy gunman was ruthless. It was a headshot. The side of Decker's face exploded in a sheen of red which spread into the puddle where he lay.

Rachel picked up the gun, swung it in both hands and fired. The shadow lurking on the roof was blown backwards and lay still.

There was a moment filled only with rain then, as if it had been waiting for this exchange of gunfire, a police hover-car, lights strobing, appeared in the black sky and slowly descended to settle on the roof.

Rachel still held the gun and stood stunned, unmoving.

Steam purged from the police vehicle, and, from this cloud, a figure appeared. Tall and thin, his long coat glistened with rain, his narrow eyes were shaded by a brimmed hat, and he leant on a cane. Without checking the fallen shadow, he walked towards Rachel. "That was Captain Byron," he said, staring at her. "You've killed a policeman in the line of duty."

Rachel managed a dismayed shake of her head, let the gun fall with a clatter, and turned to kneel where Decker lay in the puddle.

Graff joined her and prodded at the body with his stick. "I think he'll live," he said.

#   #   #

Dressed in armored battle gear, Decker joined the ranks of his fellow replicans in hanger three.

The Off World promise of utopia, much flaunted and advertised on Earth, had been won, and was maintained, at a great price. Several companies vied for control of the inhabited planetoids, with the Tanhauser Corporation claiming by far the largest share. But what they didn't advertise back on Earth, was the threat of the Attack Ships from rival corporations. That little problem was kept secret, even from the Evacuation Board, desperate to get people away from the contaminated Earth. The emigrants would discover the volatile situation for themselves – when it was too late.

The corporations all wanted the same thing: the safe continuation of the human race. The planetoids were primed for re-settlement. But it soon became clear that, without the separate countries of the world, with their separate governing agencies, whoever controlled the Off-World settlements, controlled *everything*.

The Tanhauser Corporation had the most to lose. Nobody wanted another WWT out in space with the inevitable loss of human life, so they invested in fake humans: skin-jobs; the replicans. Their nexus-8 model was the closest to human yet. An army to protect their territories, to fight and repel all aggressors, with the supreme advantage that they were expendable.

Decker was in the front row as the hanger shielding was cranked aside. Around and behind him, row upon row of fidgeting nexus-8 troupers filled the vast, girder-ribbed cavern. The shielding gave way to a series of tall, narrow windows beyond which was space. Nothing. It stretched forever, its complete blackness sucking at the senses as only a vacuum can. It took several seconds for Decker's eyes to adjust enough to see the stars. His pale left eye saw them first. The red supergiant Betelgeuse glowed faintly, dead ahead. From Earth, this star had formed the shoulder of Orion.

Decker felt the ship tilt and rotate, and beyond the windows the new configuration of constellations shifted in the blackness. There was no sense of up or down. An artificial gravity anchored him to the floor as the curve of a Tanhauser planetoid twisted into view, its cities picked out in sprawling clusters of light.

Then, beyond this small world, were specks of silver.

Attack ships.

A voice blasted through the hanger. Everyone was deployed immediately for the counterattack.

155

Decker's row filed out first, marching swiftly down a clattering ramp, into hanger three's lower level. He passed several uniformed officers urging speed and shouting encouragement. He was directed to the nearest repel craft. A black-as-space two-person tube. He glanced around to see who he'd be paired with. And there, in a distant doorway, he saw the woman from the mirror, again hunched into her fur collar. He could see a little of her face this time; dark staring eyes; the firm red line of her lips.

An order was barked into his ear. He and another trouper clambered into the repel craft and clipped themselves in. The great tube revolved towards the launch hatch. Decker saw the distant doorway swing past. He twisted his neck, but the woman he somehow knew as Rachel, had vanished again. The seat pressed suddenly into his back as the repel craft was ejected into space.

Decker was paired with Prizora. He had fought alongside her before. She was heralded, with some justification, as the best pilot in the Tanhauser fleet. She leant back in her seat, her face beneath her short-cropped black hair was grim with concentration. She gripped the flight rod and spun them away from the main ship in a curve down towards the planetoid below.

The attack ships were from the rival Floridan Corporation; they had their own planetoids but wanted more. Their ships were winged saucers, designed for close, low-level flight within the halo of surface atmosphere. Ideal for threatening off-world settlements into submission.

Prizora hurled the repel craft at the small world below like a meteor. "Saucer at grid H-14," she yelled. "Enhance."

Decker had already seen it, a lone Floridan craft sweeping down towards Tyrell City, heading for the Tyrell Gate. At this level, the main link with other cities was alive with the crisscrossing trail lights of commerce. Prizora swooped on the enemy craft, its silver wings tilting as it banked towards its target. Then she pulled up at the last moment. Decker unleashed a pulsed concussion beam. It glittered out from the repel craft, a focused reverberation of light that buckled the saucer's main dome. A direct hit. The saucer crumpled beneath the concussion, bursting into fire as Prizora whooped in triumph, flying through the ball of flame and back into the blackness.

An easy kill. They were in the first wave, with surprise on their side. It was now that the battle would get messy.

The sleek black tube of a second repel craft joined them in defense of the Tyrell Gate just as a phalanx of three saucers swept into view. Outnumbered, Prizora barked vid-screen instruction to the second pilot. Until their conspicuous c-beams were fired, their coloring might keep them hidden. Prizora swept her craft in a wide loop, circling back on her starting point where the three saucers clustered. Decker charged the concussion beam, knowing that his comrades in the repel craft behind him would be doing the same. Prizora repeated her earlier maneuver, headed straight for the nearest saucer. A second Floridan attack craft was close by. With skillful shooting, they might take out both. Decker waited for Prizora's signal, knowing she'd pull up and away at the last second. He glanced over at his pilot – and froze.

Prizora had gone. The pilot's seat revolved to face him. Sitting on it was the mysterious woman in her fur and high collar. Decker saw her, perfectly clear this time, the cascade of her curls, the paleness of her slim face and fingers, the scarlet of her lips. Their eyes locked. And Decker felt the repel craft jerk upwards, distant stars striping across the view screen. A hollow sinking sensation flipped his stomach as he realized he'd missed his chance to fire. The c-beam rod remained still in his hands.

Prizora was yelling at him. She was back in the pilot seat. There was fury in her voice, but Decker stared dumbly around the cramped craft. The ghostly image, *Rachel*, had vanished. It was impossible. She couldn't have vanished – she couldn't have appeared in the first place.

Then they were struck. Swooping close by three saucers without firing was suicidal. A blast pierced their hull, then an explosion of burning shrapnel ripped through the rear of the craft embedding shards into the navigation panel and passing through Prizora on the way. She screeched in pain, placing both hands to the right side of her neck. Blood welled between her fingers. Decker was shocked back to reality. They were spiraling up and away from the surface, now far below. But behind them, the second repel craft wasn't so fortunate. Without Decker's concussion, the three saucers veered apart, and as one, fired on the black tube. It was blown apart, ragged chunks falling down towards the city lights. Decker was at Prizora's side, calling her name. Her neck was shredded. Blood spurted in gouts, and air bubbled up through the gore as she tried desperately to keep breathing. Replican biology is deliberately simplified – and their cells designed to seek connections with each other to aid self-repair. But Prizora knew that her lacerations were too severe.

Decker knew it too. From a medical chest he grabbed at various clamps. The best he could do was to save what he could as spare parts. He reached into the exposed flapping remnants of skin and muscle, clamping the spraying vessels and closing the pale creamy pipe that burbled from the straining lungs. Finally, he injected a numbing pain killer and lay Prizora back in the pilot's chair, twitching in a glistening pool of her own blood.

Uncontrolled, the repel craft twisted in space. And Decker saw the remnants of the second black tube burn like fireworks in the planetoid's narrow layer of atmosphere. The craft's crew, two replicans, both lost. No spare parts there. He looked with his replacement eye at his own mismatched arms, and wondered, for the first time, where and who they had come from.

#   #   #

Rachel followed Graff down the corridors of what she assumed was an L.A. hospital. Despite his stick, he walked quicky and her heals clattered on the tiles behind him trying to keep up. He paused for a moment outside a closed door, then pushed it open.

Several medical staff drew back from a raised bed surrounded by monitors. Tubes and wires linked them in a web to where Decker lay unconscious, catheters and drains puncturing his body.

"Decker," Rachel gasped the name and rushed forward. There was no response from the man on the bed. She tentatively touched the skin of his shoulder, watched his chest rise and fall with shallow breaths. "Rick." Using his first name sounded odd, even to her. She turned to Graff. "Does he know I'm here?"

Graff shrugged and spread his hands. "He is deeply anaesthetized," he explained. "He may be vaguely aware of your presence – who can say?"

Rachel leant closer; her scarlet lips drawn into an anxious twist at the sight of Decker's surgery. A fluid-filled gauze lay over his left eye socket. Like a transparent blister, it magnified the new, pale blue eye that stared up at the rotating fan in the ceiling. The splints on his right hand's broken fingers had been re-dressed and his left arm lay supported on a padded ledge attached to the bed. From the elbow down, a new arm had been grafted on, replacing the one that had been shot to pieces on the roof. The join was also smothered in gauze, staples showed through the material and external veins pulsed, linking the upper arm to the paler lower limb and hand.

"He is lucky," said Graff.

"Lucky?" Rachel was incredulous.

"That such an effort should be made to save a non-human." Graff turned to her. Without his hat to shade his eyes, they were shrewd and riddled with secrets. "This surgery was sanctioned only because he, and you too my dear, are, shall we say, special cases." He leant on his cane making a circuit of the bed. "Advances are being made all the time: nexus-9, nexus-10. You two are more valuable than you know."

The ceiling fan swept shadows across Rachel's face. She gazed up at it, frowning as she tried to retrieve a memory. "This isn't a hospital," she said.

Graff's face was serious. "Excellent." He nodded to himself with appreciation as if she had just passed some test. "Where do you think you are?"

Rachel didn't need to look around. Decker's patchwork body seemed twisted into her own memories by the circling fan. "This is a replican assembly clinic."

"Interesting," said Graff. "I wondered if being here might make you remember. Your own assembly took place in a room just like this." He watched her for an emotional reaction, as if he were a living V-K empathy test. He knew that Rachel had already accepted what she was, and that she was coming to terms with what she now knew Decker to be. The fact that they were both replicans wouldn't, in itself, trigger her emotions, yet the reaction as she stared down at Decker was undeniably there: the dilation of the iris, the capillary blush-response to her cheeks. Graff was fascinated. What emotion was Rachel capable of? Could this be love?

"Body parts are manufactured in various factories." Graff watched Rachel closely. "Eyes are made here in L.A. The digestive tracts are flown in from Phoenix. There are bone synthesists almost everywhere. Assembly is a complex logistical jigsaw."

"His arm and eye?" Rachel arched a perfectly shaped eyebrow.

"Decker was tracking, or being tracked, by another replican: Rory, a mercenary-class Nexus-8. They fought on the roof of the Ellison building. But Rory had reached the end of his allotted lifespan. His brainstem was designed to last for a maximum of four years. I happened to fly past as Rory died, I heard his last words – so I knew where to source the parts we needed."

Rachel leant over Decker's body. She ignored his injuries and gently touched his lips with hers.

"Rory's arm has been stitched into place," Graff continued. "The tendons and vessels will bind with each other to bridge the gap. The eye has its fibers and nerves attached; they will seek out and root themselves into the optical centers of Decker's brain."

Rachel drew back and the pale eye seemed to follow her movement. It squirmed beneath the protective blister. "It's alive," she said.

"Rapid eye movement," confirmed Graff. "That means he's dreaming."

#   #   #

Decker roared with rage as the last fragments of his fellow repel craft were burnt in the atmosphere like the fiery streaks of a meteor shower. He swung his gunner's chair within reach of the navigation panel grasping both the steering rod and concussion-beam controls. Gritting his teeth, he snarled at the view-screen.

Star-specked space tumbled as he brought the repel craft round, swooping back towards the surface of the small world. Beside him, Prizora blinked through a sheen of blood, still alive, but too weak to assist.

"Rachel caused this!" Decker spat the words. "She appeared, here, like a phantom." A savage venom flooded through him. "Whatever she is, she won't distract me again!"

He shot the repel craft on a direct intercept course with the closest saucer. He didn't pull up. He fired the glittering concussion-beam straight ahead. The saucer shook and buckled and fell apart moments before Decker's black tube punched through the wreckage. Decker roared again, swung his battered craft around and, streaming alongside the remaining two saucers, he matched their speed and c-beamed one along its stubby wing. The saucer deformed and swerved away. Out of control, it cannoned into the other saucer. They both erupted into silent fire, debris spinning away into the blackness.

Decker tasted blood; he had bitten through his own lip; sweat dribbled down from his brow, and he tried to steady his breathing and the adrenaline-fueled shudder of his hands. He felt Prizora's eyes on him. Her head lolled, rocking against the pilot's seat, but her mouth managed a small movement. "Such emotion," she said. "Almost human."

Decker knew what she meant. In theory, replicans might develop their own emotions over time; emotions which would supersede any implanted memories or reactions. Nexus-8s were allowed only a four-year lifespan to prevent this happening.

There was suspicion in Prizora's eyes. "How long have you lived?"

Decker bunched his shaking fists. His mind raced through false recollections, boyhood, playing that piano, the image of the unicorn. He knew now that none of that was real, but he couldn't tell when his replican existence had started.

Prizora slumped, a froth of bubbles sighed from the ruin of her neck. But her eyes still glinted with fascination. "Have you ever loved?" she asked.

Decker's eyes grew wide as Prizora changed again. Perhaps it was the word 'love' that had triggered her transformation.

Rachel turned in the pilot's chair to face him, leaning closer. "Can you see me?"

#   #   #

Graff still watched Rachel with fascination as she gazed down at Decker on the assembly bed. There was a longing in her anxious dark eyes.

"Do you love him?" Graff asked.

Rachel seemed unsure. "I hurt, because he is hurt," she said. "Is that love?"

Graff considered, then nodded with some satisfaction. "I think it is," he said.

DO ANDROIDS DREAM?

"But…" Rachel frowned in confusion. "I shouldn't be capable…"

"As I said, my dear, you and Decker are special cases." Graff leant heavily on his stick. "Your brainstems are of an augmented design. And your cells have an enhanced ability to mesh with replacement organs."

On the bed, Decker's new arm twitched, his exposed new eye roved beneath its protective blister, and a name murmured from his lips, "Prizora."

"That proves that he is dreaming," said Graff. "Priz and Zora were the replicans he retired before confronting Rory on the Ellison building." He tapped the head of his cane thoughtfully against his bottom lip. "The nerves of Rory's eye are knitting themselves into Decker's brain – affecting his subconscious. Does he dream, I wonder, or does he nightmare?"

Rachel shuddered. "The eye is controlling his thoughts?"

"We tread new ground." Graff spread his hands. "Much is unknown. As I landed on that roof… As Decker watched Rory die… I overheard what Rory said – of what his eyes had witnessed." Graff stared up at the lazy whirling of the ceiling fan, as if recalling the exact words. "I've seen things you people wouldn't believe. Attack ships on fire off the shoulder of Orion. I've watched c-beams glitter in the dark over the Tyrell Gate. All these moments will be lost in time – like tears, in rain." Graff lowered his gaze to the man on the bed. "Except, those moments… Perhaps they are not lost. Perhaps they are now in Decker's dreams."

Rachel leant over Decker's face. It was disturbing to think that this new pale eye could be influencing his thoughts. She watched the roving eye settle as if it had focused on her. "Can you see me?" she asked.

#   #   #

"Yes," said Decker. His voice hardened. "I can see you."

He sprang at the image of Rachel seated in the pilot's chair. This ghostly image had caused the repel craft to be hit. Had caused the injuries to his pilot, Prizora. Had caused, too, the destruction of a second craft with the loss of two more lives. Decker didn't know who Rachel was, or how manifestations of her leaked into his life – but he knew she was the enemy – an ethereal distraction – a projection perhaps of the Floridan Corporation.

He grasped Rachel around the neck with both hands, one paler than the other, and squeezed. He felt her tendons, taught beneath his fingers; felt the compression of her throat. "Who are you?" he demanded. "What are you?"

The repel craft spiraled, uncontrolled, towards the city lights below.

Rachel's mouth flapped uselessly. A terrified horror spread from her wide eyes altering, once more, the shape of her face.

161

The surface of the planetoid expanded on the view-screen, closer and closer.

Decker realized he'd been tricked again. His hands were soaked in Prizora's sticky blood. He'd ripped away the clamps that held the pilot's life in stasis. Blood fountained from the re-opened wounds and faltering gasps escaped from burbling flaps of flesh.

Decker sprang back, realizing what he had done. Flecked with spraying gore, Prizora's eyes locked on him with accusation as their focus faded to a dull lifeless stare.

The repel craft smashed into the corner of a building. It screamed through an explosion of debris, nose down, ploughing along a street, flipping vehicles, scattering pedestrians. It thudded suddenly to a halt, raining earth and rubble over the stripes of a pedestrian crossing. "Don't walk," said an automated speaker above a flashing red light. "Don't walk. Don't walk."

#   #   #

Dials twitched and a warning beeped from the equipment surrounding the bed. A tremor shivered through Decker's body.

Rachel drew back from his face.

Graff stepped away, allowing medical staff to approach. "He's agitated," he said. "A nightmare, I think, rather than a dream."

Decker's face twisted to follow Rachel's movement. Both his eyes were now open.

The medical staff adjusted the feeds which dripped medication into the various catheters.

Rachel leant forward again. "You're waking up." She gently stroked Decker's brow, saw his eyes widen at her approach. "You're in a sort of hospital," she explained. "Don't worry. Everything's going to be OK." She leant closer, her voice a tender whisper. "I love you."

Decker's hands fastened around her throat. Eyes still wide, his fingers spasmed, his body convulsed, his mouth twisted with hate.

The medics tried to pry open his grip, but his hands shook with a more-than-human pressure, relentlessly squeezing as Rachel's astonished face turned pale then a slack sickly cyan.

The warning beeps were louder now. A medic opened a valve, releasing a sedative, which closed Decker's eyes and caused him to slump back on the bed. But his hands still had to be levered from around Rachel's neck.

Graff raised an eyebrow, sighed, and touched Rachel's fallen body with the tip of his cane. Nexus-9 spare parts, he thought. She'd not be wasted. And yes, she had been a success; a special case. She had lived beyond the four-year limit. She'd developed burgeoning emotions. She had loved.

And as for Decker...

Graff narrowed his eyes, watching the medical staff fuss over the sedated body. Decker was a work in progress. Every new model had its problems to be overcome. He had made a decent blade runner – a dangerous job, better not to risk a true human. *Decker.* There was a clue in his name. Dec as in decimal; the first Nexus-10. Long lived, and with an advanced cortex capable of dreaming. Not bad for a prototype.

Graff turned his cane towards the door, tapping his way out into the corridor. The brain designers would need to be told of this incident. He was already planning his report. ♜

LIFE FORM: A RETURN TO FOUKE

By Heath W. Shelby

9:35am
Friday, August 29, 1986

JESSICA HODGES HADN'T SLEPT IN at least 24 hours. Her lack of sleep wasn't due to insomnia, but rather a childlike excitement she hadn't felt since she was a kid waking up on Christmas morning to see what Santa Claus had left under the tree.

This weekend was her and her husband David's tenth anniversary. However, that wasn't the source of her excitement. That stemmed from David's anniversary gift to her.

Yesterday, when he returned from work, David surprised Jessica with a brand-new RCA VHS camcorder and news that he was taking her and their sons, Loyd and Eric, on a weekend getaway to Fouke, Arkansas.

Now, for most folks, a weekend getaway to Fouke wouldn't be considered a vacation worthy of a 10th anniversary, but for Jessica Hodges, this trip was a dream come true.

For over ten years, Jessica had been fascinated by the movie "The Legend of Boggy Creek." Jessica's fascination with the movie and the mysterious creature featured within the film bordered on obsession. David and her kids knew better than anyone else that Jessica's big dream was to go to Fouke and see the infamous Boggy Creek Monster for herself. David even spent his bonus check on a top-of-the-line camcorder, batteries, and blank tapes so Jessica could hopefully capture the monster on film.

Jessica was packed and ready to leave her family's home in Higginson, Arkansas before five a.m., but her family slept in, delaying the departure until almost six. Jessica grabbed a couple of boxes of Cookie Crisp and a few cartons of Foremost Milk for an on-the-go breakfast, helped the family pile into their 1983 Z28 Camaro and hit the road.

Jessica volunteered to drive because she was simply too excited to doze off. For most of the three-and-a-half-hour trip, David and the boys slept while Jessica counted down the miles while listening to Alabama's *Roll On* cassette that she had borrowed from her mom. When Randy Owens wasn't serenading her, Jessica was soaking up the sounds of her family snoring and their two black cats, Cocoa and Midnight, purring.

Jessica felt her heartbeat quicken as she approached a grass covered hill with a sign that read, "WELCOME TO FOUKE."

"David! Wake up! We're here!"

When David didn't stir, Jessica slapped her husband's arm with her right hand.

"Huh?! What?!"

"David, we're here! We just passed the 'Welcome to Fouke' sign. I need you to tell me where we are supposed to go."

David sat up, unbuckled his seat belt, and fished his wallet from his back pocket. David quickly found the folded-up yellow sheet of paper he was looking for.

"It says here that we are supposed to go to the Fouke Filling Station on Main Street and talk to a Mr. John Smith. He's supposed to have the keys to the place we're staying at this weekend."

"Have you got an address for me?"

David looked at his wife and smiled. "How big do you think Fouke is? This ain't Little Rock. You ain't gonna get lost. Get on Main Street. I'm sure we can't miss it."

Minutes later, Jessica spotted their destination on the right-hand side of Fouke's Main Street. Jessica parked their Camaro next to the Fouke Filling Station's lone gas pump, climbed out of the car and stretched her legs. Jessica was startled in mid-stretch by a heavy-set man wearing a black ball cap and greasy overalls.

"Howdy! You folks need a fill up?"

Jessica chuckled to herself and replied, "Yes, sir!"

Greasy Overalls removed the nozzle from the gas pump and went about filling up the Hodges' Camaro.

"You folks ain't from around here."

David climbed out of the car and answered Greasy Overalls' inquiry,

"No, sir. We're just here for the weekend. We were supposed to meet a Mr. John Smith here to get the keys to the place we're staying at this weekend. Would that be you?"

"I'm afraid not. John Smith would be the boss man around here. Me? I'm Elmer. I'm ole John's helper and—"

"The reason why I'm always out of Dr. Peppers and Moon Pies."

David and Jessica turned to see a man wearing khakis and a blue work shirt with the word *Smith* embroidered above the right pocket.

"I believe I'm the man y'all are lookin' for."

David walked over to the newcomer and shook his hand. "Mr. Smith, it's good to meet you. I'm David. That's my wife Jessica. In the backseat there you'll find our boys Eric and Loyd, and their two cats, Cocoa and Midnight."

John Smith leaned down to look through the Camaro's windshield.

"Whee! You've got yerselves a carload, dontcha?"

Jessica leaned into the car and told her sons, "Boys, say 'hi' to Mr. Smith."

Eric and Loyd raised their hands and tentatively waved at the stranger gazing into the car's windshield.

"The boys are a little shy."

"Oh, that's okay! I'd be shy around a scary old man like me, too."

"Mr. Smith, we really appreciate you giving us a place to stay this weekend."

"Oh, no trouble at all! Here are the keys and ole Elmer there will show y'all where the place is."

Elmer replaced the nozzle on the gas pump and walked toward the front door of the Fouke Filling Station.

"Y'all give me just a minute to grab me a Dr. Pepper or two and we will be on our way!"

A few minutes later, the Hodges had successfully followed Elmer's beat up blue Dodge pickup to their weekend getaway.

The Ford House wasn't exactly a Best Western, but David knew that his wife would forgo swimming pools and room service for a weekend stay in the countryside of Fouke with the chance to encounter the area's mysterious monster for herself.

The Ford House wasn't anything extravagant: a single-story wood structure located at the end of a dirt road with a big picture window and a huge front porch, shaded by a couple of big oak trees and almost completely surrounded by woods.

"Y'all need some help with your suitcases?"

"No, Mr. Elmer. I think we've got it."

"Okay, ma'am. If there's anything y'all need, just give me a call at the fillin' station. You guys have a list of emergency numbers by the phone in the kitchen. You'll find the fillin' station's number right there. Y'all have a microwave in that kitchen, plus three bedrooms and a bathroom. And, if y'all get bored, there's a TV with one of them vee-see-auras in there."

"Thank you, Mr. Elmer. That's sounds perfect."

As Jessica went to help the kids and their cats get out of the car, David walked over to Elmer.

"Are you guys expecting a big crowd in town this weekend?"

Elmer laughed and took a swig of his Dr. Pepper.

"Son, we ain't exactly a tourist destination. Folks celebrating Labor Day weekend will be heading to the Gulf Coast, not the banks of Boggy Creek!"

Elmer could see David blushing a little from embarrassment.

"But we do have a few touristy things around town...lemme guess... you guys are fans of that movie..."

"Well, yeah...Jessica is a huge fan. That's why I booked this place for our 10th anniversary...for Jess to get the whole 'Boggy Creek Experience.'"

Elmer took another swig off his Dr. Pepper.

"The 'Boggy Creek Experience,' huh? Well, I don't know what that is, but if you want an 'experience,' y'all go by and visit The Monster Mart over on Main Street. It's right next door to The Monster Cafe, if y'all are hungry."

"Cool! Are there any other places or maybe sites from the movie we can go see?"

Elmer slowly shook his head.

"Folks who were part of that movie don't like folks tramping around their properties. It got real bad in the late 70s. Sheriff Vines had to go hire himself another deputy just to help him run off all the trespassers."

"We don't want to get in trouble with the law..."

Elmer walked back to his pickup truck, opened the driver's door, and started to get in.

"Y'all just go to The Monster Mart. Go get y'all a Monster Burger at the cafe. If y'all need some groceries, the store is right across the road from the cafe."

Before he turned the key in the pickup's ignition, Elmer watched the Hodges' kids playing on the tire swing in the front yard, while their two black cats scampered nearby. Elmer rolled down his window and waved David over to his pickup.

"Mr. Hodges, do yourself a favor and keep those cats in at night. There are all kinds of critters roaming around these woods that would make a quick meal outta those little kitties."

"Critters? What kind of critters?"

"Oh, you know…coyotes…maybe a bear or a panther."

"Well, I've got shotgun and some shells in the back of the car…"

Elmer started up his pickup, nodded to David and said, "I'd keep 'em handy, if I were you."

As Elmer's pickup truck rumbled away down the dirt road, David walked over to his wife, who was watching Eric and Loyd having the time of their lives on the tire swing.

"What did Mr. Elmer say?"

"Nothing much. He just told me to keep the cats in at night. He said there were 'critters' roaming around here at night."

Jessica's eyes lit up and a big smile swept across her face.

"Critters, you say? You mean…like…Bigfoot?!"

"Calm down, honey. He was talking about critters like coyotes…"

"MOM! DAD! Look! Big kitty!"

David and Jessica turned to see their six-year-old son pointing excitedly at something behind the house.

"Eric, what is it?"

As Jessica picked up Eric, David ran to the back of the house where he saw what appeared to be a big cat sitting at the edge of the backyard.

"Jess, get the kids in the house!"

David walked back to the Camaro and retrieved his shotgun and a couple of shells. When he returned to the backyard, David saw that the big cat was now laying on its side. David slowly approached the cat with his shotgun raised. David soon discovered there was no reason for the shotgun.

The source of Eric's fascination was a now-dead panther. The large feline's hind quarters were covered in blood and most of its left hind leg was missing as the result of what appeared to be a massive bite wound.

David heard footsteps behind him.

"Honey…what is it?"

"Jess, go get your camcorder while I make a phone call."

"Miller County Sheriff's Department. Wreneta Tubbs speaking. How can I help you?"

"Yes, ma'am. My name is David Hodges. My family and I are staying in Fouke at the old Ford house…I don't know the actual address…but we have a dead panther in the backyard."

"Sir, you've killed a panther at the Ford house?"

"No, ma'am. I didn't kill the panther. It just walked up into the yard…

and died…"

"…"

"Ma'am? Are you there?"

"Sir, let me get this straight…you're saying a panther walked up into the yard - in broad daylight - and just died?"

"Yes, ma'am. Apparently, something tried to chew its leg off."

"Sir, is this a joke? Are you messin' with me? You do know it's a crime to make a false police report?"

"I know how it sounds, but I'm serious. We haven't touched the big cat. It's still laying in the backyard."

"Sir, I am going to dispatch a couple of deputies and I will see if I can also get a game warden out there. Y'all hang tight. Someone should be out there in 10 to 15 minutes."

Ten minutes after David hung up the phone, a Miller County Sheriff's car pulled up next to the Hodges' Camaro. Two officers exited the vehicle and walked to the backyard where David and Jessica were solemnly standing over the dead cat.

"Mr. Hodges? I'm Deputy William McCartney and this is Deputy Michael Little. Wreneta sent us out here to check out a dead panther. I take it this is the cat?"

"Yes, sir."

Deputy Little crouched down close to the cat to examine the corpse.

"It looks like something tried to bite its leg off…what in the world would leave a bite mark like that?"

"That would be a bear, Deputy. A big bear."

The deputies and the Hodges turned to see a game warden walking across the yard toward them.

"Howdy, folks. I'm John Miser. I'm the game warden around these here parts and I'll take care of things now."

As Game Warden Miser spread out what appeared to be a body bag next to the feline's corpse, Deputy Little asked, "Did you say a big bear did this?"

Game Warden Miser continued placing the panther's corpse in the bag and answered the deputy without ever turning around to acknowledge him, "Yes, sir. A really big bear."

Deputy McCartney stepped forward and asked, "When have we ever had a bear that big around here? And I've never heard of a bear attacking a panther at all."

Game Warden Miser zipped the bag closed, threw it over his left shoulder and began walking toward his truck that was parked behind the

169

deputies' car.

"You'd be surprised by what's actually out there in them woods around Boggy Creek."

John Miser waited until he was back on the highway before he picked up the receiver of the CB in his truck, selected channel 11 and checked in with his boss.

"This is Game Warden Miser. Smith, are you there? Smith, come back."

"Smith here. Did you acquire the package?"

"Yes, sir. The cat is in a bag in the back of the truck. I'll drop it off at the filling station in a few minutes."

"Could you tell what happened to the cat?

"Well, judging by the fatal bite wound, I would say your AR1 is responsible."

"We're going to have to bring the AR1 in for a diagnosis. Its ferocity is getting completely out of control."

"Mom, what happened to the big kitty?"

Jessica walked over to the couch where Eric and his brother were leaning over the back of the couch, watching the game warden's truck carry the big kitty's corpse down the road in a cloud of dust.

"Honey, the kitty...was sick..."

"Something chomped on him!"

Jessica gently pinched her elder son's arm and delivered the much-feared full-name warning, "David Loyd Hodges!"

Eric turned away from the window and looked excitedly at his mom.

"You mean like Pac-Man?"

"No...more like that killer crate monster in that *Creepshow* movie Dad let us watch!"

David walked into the living room just in time to catch the end of his family's conversation and the catch the glare Jessica leveled at him.

"Hey, guys...what do y'all say we get out of here and go to town and get something to eat?"

11:35am

David parked the family's Camaro in front of the largest building on Main Street in Fouke: the Monster Mart. If the large letters "MONSTER MART" didn't catch your attention, the seven-foot-tall Fouke Monster statue guarding the front door would.

Jessica helped her sons out of the back seat of the Camaro, all the while glancing over her shoulder at the immense Fouke Monster statue. David knew his wife well enough to recognize the childlike look in her eyes that let him know that Jessica wanted nothing more than to explore the Monster Mart thoroughly.

"Honey, let's get something to eat before we let you loose in the Monster Mart, okay?"

Jessica nodded, never taking her eyes off the Fouke Monster statue.

To the left of the Monster Mart was the smaller Monster Cafe, a quaint little restaurant with a big empty parking lot.

"David, are you sure it's open?"

"The sign says 'OPEN.'"

A bell rang as David ushered his family through the front door.

"Y'all just grab yerselves a table anywhere and I'll be right with you!"

A tall gentleman wearing a greasy apron and a red and black ball cap walked from the kitchen with menus in his hand and a big smile on his face.

"Howdy, folks! My name is LV Wilson and I'd like to welcome you to the Monster Cafe, home of the world-famous Monster Burger. Y'all want a Monster Burger, or do y'all need to check out a menu?"

"How big of a 'monster' is this Monster Burger?"

LV grabbed an empty plate off a nearby table and held it up for the Hodges to see.

"The Monster Burger is as big as this plate. If you want French fries to go with it, they'll have to come on a second plate."

Eric stared wide-eyed at LV and the plate.

"Mom! I want a Monster Burger!"

LV laughed out loud at the youngster's enthusiasm.

"Young man, I'd be glad to get you a Monster Burger, but I'm not sure you could eat it all. We'd probably have to get you a doggy bag!"

"No, sir. We'd need a kitty bag."

LV laughed again, while David and Jessica just shook their heads.

"Young man, what's a kitty bag?"

"We don't have doggies. We have two kitties back at the house, so we need a kitty bag."

LV placed the plate back on the table and picked up a pencil and order pad.

"Well, he's got a point. A 'kitty bag' it shall be then. What can I get you guys?"

David handed the menus back to LV and said, "I guess make it four Monster Burgers, four Dr. Peppers and we'll take any leftovers home in a 'kitty bag.'"

LV walked back to the kitchen and hollered over his shoulder, "So, what brings you folks to our big town of Fouke, Arkansas?"

"We're actually celebrating our tenth wedding anniversary."

"In Fouke?"

"Well, the wife here is a big fan of that *Boggy Creek* movie -"

"But not the sequels! Just the original."

LV waved a spatula at Jessica from the kitchen.

"Hey, now! That first sequel wasn't that good, but it had Mary Ann from *Gilligan's Island* in it!"

"I'll stick with the original movie. Plus, I always preferred Ginger."

LV laughed and went back to frying Monster Burgers.

"So, where are you folks from?"

David replied, "Higginson. It's a little place right outside of -"

"Searcy! I graduated from high school there."

LV leaned forward and tapped the ball cap he was wearing, which had a red lion in the center of it.

"I played football there and still keep up with the team. I have been holding out hope that the football team will win a state championship sometime before I die."

"Well, maybe sometime in the next 30 to 35 years…"

LV carried a tray with four glasses of Dr. Pepper over to the Hodges' table.

"Y'all's burgers will be up in a minute."

Jessica took a sip of her Dr. Pepper and asked LV, "Mr. Wilson, are there any…sites or things we could look at around town related to the movie?"

"Well, when y'all finish y'all's meal, y'all should definitely go next door and see my wife. Miss Danielle runs the Monster Mart. We've got all kinds of souvenirs in there and, if you go to the back of the building, we have a Fouke museum set up in there. We have stuff from the movie and, yes, even the sequels. You'll also find some footprint casts and other real evidence of our famous monster…or monsters."

Jessica's eyes widened and a big smile appeared on her face.

"And if you really want the Fouke experience, go over to Butch's Barber Shop and get yerself one of his world famous Monster Mullets!"

"Mom! Can I -"

"David Loyd Hodges! Absolutely not!"

Once the "kitty bags" full of leftovers were stowed in the Camaro, the Hodges made their way into the Monster Mart. The sounds of Dokken's "Into the Fire" and an overwhelming amount of Fouke Monster goodies greeted the Hodges as they entered Fouke's most famous establishment.

"Welcome to the Monster Mart!"

A striking woman with a big welcoming smile waved at the Hodges from behind the checkout counter.

"Mr. Wilson next door told us we had to check this place out."

"That's my husband. I'm Danielle. LV is the reason for this music. A friend of his is the Program Director at KTFS. They started playing this music a couple of years ago and LV loves it, so that's all we listen to in here."

"Hey, there ain't nothin' wrong with rockin' with Dokken!"

Jessica looked at her husband like he was speaking a foreign language before turning her attention back to the Monster Mart's proprietor.

"Mrs. Wilson, I love your shirt!"

Danielle was wearing a black shirt that featured a silhouette of the Fouke Monster surrounded by the words "The Fouke Monster Saw Me, But No One Believes Him!"

"Call me Danielle. If you like this shirt, we have a whole rack of them over there."

While Jessica looked for a shirt in her size, David discovered what he thought was a Rubik's Cube. However, instead of colored squares, this puzzle cube had colored Fouke Monster footprints and had the appropriate name of Creature Cube.

"Dad, can we have some quarters to play Donkey Kong?"

David fished a handful of quarters out of his pants pocket and walked over to the arcade machine that held his sons' attention. David saw that the arcade machine was in fact not Donkey Kong, but rather a knock-off called "Boggy Kong."

David turned around to notice that his wife had not only had found the shirt she was looking for, but she had also discovered a half dozen more, as well as a movie poster, a mirror with an etched Fouke Monster and a Creature Cube.

"Honey, how much is this stop going to cost me?"

"Hey, at least admission to the museum is free!"

10:24pm

"Honey, you've got to go to bed."

Jessica yawned, stretched, and resumed laying across the back of the couch, looking out the picture window into the darkness hoping to see something...anything.

"I will. It was just such a good day. Thank you for the best anniversary gift I could ever ask for."

173

"You're welcome. But, babe, you've got to get some sleep. You didn't sleep at all last night, and you've been going full tilt all day."

Jessica got up off the couch, walked over to her husband and hugged him.

"Sweetie, I will go to bed in just a bit. I think I might pop the movie into the VCR before I turn in."

"Well, we didn't pack any popcorn, but there is still some Monster Burger leftovers in the kitchen."

"Oh, no! Monster Burgers for lunch AND Monster Burgers for supper… if I don't eat another hamburger for the next year, it will be too soon!"

12:22am
Saturday, August 30, 1986

As the credits of her favorite movie rolled across the screen of the large console television, Jessica stood up, stretched, and hit the "STOP" button on the VCR remote control. The TV's blue screen cast an eerie light across the quiet living room.

Jessica walked over to turn off the television and noticed her new camcorder sitting at the end of the couch. Jessica bypassed the television, picked up the camcorder and looked back to the picture window.

"Hmm…I wonder…"

Leaving the blue light illuminating the living room, Jessica unlocked the front door and stepped out into the Fouke darkness with camcorder in hand.

1:05am

"Hon? Did you finally decide to come to bed?"

Jessica had tried to be as quiet as possible as she climbed into bed, but she still managed to wake her husband.

"Yeah. Go back to sleep."

"What took you so long?"

"I just had…some business to take care of…"

8:22am

David walked into the living room to find Loyd and Eric sitting on the couch, each working on a bowl of Cookie Crisp, while his wife was sitting on the floor in front of the television, watching something on the VCR.

"Cereal for breakfast?"

Without turning her attention from the television, Jessica replied, "Sorry, Sweetie. I didn't get a chance to cook anything. There's plenty of milk, Cookie Crisp and Frosted Flakes in the kitchen."

"Mom, can we watch cartoons?"

"Eric, not right now...maybe later. Loyd, can you get the cats some milk?"

Loyd carried his now-empty bowl into the kitchen where his dad was enjoying his own bowl of cereal.

"Dad, can you hand me the milk for Cocoa and Midnight?"

David handed his son a carton of milk and watched as he filled his empty bowl and placed it on the floor for their two eager cats.

"Dad, can me and Eric take the pellet gun and go exploring?"

"You brought your pellet gun?"

"Yessir. It's under the blanket in the back of the car with a box of pellets."

"If it's okay with your mom, it's okay with me. Just don't shoot your brother."

"I won't! I promise! MOM!!"

"David Loyd Hodges, you don't have to yell across the house! Just walk in here and talk to me."

"Mom, can me and Eric go outside and walk around with the pellet gun? Dad said it was okay if it was okay with you."

Jessica turned away from the television and looked at Loyd, who was now joined by Eric at his side.

"On three conditions: you stay out of the woods, you be careful and you don't -"

"I know! Don't shoot my brother..."

David walked into the living room just as Loyd and Eric were rushing out the front door. David sat on the couch and watched out the window as his sons dug around in the back of the Camaro for the pellet gun and pellets.

"Hon, are you going to tell me what you've been watching all morning?"

Jessica turned around and greeted her husband with a gleam in her eye and a big smile across her face.

"You are not going to believe it!"

"Believe what?"

"Last night before I came to bed, I put the camcorder out on the hood of the car, hit "RECORD" and aimed it at the front porch. I got up this morning and brought the camcorder in. I ended up with three hours of footage…and I got…something…on this tape. Watch this."

Jessica hit "PLAY" on the VCR remote. On the television, David could see the house they were all asleep in the previous night. David could barely make out the front porch thanks to a full moon that lit up the yard to the left of the house.

"Look at this!"

Jessica pointed to a tall, stocky shadow that moved from the darkness at the right side of the house onto the porch. The shadow had to be at least seven feet tall, and it appeared to bend slightly and look in the big picture window.

"Is that some…guy…snooping around?"

"I don't think so. Keep watching."

The shadow continued moving down the porch until it came to the front door. The shadow stopped and David could see an arm reach for the doorknob.

"*Huff*!!"

"What was that noise?"

Jessica paused the tape.

"Watch this part very closely."

Jessica hit "PLAY" and something dark covered the camcorder's lens. Jessica hit "REWIND" and then "PLAY." As soon as the dark object appeared on the screen, Jessica paused the tape again.

"Look!"

The paused image appeared to be a large hand.

"Something grabbed the camcorder!"

"And that's not all. Keep watching."

The screen continued to be dark as the mysterious hand continued to cover the lens.

Sniff! Sniff! Sniff!

"Is it smelling the cam -"

"*ArrOOOOOOOO!!!!*"

David broke out in goosebumps.

"What is that?!"

"*CLUNK!*"

The mysterious hand disappeared from the screen as it apparently dropped the camcorder on its side. David cocked his head sideways to see the tall shadow run across the porch and disappear into the darkness from whence it came.

David stared at the screen in disbelief, as Jessica ejected the videotape from the VCR.

"It's real…"

Jessica kissed her husband on the cheek, hugged him and whispered in his right ear, "Yes, Hon. It's real."

"Loyd! Slow down!"

Since their mom told them they couldn't go exploring in the woods, Loyd was instead leading his little brother down the dirt road in front of the house. Loyd had his Crossman pellet gun propped up on his right shoulder as he was on the lookout for something to shoot…a snake, a bird, maybe even a rabbit.

"Loyd, you need another pellet?"

Loyd always let Eric carry the box of pellets when he had his pellet gun. The Crossman pellet gun wasn't like his old Daisy BB gun. With the BB gun, you could automatically load BB after BB. With the pellet gun, you had to manually load a single pellet after each shot. Eric was always quick to hand Loyd a pellet, plus with Eric carrying the pellets, that's one less thing Loyd had to keep up with.

"I haven't shot this one yet. I can't find anything to shoot down this ole road."

"How 'bout that!"

Eric was pointing at something on the other side of the ditch off the left side of the road. Loyd walked to the edge of the road and looked into the woods on the other side of the ditch. Just inside the woods, Loyd could make out some kind of large animal with brown hair. The animal was hunkered down with its back to the boys.

"Shoot it, Loyd!"

"Shhh! I've gotta pump up this gun more first."

Loyd's dad had always told him to pump up his pellet gun ten times, but if ten times was good, 20 times would be better, especially for a big animal like this.

Ten extra pumps of the gun's faux wood stock later, Loyd took aim at the animal that was up until now completely unaware of its would be hunter.

PFFFTTT!

As the pellet hit the animal in its back, it stood up and whirled around to face its attacker. Neither Loyd nor Eric had ever seen anything like what was staring back at them.

The creature was about as tall as Loyd. It was covered head to toe with thick brown hair. It had long arms and appeared to be holding something covered in blood. Blood also dripped from its long snout. Two jet black eyes conveyed nothing but hatred as it started moving out of the woods toward Loyd and Eric.

"Eric, give me another pellet!"

With unsteady hands, Eric popped open the plastic container of pellets only to dump the entire contents of the container on the ground.

"Loyd…"

The creature reached the ditch bank and opened its blood covered snout.

"RAAAAAGGHHHH!"

Loyd and Eric backed away from the ditch as the creature jumped over the stagnant water and landed on the road between the boys and the perceived safety of their parents.

Loyd looked down the other end of the road and saw an old house not too far away.

The creature started walking toward the brothers, raising its long arms above its head and emitting a bone chilling howl.

"ROOOOHHHHHH!!!"

Loyd grabbed his younger brother's left hand and screamed, "Run, Eric! Run!!"

KNOCK! KNOCK! KNOCK!

"Help us!!"

The sudden noise startled Jack Prince as he was dozing off in his recliner.

"What in tarnation?!"

Jack walked into the kitchen and saw two terrified young boys beating frantically on his screen door.

"Mister! Please, help us! Please let us in before it gets us!"

"Before what gets you?"

"The monster!"

Jack opened the door and the two boys barreled into the room. Jack looked around his front yard but didn't see anything out of the ordinary.

"A monster, you say?"

"Yes, sir! It was chasing us down the road. I shot it with my gun here."

Jack took the pellet gun from Loyd's trembling hands and looked it over.

"Nice gun. I don't think it's made for monster hunting, though. Where's your mom and dad?"

"They're down the road. We're staying in that house down there."

"The old Ford house? Hmm…I think I know the phone number for that ole place. Y'all get yerselves a sodee pop out of the fridge and I'll give your parents a call."

Jack Prince was waiting on his front porch as the Hodges jumped out of

178

their Camaro and ran across his front yard.

"My boys?!"

"They're okay, ma'am. Them boys are sitting inside watching cartoons and eating all of my Mallo Cups."

Jessica ran into the house, while David stopped to shake Jack's hand.

"Thank you, Mister…"

"Prince, Jack Prince. No need to thank me."

Jack held open the screen door for David.

"I'm David Hodges. That's my wife Jessica."

Jack nodded at Jessica as she was smothering her boys in a huge, frantic hug.

"Mr. Prince, can you tell us what happened?"

"Well, sir…your boys said they had a monster hot on their heels."

Jessica left her sons and walked into the kitchen to join her husband.

"Mr. Prince, did you say 'monster?'"

Jack laughed and shook his head.

"Well, that's what your boys said, but I'm afraid they just spotted the Fouke Monkey."

Jessica looked at her husband and then back to Jack with a look of disbelief all over her face.

"The Fouke…Monkey?"

Jack laughed again.

"Yeah, it seems that Fouke has had a monkey roaming the area for a couple of years now. You see, there's this woman who lives just outside of town. What's her name? Sue Ellen? No, that's the lady on the TV show I watch on Friday nights after *The Dukes of Hazzard.* Oh! Her name is Susan Keller. She's a bit eccentric. A couple of years ago, she got herself a monkey. Not long after that, that ole monkey got out of its cage, and it's been runnin' free ever since."

"A monkey?"

"What? Did you think it was the Fouke Monster?"

Jack laughed so hard he started coughing.

"Boys, we need to go and let Mr. Prince get back to his business."

Jack collected himself as he returned to his recliner.

"Oh, yeah. *Championship Wrestling* is on at 11."

"Mr. Prince, we really appreciate you. Do we owe you anything?"

"No, sir. You guys don't owe me a thing…unless…"

"Anything. Just name it.'

"I've got some money here…if you guys happen to be going into town any time soon, I could use some of those Hawken pouches."

As soon as the Hodges left, Jack Prince got up from his recliner, walked over to the phone on his kitchen wall and dialed the number he never liked to dial.

"*Yes.*"

"Mr. Smith?"

"*Yes?*"

"This is Jack Prince. I just thought you'd like to know that the family you've got set up in the ole Ford place had a run in with the AR1."

"*Is that so?*"

"Yes, sir. But I handled it."

"*How so?*"

"I told them it was Susan Keller's ole monkey."

"*Did they buy it?*"

"Oh, I'm sure the parents did, but you know kids and their imaginations."

"Mom, we didn't see a monkey. It was some kinda monster."

"Yeah! If it was a monkey, it was the ugliest, scariest monkey in the whole world!"

Jessica and David had decided to go into town and grab some groceries at the Fouke Supermarket. As soon as the trip began, Loyd and Eric had been doing their best to convince their parents that what they had encountered was definitely not a monkey.

"We believe y'all."

"You do?"

Jessica cast a knowing look to her husband as he replied, "Yes, we do, boys. We know that there's...something other than a monkey out in those woods."

11:03am

"Boys! We've got enough junk food in the basket!"

When they had entered the Fouke Supermarket, Jessica had instructed her sons to go get something they would like for lunch and supper. Now, Jessica's grocery basket was full of Big League Chew, Mallo Cups, candy cigarettes and Zagnut bars.

David walked around the corner with an arm full of Totino's frozen pizzas.

"This should cover us for the rest of the weekend."

"Well, let's check out before the boys put every package of candy in this store either into this basket or into their mouths."

As Jessica began unloading their groceries onto a conveyor belt, a petite lady with light brown hair, glasses and a friendly smile greeted them.

"Howdy! Did y'all find everything you needed?"

David remembered Mr. Prince's request.

"Actually, no. Do y'all have any Hawken Pouches?"

"That's a nasty habit."

"Oh, it's not for me. I'm running an errand for Mr. Jack Prince."

"Well, tell ole Jackie that Nina said, 'Hi!'"

Nina walked to the wall behind the cash register and found a can of Hawken Pouches to add to the Hodges' haul.

"Are y'all new to our little town?"

"No, ma'am. We are just here for the weekend. I'm a big fan of the Boggy Creek movie and David here surprised me with a weekend getaway for a 10th anniversary gift."

"Well, happy anniversary! In all my years, I don't think I've ever heard of anyone taking a trip to Fouke for an anniversary getaway."

"Well, we're here through Labor Day so we can get the 'Fouke Experience.'"

"Well, if y'all want the complete 'Fouke Experience,' y'all need to go see my husband over at Butch's Barber Shop and get yourselves one of those 'Monster Mullets.'"

"Mom! Can we -"

"David Loyd Hodges! Absolutely not!"

9:11pm

"Overall, it's been a good day."

"Well, it started off a little rough."

After returning from the Fouke Supermarket, the Hodges dropped off Jack Prince's Hawken Pouches, came back to the Ford place and enjoyed Totino's pizzas for lunch. While David and the boys napped the afternoon away, Jessica poured over her videotape containing the footage of something mysterious that was definitely not a monkey.

The Hodges capped off the day with a Totino's pizza supper. Now, with their sons in bed asleep, David and Jessica were crashed on the couch with Cocoa and Midnight.

"Can we watch the movie again?"

"Really, Hon?"

"Just one more time?"

"One more time…today."

181

Jessica gave her husband a smile he had never been able to refuse.

"Okay…let me get up and I'll put the tape in."

Jessica waved the VCR remote at her husband.

"No need! The tape is already in and ready to roll!"

10:05pm

As her favorite movie was playing out again on TV, Jessica had joined her husband in a deep slumber on the couch. So deep was the Hodges' slumber that neither of them saw the large hand that was pressed against the picture window above the couch. The Hodges also didn't hear the sound of the hand slowly raising the window.

Cocoa climbed off the top of the couch and laid down beside Jessica, while Midnight slept on. A large hand covered in long brown hair slowly reached through the window and grabbed the sleeping cat.

"REEEAAAARRRRR!"

Cocoa ran to the back bedroom as David and Jessica woke up, startled by the chilling cry of their cat.

"David! Midnight!"

"REEEAAAARRR-"

Midnight's cries suddenly stopped and the only sound the Hodges heard came from the movie on the television.

"Hon, stay here! I'm gonna go get my gun."

"Mom? Dad? What's going on?"

Loyd and Eric began to walk into the living room when Jessica ran to head them off.

"Boys! Take Cocoa and go to your room! Don't come out 'til me or your dad come to get you!"

David came back into the living room with his shotgun.

"Everyone stay in the house! I'm going outside to find Midnight."

As David bolted out the front door, Jessica grabbed her camcorder.

"David! Wait up!"

Jessica ran into David as she ran out the front door. David had stopped to investigate a trail of blood that ran from the window to the end of the porch.

"What is it?"

"It's…blood…Jess. You really shouldn't be out here."

Jessica turned on the light on her camcorder, raised the device to her shoulder and looked through the viewfinder.

"Jess…"

"David, just follow me. And keep your shotgun ready."

Jessica followed the blood trail to the end of the porch where she saw something laying at the edge of the porch. It was black and furry. Jess leaned over and picked up the object.

"It's Midnight's tail...Oh, my God! David!"

David ran around his wife to see what had frightened her so bad. David glanced out into the yard where the blood trail continued. The trail seemed to end in the middle of the yard where David could see something crouched with its back to the Hodges.

"Jess, bring that light around here..."

Jessica aimed her camcorder at the object in the yard. A creature about four feet tall and covered in brown hair turned to look at the Hodges. Its long snout was covered in blood. Its soulless jet-black eyes settled on its observers. The creature raised one of its long arms and threw what was left of Midnight toward the Hodges and then unleashed an unearthly cry.

"RAAAUURRRRRRRRRRRRRR!"

"Jess, run!!"

David and Jessica turned to run back into the house, but as they ran back onto the porch, their escape was cut off by a much larger creature standing between them and the front door. This hairy creature was at least seven feet tall and looked like it had no intention of moving. Slowly, the larger creature walked toward the Hodges as it unleashed a guttural growl.

"GrrrrAWWWRRR!"

David raised his shotgun and fired. The big creature staggered back down the porch and disappeared into the darkness.

"Jess! Now! Get in the house!"

Jessica began running toward the front door when all of a sudden something slammed into her back. The camcorder went bouncing across the porch as Jessica tried to catch her breath. When her breath wouldn't come, Jessica realized that something was on her back.

"JESS!"

Jessica felt the searing, sharp pain of the creature's fangs as they sank into her left shoulder.

"DAVID!!! OH, MY GOD!!! HELP ME!!!"

Jessica could feel the creature's claws tear through her shirt and into the flesh on her back.

BLAMMMMM!

David fired his shotgun at almost point-blank range into the face of the savage creature attacking his wife. Blood, teeth, and bits of hairy flesh covered the walls of the Ford house, as the creature fell to the ground next to Jessica.

183

"Jess?!"

"David…get the kids…and Cocoa…I think I need to go to the hospital."

As her husband ran to get their kids and their cat, Jessica raised her head off the bloody porch.

"And don't forget the camcorder!"

As the Hodges sped away in the Camaro, the large creature stepped out of the shadows from the back of the house. The creature walked across the porch to where the corpse of the smaller creature was laying. The large creature cocked its head as if it was listening to something. The creature then bent down, picked up the mangled corpse and carried it into the dark Fouke woods.

3:05am
Sunday, August 31, 1986

"Smith?"

"It's early, Prince. What's going on?"

"I just thought you would want a heads up that the family you rented the Ford house to left out around midnight."

"Do you know what happened?"

"What do you think happened? It was a night full of gunshots and your Hairy Scaries."

6:00am

John Smith prided himself on being prompt. Seven days a week, Smith opened the Fouke Filling Station at 6am sharp. However, today Smith would have to miss the early churchgoers heading to the Fouke Church of Christ. Today, Smith had more serious issues to deal with.

Smith approached a large metal cabinet at the back of the filling station and turned a handle on the cabinet's door to the right. The metal cabinet slowly slid away from the wall, revealing a set of shiny metal doors. After punching in a series of numbers on a nearby keypad, the doors slid open, and Smith stepped into a large elevator.

Smith inserted a key into a panel on the inside of the elevator. In moments, the elevator transported Smith to a secret facility that had been beneath Fouke for well over 20 years now.

As the doors opened, Smith was immediately greeted by the salutes from two armed guards. Smith didn't even acknowledge the guards, breezing past them into a busy laboratory.

"Status report, Colonel Tapp. Now!"

Colonel JoAnn Tapp opened her clipboard and approached Smith.

"Commander, the AR1 was in really bad shape when the AR2 brought it in, but the scientists here have done wonders in just a matter of hours. Would you like to speak with Dr. Hammonds?"

There was no one in the word Smith trusted more than his longtime colleague and if Colonel Tapp said wonders were worked, he believed her.

"Yes. Absolutely. Thank you, Colonel."

Colonel Tapp walked over to the pair of scientists who were working on the AR1 at a nearby operating table. The tall scientist with the shaved head and white beard approached Smith.

"Commander, Dr. Henderson and I have been hard at work on the AR1 for several hours now."

Dr. Grant Henderson joined his colleague.

"Commander, I have a question."

"If you must, Dr. Henderson."

"Dr. Hammonds and I have worked nonstop this morning on this… thing. Out of all the projects that we have utilized here, this one seems to be somewhat useless. It's too *small* to be considered one of those so-called Bigfoot creatures. It's too violent. It's honestly more trouble than it's worth. What's the big deal with this thing?"

"It's a big deal because it's important to me."

Everyone in the laboratory turned to see the source of the deep voice. No one said a word as a tall man decked out in military dress and mirrored sunglasses stepped to the group. It seemed as if time stood still and the temperature in the room suddenly dropped twenty degrees. Unfazed, Smith extended his right hand to greet the imposing man.

"Mr. Jones, what brings you here?"

Jones ignored Smith's outstretched hand and walked over to the operating table that contained the AR1.

"The big deal is it…he came here when I did."

Everyone stared at Mr. Jones with confusion in their eyes. For most of those in the laboratory, little was known about Mr. Jones other than he was the mysterious man who was in charge of everything. No one knew where he came from, but everyone knew Mr. Jones was the big boss and he was intimidating.

Ignoring the unspoken questions, Mr. Jones turned to the scientists.

"Status report."

Dr. Hammonds stepped forward and nervously cleared his throat.

185

"Sir, I've got some good news and I've got some bad news."

"Give it to me straight. What's the bad news, Dr. Hammonds?"

"Well, there was a lot of damage to the AR1. It took a direct shotgun blast to the face. As a result of that, the AR1 no longer has its fangs. Its eyes and ears were undamaged, but there was some internal damage."

"What do you mean 'internal damage?'"

"We lost its inhibitors and its primary drive. Those chips are irreplaceable."

"In English?"

"The ferocity the AR1 has been exhibiting? Gone. It's practically docile now. And it appears that it has a partial loss of memory."

"Can you tell how much memory loss that we are looking at?"

"Well, it appears that the AR1 doesn't recall its time with our facility... but it now recalls...everything that came before."

Jones almost appeared to smile.

"The good news?"

"Dr, Henderson and I were able to replace all of the organic damage. The AR1's face now shows no damage from its run in with the Hodges family. We just had one really unexpected side effect from the whole incident..."

"Which is?"

"Did you know the AR1 could speak?"

"I did, which was one of the reasons I had the inhibitors implanted in its brain."

"Well, it was speaking...and laughing...until we sedated it to complete the work on its cybernetics."

Mr. Jones walked back over to the AR1, leaned down near its ear, and whispered, "Friend."

Smith stepped toward the operating table and asked, "Mr. Jones, did you say something?"

"Excuse me, Commander! We have a problem!"

Major Karen Eddington startled the gathered group when she entered the laboratory. When she saw the group included Mr. Jones, Major Eddington was startled herself.

"I'm sorry...I wasn't aware -"

"Major, what seems to be the immediate problem?"

"Uh...Mr. Jones, sir...it would be best if you and Commander Smith would join us in the Control Room."

Mr. Jones and Smith followed Major Eddington, who left the room as quick as she could. Once in the Control Room, Mr. Jones and Smith were greeted by a paused image on the big screen of a young lady with long brown hair on the set of what appeared to be a local newscast.

Major Eddington approached a gentleman sitting at the controls in front of the large screen.

"Corporal Baty, they're here."

Corporal Daniel Baty turned to address his superiors.

"Sirs, we have an issue. This was recorded at 6am this morning off of KTAL Channel 6."

"What is it, Corporal?"

"An early morning news report that could mean...bad news for this project."

Corporal Baty felt a sudden chill as Mr. Jones placed a large hand on his shoulder.

"Let's see it, Corporal."

Nervously, Corporal Baty hit "ENTER" on his computer keypad and the recording came to life.

"Good morning! I'm Sarah Reed. Welcome to the Sunday morning edition of 'Wake Up, South Arkansas.' Coming up, we'll check out 'Wake Up Weather' with Ronnie. Bud Black has an update on the Razorbacks as they prepare for their September 13th opener against Ole Miss. But first..."

The young lady with the long brown hair turned her smiling face to a closeup camera.

"...we have breaking news out of Fouke. A woman is in a Texarkana hospital with severe injuries after she claims she and her family were attacked by a mysterious creature in Fouke. With more details, let's go live on the scene with Channel 6's Misty Riley. Misty, what happened overnight in Fouke?"

"Sarah, the details and images we are about to share with you are simply horrific. Jessica Hodges, her husband David, their two sons and two cats were staying at the Ford house in Fouke, which you can see behind me."

The camera panned away from Misty to show the Ford house in the distance, at the end of a dirt road.

"This is as close as the Miller County Sheriff's Department would allow us to get to the house where the incident allegedly took place. Law enforcement will not comment at this time on this incident, but earlier this morning, Channel 6's Dana Daniels was able to speak with the Hodges family at the hospital."

The live report was replaced with a shot of a young blue-eyed reporter standing outside of a hospital room next to David Hodges.

"Mr. Hodges, Dana Daniels with Channel 6 News. Can you tell us what happened last night in Fouke?"

"We were attacked."

"Attacked? By what?"

"Monsters!"

"Monsters?"

"Yeah…monsters."

"What kind of monsters?"

"The kind in that Boggy Creek movie."

The camera zoomed in on Dana, who couldn't say a word.

"Yes, ma'am…I know what you're thinking, but they are real."

The live report returned.

"Thank you, Dana. Normally, we would chalk up claims like Mr. Hodges' to hallucinations or misidentification. But in this instance, the Hodges have proof. David Hodges has given Channel 6 a damaged videotape that his wife shot during their time in Fouke. The images you are about to see are from last night's attack. A warning: the clip you are about to see contains graphic and violent images."

The report shifted to a skewed recording captured by a camcorder laying on its side. The camera showed Jessica Hodges bloodied and laying face first on the porch of the Ford House. David Hodges could be heard yelling off camera.

"*JESS!*"

A short, hairy creature leapt onto Jessica's back. The creature moved so quickly, it was hard to make out specific features, but its ferocity could be seen clearly.

The creature sank its teeth into Jessica's shoulder.

"*DAVID!! OH, MY GOD!!! HELP ME!!!*"

The creature then began slashing at Jessica with its claws, as bits of clothing along with flesh and blood flew all over the porch.

David stepped in front of the camera, obscuring the view of what came next.

BLAMMMMM!

The screen went dark for a second before Misty appeared again standing down the road from the Ford house.

"That was all we were able to pull from the damaged videotape provided to us by David Hodges. Jessica Hodges remains in serious but stable condition at a Texarkana hospital. We will remain on the scene and attempt to talk with the Miller County Sheriff's Office about this developing story. Sarah, back to you,"

"Thank you, Misty. Channel 6 will continue to follow this story and bring you updates as we receive them. Right now, let's check out 'Wake Up Weather' with Ronnie Bright."

"Thanks, Sarah. The remainder of the weekend will be nice, but you'd have to have duck bite fever to like the wet forecast that's heading to South Arkansas next week -"

The screen went black, silence filled the room, and everyone did their best not to attract the attention of the clearly agitated Mr. Jones.

"Smith."

"Yes, sir, Mr. Jones."

"Have Colonel Tapp dispatch a team to retrieve the evidence given to this television station. If we secure this tape quick enough, national outlets won't pick up this story. Right now, a very small Sunday morning audience has seen this. Act quick enough, and we can contain this."

Smith turned and left the room as quickly as he could.

Mr. Jones leaned over Corporal Baty's shoulder and placed his hand on a red button that was sealed and locked under thick lucite.

"I'm sorry, sir. That control is locked, and we don't have a key for -"

Corporal Baty's jaw dropped when he saw the lucite container slide open at Mr. Jones' touch. Jones hit the button and a wall at the back of the control room slid open to reveal a large, metallic pod.

"Major Eddington, inform the scientists to prep and load the life form into this transport."

"The 'life form,' sir?"

Mr. Jones turned his mirrored gaze to Major Karen Eddington.

"The AR1."

"Yes, sir."

Major Eddington left the room and left Corporal Daniel Baty alone with Mr. Jones.

"Corporal, I will give you a set of coordinates when the time is right."

"Coordinates, sir?"

"We are sending the life form...home..."

"Home, sir?"

Ignoring Corporal Baty's question, Mr. Jones walked toward the laboratory door.

"I will return, Corporal. We will launch when night falls."

9:05pm

Corporal Daniel Baty's shift should have ended hours earlier. However, aside from a few trips to the latrine, Corporal Baty was too afraid to leave his post in the Control Room until he was relieved of his post by Mr. Jones himself.

"Corporal, I have entered the coordinates. Please, begin the launch sequence."

Corporal Baty tried not to show his surprise at the arrival of Mr. Jones but failed miserably.

"Sir...uh...how long -"

"We're not putting on a big production here. Speed is of the essence."

Corporal Baty began a short launch sequence countdown of 30 seconds.

"Won't the launch still be visible to the locals?"

John Smith entered the room, startling Corporal Baty even more, but his question didn't even faze Mr. Jones.

"With the technology I have brought here, we will have a silent launch. No fire trail at all. No one will hear a thing and, now that it's dark, no one should see anything."

A digital clock above the large screen reached 5...4...3...2...1.

The screen showed an underground silo open in a nearby field, followed by a metallic pod rising out of the newly opened hole in the ground and slowly gaining altitude.

Mr. Jones turned and left the control room without uttering another word.

9:07pm

Sharon Kay Wheeler looked forward to Labor Day weekend every year. The last hurrah of the summer always meant a family get together at her farm on the outskirts of Fouke. The only thing Sharon didn't like about the Labor Day weekend was when her brothers Jack and Leon would take off with Jack's best friend, John Burgin, and get into the trouble only three rowdy guys could get into.

Sharon had left the wives back at the farm while she headed out in her pickup truck to find the guys, who were supposed to be home before dark. Sharon had driven around town and couldn't find a sign of the guys. An hour later, Sharon was now traveling the dirt roads around the fields and woods of Fouke.

As she rounded a corner near an open field, Sharon could see in the truck's headlights three guys with guns standing in the field. Sharon pulled over, parked the truck, and ran over to give the guys a piece of her mind.

"What in the world are you idiots doing?!"

The three guys laughed and looked at the small, angry woman stomping across the field toward them.

"Hey, sis! Would you believe we're hunting the Fouke monster?"

"Jack, I believe the only thing you guys have been hunting is the bottom of another bottle!"

The three guys all shared a laugh as Sharon noticed something in the night sky above their heads.

"Sis? Whatcha lookin' at?"

Sharon couldn't find the words, so she just pointed at the object rising slowly into the moonlit sky above Fouke.

The laughter stopped as the guys followed Sharon's gaze.

"Is that...a...UFO?"

Without another word, Jack raised his rifle to his shoulder and fired a shot at the strange object.

BLAMM!

WHANG!

"You hit it, Jack! You hit it!"

Instead of falling back to Earth, the strange object picked up speed and disappeared into the night sky.

11:27pm

"Commander, we have a problem...you may need to call Mr. Jones..."

"What is it, Corporal Baty?"

"Well, sir, it appears that the transport never reached the atmosphere..."

"WHAT?!!!"

Smith and Corporal Baty both jumped at the angry arrival of Mr. Jones.

"Corporal, what do you mean 'the transport never reached the atmosphere?' Where is the transport now?!"

The commotion drew the attention of Doctors Stephen Hammonds and Grant Henderson, who slowly entered the control room to see what was going on.

"Sir, it appears that the transport has crash landed in California...the San Fernando Valley to be exact."

"Status on...the passenger. Is he...dead?"

"No, sir. It appears he is alive and well...and out of sedation. From what I can tell, he has taken up refuge in a family's home"

"Is the family aware he's there?"

Corporal Baty put on a pair of headphones and listened intently.

"Yes. Yes, they are aware. They are referring to the life form as an 'alien.'"

"Smith...have Colonel Tapp dispatch a...oh, I don't know...if they are going to call the life form an 'alien,' let's call it the 'Alien Task Force.' Have Colonel Tapp dispatch 'The Alien Task Force' to retrieve the AR1."

191

"Yes, sir. I have to ask…until our task force can retrieve the AR1, is this family in any kind of danger, considering the AR1's previous level of ferocity?"

Dr. Hammonds stepped forward.

"Sirs, there shouldn't be anything to worry about. The family should be safe. I just hope they don't have a cat…" ♜

FLOODWATER

By Jason Henderson

1.

IF YOU WERE WATCHING THEM from above, they would make a kind of kinetic art. The girls of Landover Academy flitted in and out of the dormitory sitting room like molecules given heat, bouncing against each other, out the door, in the door, into the kitchen and out of it, onto the couch and off it, up the stairs, down the stairs, a constant energy of maroon jackets and pleated skirts.

Claire was going to be late. She hated that. She hated the effect it would have on her already shoddy credibility with the school, and it mattered to her, even if the thing she was late for was punishment. She made it back from the stables in record time, but when she got to the cafeteria where she was supposed to be working, she realized her partner Molly wasn't there.

And that wouldn't do, because the girls were being punished together, so an extra amount of accountability had been thrown into the mix. They had to show up together. They had to work together.

Claire turned around and stepped onto the green mall that stretched across campus. The cafeteria was close to the lecture halls but getting back to the dorm meant crossing the mall. This would be her third time traipsing across the campus this morning.

As she hurried across the well-manicured lawns, she noticed glumly that the day had grown darker rather than lighter since dawn. Clouds hung pregnant in the sky and there was a heavy mist. The whole atmosphere was gross.

She burst into the sitting room and headed for the stairs, stopping a moment when she saw Nancy with her feet up on the coffee table as she watched TV with Taffy and Tootie. Claire smacked Nancy's boot lightly. "Feet off the coffee table."

Nancy scoffed. "Who do you think you are, Mrs. Tarrant?"

"It's tacky," Claire said. "Have some class." All this in just a moment, after which she spun and ran up the stairs to the main part of the dormitory, the three-story dormitory with its dark wood coffers in the ceilings and hundred-year-old lamps at every landing. She made it to the tiny room she shared with Molly, slapping the chalkboard hanging on the door. In pink and blue chalk Taffy had labeled it:

CLAIRE *AND MOLLY*
(GOOD LUCK! HA HA)

The door swung open. Molly wasn't ready at all.

Molly Polniaczek lay on her stomach on her side of the room—the window, won in a coin toss—reading a Connie Claire mystery, *Mystery of the Green River*. Claire recognized it by the green paperback cover and the ponytailed sleuth Connie on the cover. She was wearing a pair of soccer shorts and a T-shirt, her hair down and falling around her face.

"Are you reading my book?"

"Is this your book?" Molly turned it over. "It's twenty years old."

"It's a *collector's item* if you don't mind." Claire snatched it from Molly's hand as Molly gaped in annoyance. Claire looked down at the book and placed it back on her shelf, with the other twenty-year-old books she kept there.

Molly shrugged. "It's good, have you read it?"

"Of course I have, but not *this* one because I don't open these. I got it at the library."

"What?" Molly sat up. "Why?" Molly was able to make the word *why* sound like she was seeing the dumbest thing ever.

"Just…" Claire remembered why she was there. "Molly! God… we're late. Can you get dressed? We have to go *together*."

Molly looked at the clock. "Oh, right." She seemed for a moment like she was going to apologize but instead she shook her head. "They won't notice."

"They'll…"

"They won't notice," Molly said again as she lost the shorts and put

194

on her skirt, which she had conveniently draped in her classless way over the top of her bookshelf and pulled on her blouse and jacket. She set about buttoning the shirt as she joined Claire heading out the door. "Believe me, these guys don't notice anything."

"Yeah, well, if that were true, we wouldn't have to work the cafeteria."

"Oh, that's different."

Claire had to acknowledge that their cafeteria duty was heavily her own fault. In the first week after Molly had arrived. Molly had convinced some of the other girls to go on a joyride with her in a borrowed maintenance pickup. They were taking it to town to try and get into a bar. Claire had, in as classy a way as she could manage, told Mrs. Tarrant. Molly was brought back and punished, but surprisingly, so was Claire. That was something she didn't expect, that Mrs. Tarrant was going to decide that the way to solve their problems was to make them share a room hardly big enough for Claire on her own to be comfortable. Princess and pauper. Southern belle and grease monkeyette.

When they got out on the mall Molly looked up. "Gonna rain."

"No kidding," Claire said. By the time they reached the cafeteria, the first droplets had begun.

They prepped the cafeteria and served breakfast. It was a whole ritual—sack breakfasts for some students who had to dart in and then out to class, sit-down for those who had a later start. When breakfast was half-done, Claire put out her hand for a fresh stack of silverware and Molly landed them there expertly, but when Claire glanced at Molly's eyes, the girl was watching the big cafeteria windows.

Thunder rolled through the building. It was now pouring outside. The last girls who came in for breakfast grabbed sacks and darted out, holding the paper bags over their heads and running back towards the lecture halls.

The rain outside chilled Claire to the bone just to look at, coming down in silky gray waves pushed by the wind. It looked to her like translucent curtains over the green lawns.

"Brrr," she said.

"Mm hmm," Molly hummed in agreement.

"Girls?" Ms. Mittank, the Food Services Manager called to them. Both girls turned. The woman was standing in the door to the kitchen, taking off a green apron and hanging it on a hook as she talked. "That's it, you should get to class. The rain's pretty bad." She looked at them both. "You don't have umbrellas?"

They didn't. Ms. Mittank pointed them to the Lost & Found Box by one of the doors and they rummaged around, choosing from a surprisingly plentiful collection of abandoned umbrellas. They picked an ugly but big yellow one, big enough for both of them.

They stepped out onto the lawn, sticking close together.

"How long do we have til class?" Molly asked.

Claire glanced up at the clock tower, which was a little hard to see in the rain. "About twenty."

"You want a cigarette?"

"Ew," Claire said.

Molly rolled her eyes.

"Okay, a drag."

They headed away from the cafeteria into the woods and found a spot under a big tree, right at the top of the hill that rolled down to the highway. As Claire held the umbrella, Molly fished out a pack of Chesterfields and lit one of them with an Army Zippo she had gotten from her dad. Molly had told Claire that her dad was a tank commander in Korea and had carried this lighter all through the war. It was her greatest treasure.

Molly took a drag from the cigarette and then offered it to Claire, who hesitantly took a drag as well and handed it back.

Something seemed to catch Molly's eye. The girl scowled as though confused, which for Molly always looked like annoyance.

"What is it?"

Molly pulled away from the tree, gesturing for Claire to follow as she took the cigarette back. Molly held the umbrella as they walked closer to where the hill began a steady, shallow incline to the road about an eighth of a mile away. From here, Claire was able to catch a flicker of red light bouncing off some wet maple leaves.

They looked down the hill to find a scene of flickering lights and disaster.

Past the trees, through drifts of soaked leaves that clattered loudly with the rain, a number of men in heavy coats scurried around the two-lane highway, emergency lights dancing off the rainy road. Their black leather shoulders flashed with reflections of the blue and red lights of a pair of police cars blocking the road. An ambulance, its own lights swirling, was just now pulling ahead of the police cars and stopping. Claire heard distant shouts of the men as the officers waved the ambulance into place.

What they were gathering around was another ambulance—this one with no lights at all, turned on its side, its rear doors laying open. A constellation of objects Claire couldn't see were spilled out over the road.

"What's that on the road?"

Molly blinked. "Looks like… medical supplies. Boxes of bandages. Blankets. Stuff like that."

Now a paramedic ran out of the ambulance that had just parked and was jumping to look through the windshield of the ambulance. Claire heard one of the cops shout, "We got someone back here!"

"Good Lord," Molly said as she offered Claire the cigarette.

"Is there anything we need to…" She stopped, watching two of the cops drag a man in a white paramedic's uniform out of the back of the ambulance. Two more paramedics immediately swarmed over him.

"What would we do?" Molly asked. "Call the police? They're already here." A huge drop of rain landed on the cigarette, ruining it, and Molly let it drop with a sigh. She shivered and Claire instantly did the same. The rain was getting worse, if that was even possible.

"We should tell Mrs. Tarrant at least."

"Sure," Molly said. "Come on, let's get in."

The girls ran back to the campus in time for class, but just as Molly put her hands on the heavy wooden handles of the door into Lecture Hall A, Claire stopped her. "Something's going on at the cafeteria."

They looked across the mall and back to the cafeteria they'd just left twenty minutes earlier. Through swirls of color from the falling rain, they could see hundreds of people gathered and looking towards the proscenium stage at the end of the room opposite the kitchen.

"Huh," Molly said.

2.

The girls ran to the cafeteria once more and went in a side door, finding a place behind the sea of white socks and pleated skirts. Claire was taller than Molly, and in fact was taller than most of the other girls here, so she had a slight advantage seeing through the crowd. Up at the stage, Headmaster Lyman and Mrs. Tarrant were standing and shouting, their heads craned upwards to aid in the projection of their voices.

"… most likely the rain is going to continue. We're hearing now that we're getting more than we thought. Very likely we're looking at flooding in the afternoon."

"Including here? Aren't we on a hill?" That was Taffy. She was a large, gregarious girl, full of practical jokes, but Claire heard in her voice a solid concern.

"Including here," the Headmaster said, nodding. "We're higher than the road but not by much."

"The point is," said Mrs. Tarrant, "we can't stay here. We're evacuating."

Claire and Molly both leaned forward. They glanced at one another. Claire then looked back out at the sheets of rain, but Molly had her eyes cast down. Claire promptly realized the girl was looking at Claire's boots, which she always wore when she went out to the stables.

Molly spoke up from their spot in the back. "What about the stables? Don't we need someone to stay to tend the animals?"

"Thank you," Claire said.

"You never stop going on about the things," Molly said.

"That's…" the Headmaster started to answer and then stopped, working his jaw. Claire got the idea he had no idea what to say next. Like it hadn't occurred to him. Which was possible; there was a lot going on. Finally, he started again the way Claire had already decided that men like to start statements that don't have a lot of fact or even certainty behind them. "Look. We need to get moving. The staff will work on evacuating the animals. But what we need from everyone here is to go back to your dorm rooms, pack, and be at the flagpole in an hour."

That was the answer. Be ready to be out in an hour. Mrs. Tarrant spoke next as Molly and Claire listened, but it was like a lot of big meetings, the rest of it was just the same as before, in more and different words.

The meeting broke and the students wandered out into the mall under umbrellas, chattering, their voices lost and blurred together in the pattering of the rain.

Beside her under the umbrella, Molly shook her head as the students ran around them.

"What do you want to do?"

"I'm hoping they have a horse trailer," Claire said. "If they're going to have buses, they can have a truck with a horse trailer."

"What else do they have in the stable?" Molly asked.

Claire thought. "Besides two horses, we have a rabbit pen and a goat."

They had stopped. Molly looked past Claire at the cafeteria and Claire followed her gaze. The Headmaster and Mrs. Tarrant were still in there, answering questions from stragglers.

Claire asked, "So… did Lyman look like he had trailers lined up for the animals?"

"I think he looked like he hadn't given it a thought in the first place."

Claire shook her heard. She looked back at Molly. "I'm not crazy, you know. I just don't want to see my favorite horse get swept away if we're going to be driving out."

"Yeah," Molly said. "But it doesn't matter how 'not crazy' you are. We gotta hustle. You have a truck bed's worth of clothes and you're gonna need to pack something."

Claire was thinking. "The flagpole is the highest point on the campus." Molly nodded as Claire pictured it in her mind. Circular driveway, at the end of a drive that ran back to the main campus. About fifty yards of grassy clearing before some woods.

"I'm gonna get the horses and walk them to the flagpole," she said. "It shouldn't take ten minutes. Then we can head back to the dorm and grab what we want."

"We?"

"I could use your help," Claire said.

Molly grimaced and lit another cigarette. "Yeah, okay."

They set off down a wide drive that had been carved into the woods. As Claire walked along it in her tennis shoes, they started to try to figure where they could step. The tires of trucks used to make the trip back and forth had dug deep, and now the dirt path was turning to mud. The girls moved to the edge where there was more grass to walk on, but it made moving side by side with the one umbrella a chore. They were about fifty yards into the path in the woods to the stables when they heard a girl calling from being them.

They turned around, peering through the rain. It was Taffy, younger and taller than any of them, galumphing along fast in thick black rubbers, with a big yellow wagon in tow. "Wait up!"

"What's that?" Molly asked, pointing with her cigarette.

"You guys are looking to get the animals, right?"

"Horses," Claire specified.

"Well, okay," Taffy said, "but I can fit a rabbit pen on here."

The stables stood in a clearing in the woods, lit up by enormous floodlights on telephone poles on either end of the barn-like structure. With the rain pouring down, the lights cast strange shadows, distributed oddly and unevenly under their cage of clouds. As the three girls approached the stables, Claire had the uncanny feeling of not being sure if it were night or day.

Even with the umbrella keeping some of the rain off, Claire was feeling numbing cold. Her clothes were damp, and every movement felt thick and awkward. Stepping into the stables, the rain was gone but she was so soaked it didn't matter, and they had to shout over the rain beating against the tin roof.

The horses were in a nervous state, and Molly and Claire spent a moment consoling them, patting their sides and jaws before harnessing them. Taffy made quick work of putting a rabbit hutch on the large yellow wagon and putting all the rabbits into it.

"What about the goat?" Molly asked, looking back at the small, white creature.

Claire found a lead and attached it with a collar to the goat's neck and tied this to Taffy's wagon. "It'll do." Taffy nodded and looked around.

199

"Where's my umbrella?"

Claire shrugged and Taffy wandered off towards the goat pen. When she turned a corner out of sight, Claire looked up at the ceiling. "Boy, I've never heard rain like that."

Molly didn't respond, just worked her jaw and nodded so imperceptibly that Claire felt she was the only one who could notice it. "Hey Taffy, you find it?" Molly called.

No answer. "Look, you're gonna just have to deal with no umbrella."

They heard a heavy *thunk* of wood and Claire looked at Molly. And another *thunk*.

They stepped away from the wagon. Walking towards the goat's pen. Turned a corner and looked inside.

Claire took it in. Beds of straw. Wooden walls on either side and old tools hanging, and an open window with rain spattering in, and she immediately realized one of the sounds they'd heard was the window being thrown open, fast.

And one more thing.

Taffy was stuck to the wall with a pitchfork that ran straight through her neck, her body hanging by the head, her neck distending around the prongs of the pitchfork.

3.

"Do we…" Molly stopped. Her mouth hung open, her cigarette dropping and dying in damp dirt. She tried to start again, spinning around to look into the rest of the stables. "What…"

"Taf…" Claire said. Her brain wasn't working. Taffy was dead and someone had stabbed her, pitchforked her, through the neck, and they were…

Molly touched Claire's arm as her voice shook. "Let's go." And they began to run.

In the stables they reached the horses when the roar of a large engine filled the room. Headlights swept through the rain and the wide entrance to the stables.

Molly stepped to the front of the stables and looked out, shielding her eyes against the glare of the headlights. Soon, she looked back at Claire. "It's Lyman!"

Claire joined Molly, looking out at the source of the lights and gasped. It was Lyman's school Suburban all right, but the water outside was flowing high, perilously close to the vehicle's bumper. That was way worse than she thought it was.

She and Molly looked back over their shoulders. They saw nobody. But the killer could be here in one of the stalls. Right now. Claire's head swam. "I don't know what to be more afraid of," she said. "The water or a-, you know, someone."

"Hey," Molly said, clutching Claire's hand. "One thing at a time." She waved at the suburban. "Heyyyy!"

Lyman shouted back as he opened the Suburban door, dropping out of it and sliding down into the water. It came up to his thighs and he clutched the milk-chocolate door handle. "Can you make it?" he cried.

"Mr. Lyman, something's happened!" Claire called. "Taffy…"

"We have to go!" Lyman called back, and Claire had no idea if he had heard her or not. The headmaster wasn't listening anyway, and in the roar of the rain he was a silent movie figure. Lyman reached back into the vehicle and produced a coil of rope, which he tied to the Suburban's door handle. Then he started wading towards them.

He was about a yard and a half from the vehicle when two things happened at once. Lyman called, "this will help keep us steady—" and then the vehicle itself slid several feet. Lyman looked back, his mouth open in shock, and then set his face firmly as he looked back. He continued wading.

And then a figure in a jumpsuit emerged from the water and grabbed Lyman by the collar, disappearing just as quickly and dragging him into the floodwaters.

Molly and Claire screamed. All that remained was the rope.

"That was the…"

"What the *fuck* is going on," Molly asked. She stepped forward into the slope, the water coming up to her shins. "Where did they—no, no, no…"

"Molly, get out, he was under the water!"

"The guy in the jumpsuit? The one who killed Taffy?" Molly waded further, reaching for the rope as the water came to her waste. The rope was trailing at an angle from the truck and she lept, letting the water carry her a few feet before she grabbed it. Claire watched Molly struggle for a few seconds until she was up, the water at her stomach, clutching the rope as she waded back towards Claire. "I don't care if he was fucking Superman, if he was swimming, he's a hundred yards that way now."

"He killed Mister Lyman!"

"Come on, Claire," Molly said, moving forward. The water was so thick on her face, the rain so heavy, she was almost hidden under it. "Take my hand and hurry up."

Claire stepped forward, reaching as she felt the water build in momentum and strength the higher it rose around her. Stretching out her arm, she felt for a moment that she would be swept away, and then Molly had her hand.

They followed the rope back a yard or two to the Suburban and crawled in. The keys were still in the ignition. "Lemme drive," Molly said. She gave Claire a slight shove and Claire crawled over to the passenger seat. Molly pulled at the door to close it, but it wouldn't budge, the water shoving it open.

Claire said, "Maybe go forward and you can shut it as you move."

"Nah," Molly said. "We have to back up." She put the selector in Reverse and backed up onto the path that Mr. Lyman had driven down, the door staying open as water sloshed in. But after a few more yards, the water was lower, and Molly found a place to spin around. She slammed the door as she drove slowly along the dirt road towards the school.

It had been several minutes since either of them had said anything when Molly spoke again. "Who would do that," she said. Her voice was almost lost amid the pounding of the water and the thump of the Suburban's windshield wipers. "Who would... in that way... and leap out of the water like a... shark."

They stopped at a fork, the path on the right heading towards the flagpole cul-de-sac, the left headed to the dorms.

"Forget the dorm," Claire said as she watched the water outside. "Everyone's gathering at the flagpole. ...Oh my god, we forgot the animals."

Molly nodded slowly as though listening to Claire but also having a conversation inside her own head. "Yeah. Yeah, you're right. Plus, we gotta tell Mrs. Tarrant that... what we saw."

"Yes," Claire said. "Yes."

Molly turned right and they drove another thirty yards down the path and then met a creek that wasn't there before. It swept across the road before them like a river, rushing in foam and sticks and litter. Claire saw an old hair dryer surfing by, its long, ribbed tube flopping in the water behind the hair cover, so that it looked like a weird little manta ray making a break for it.

"I..." Molly flexed her fingers on the steering wheel.

"You can't drive through that," Claire said.

"Maybe I could," Molly said.

"You can't," Claire said. "Remember the safety films? You'll get tossed like a toy boat. Nothing beats the power of water." She shivered, looking out at the high water around them. "We shouldn't even be in this."

"I know!" Molly hissed. "What... okay, what do you want to do?"

"Dorms," Claire said. "We have to go back."

"What if they're flooded?"

"That building is three stories tall," Claire said.

Molly nodded and threw the vehicle into reverse again. For a moment the Suburban refused to cooperate and slid sideways, and then they were moving, the two girls looking back through the rear window until they reached the fork in the road again. They backed all the way up until the sign was before them again, because there was no opportunity to just plow down into the ditch or cut through trees. The road was the safest and even it ran with a foot of water.

4.

When they reached the dorm, it was bad. The water was lapping up over the lower steps of the porch and Molly brought the vehicle to a stop right at it.

"No power on," Claire said. She couldn't see any lights.

"The basement's flooded." In the dark day, the headlights lit up the front door of the dorm. The top floor was raised off the ground. It looked like that wasn't flooded.

They had to wade through the water, running, and Claire had the image over and over again of the man raising from the water to grab Mr. Lyman. She looked down, shuddering. Molly said, "that won't happen again. You're more likely to be bitten by a snake."

It was dark inside, the windows doing nothing for light except to make the whole place a shadow. "We should look for flashlights," she said.

Molly had disappeared into the first-floor bathroom and emerged with towels, throwing one to Claire silently. She dried her hair as she walked into the kitchen. "Do we have any in the cupboard?" As she opened it, Claire looked under the sink. Down there she found an old green L-shaped Army flashlight and flicked it on.

"No flashlights in here," Molly said. She looked out, saw Claire's, and gave the thumbs-up. "Winner. Oh!" she ducked back into the cupboard and emerged with a little gray transistor radio.

They put these two prizes on the tile of the kitchen counter.

Claire set the flashlight against a banana so that it aimed up into the ceiling, giving them some light. Molly was about to turn on the radio and Claire stopped her. "Wait, wait."

"What?" Molly asked. "I want to hear about it."

"I just…" Claire waved her hands. "Just, wait. Slow down. Please?"

"We can slow down," Molly said. "But I'm gonna see what I can get." She turned on the radio and static filled the air. Then she began tuning.

"Taffy's dead. Someone killed her…"

"Trying not to think about it," Molly said.

"Are you trying not to think about Mister Lyman being pulled into the water like Captain Queeg?"

203

Molly found a clear station that was droning on about a car wash in town. She looked out. "Captain who?"

"Captain Queeg, you know, the tough guy, gets bitten in half by Jaws."

"Captain Quint," Molly said. She set the radio down and let the advertisement drone on. "I'm not..." She looked down. "I don't understand it."

Claire saw the two images in her mind, Mr. Lyman being sucked under, the pitchfork in Taffy's neck, and suddenly her body started to shake. "We're going to die. No one knows where we are. *We're going to die!*"

Molly came over to her and grabbed her by the shoulders. "Hey." She took Claire's chin in her strong hand. "Hey. Look at me. We're not. We're gonna take it one step at a time."

There was another commercial playing and then at once it stopped, and a man's voice broke in.

"Hello... ugh, sorry. We interrupt this broadcast with an alert to citizens living in the Peekskill area. We've been notified that the Trifle River Dam has been breached, and those in the following towns and surrounding parts should seek high ground immediately."

Claire and Molly listened to the list roll out, and Claire thought for a moment that it reminded her of listening for the name of her school in announcements of closing on snow days.

"Canfield...."

Molly was the one who shook then, her mouth quivering. "Okay."

"... repeat, all citizens in the affected areas should go to high ground immediately."

"Aren't we on a hill?" Claire said. She was thinking just then of the ambulance wreck, which was down the slope in the highway."

"Not enough," Molly said. "Bring the flashlight."

They high tailed it up the stairs. When they reached the second story, Claire pointed to their room, but Molly was insistent. "We should go in the attic." They found the hatch and pulled the rope that hung there at the end of the top floor hall. As Molly unfolded the ladder, Claire looked out the window.

Water was lapping in waves next to the truck's hood. There was no driving out now.

The attic of the dorm was barely visible in the Army flashlight. The place flickered with ribbons and streamers and old Christmas decorations.

"There's gotta be a trunk with blankets, maybe?" Molly was stretching. But then she added something that makes sense. "Maybe people would use them to wrap up old photo frames?"

They set about searching. They found a trunk with old hockey equipment, and a trunk with play costumes.

Finally, the found a trunk near the corner. Molly was unlatching it when Claire said, "Whoa."

"What?" Molly got it open and said, "Bingo," as she unwrapped a blanket from around an old school portrait. "Told ya."

"Look at this," Claire said."

Next to the trunk was a long line of streaked dust—where the trunk itself had been moved. And behind it was a square hatch leading to the top of a ladder.

Molly looked. "Huh. Oh. Well, that would lead to over the sitting room. A second attic."

"But why would it be blocked by this trunk... which it... was. Because it's been moved."

In the dimness, Molly nodded.

"We should block it," Claire said., suddenly sure.

"What are you thinking? Someone had a reason to sneak into our attic? Uncover an old ladder? And then what, swim out to kill Taffy and Mister Lyman?"

"Maybe not in that order," Claire said, her voice dropping. "Molly, what if he's in there. What if he likes it here? Maybe he was always here."

"Jesus, you're creeping me out," Molly said. "Okay, yeah, you don't have to ask me twice." Claire set down the flashlight and they each grabbed part of the trunk and began trying to move it.

"Man, it's heavy," Molly said.

And then they heard the clattering of the flimsy the ladder they'd come up—the clatter of the flimsy letter under heavy footfall.

5.

They moved down the ladder swiftly, as silently as they could. Claire found herself straining in the dark to keep silent and listen as she finally reached the floor of the lower attic. She clicked off the flashlight and it sounded like a rifle shot, and then she and Molly stood in the dark at the bottom of the ladder.

There were footsteps in the main attic. Still at the far end, where the girls had come up.

Claire thought, we should have pulled the crate back over the hole. But of course, there was no way she could have, for both its weight and the awkwardness of trying to pull it in place from the ladder.

So, they listened.

"Do you think it's..." Molly whispered.

Claire shook her head. Molly had said exactly what she was thinking and there was no answer.

Whoever it was moved in the dark as they heard heavy footsteps moving across the attic—and stop, move again, stop.

Then a click. Claire saw a light turn on, a flashlight sweeping in the dark attic above at the top of the ladder.

And then off. More footsteps, and Claire listened, trying to imagine the person moving around in the attic. Then they disappeared down the main ladder and back into the house.

Finally, they heard the attic ladder close up, its hinges creaking, and the attic trap door closed with a solid *whack*.

In the lower attic, Claire and Molly looked at one another in the dark and finally allowed themselves to breathe.

"Oh, my God," Molly whispered as she doubled over, her hands on her knees.

"Why do you think he turned around?" Claire asked. She was shaking with fear still.

"I don't know." Molly stood up, stretching in the dark. She turned around and looked out at the dark lower attic. She stopped, folding her arms and tilting her head. She was a silhouette of a Molly that Claire had seen a hundred times this year; the *what am I looking at* Molly.

Claire looked across the attic and couldn't make sense of the shapes. Molly touched her arm, flexing her fingers, *gimme*.

Claire handed her the flashlight and Molly flicked it on.

The room was twice as long as it was wide, exactly the size of the sitting room, and the attic ended at the edge where, below, the sitting room ended, and the kitchen began.

There was a round, brown and yellow rug laid down in the center of the room. At one edge of the rug was a tea table with a candlestick, a plate and a cup, and a cushion for sitting on.

The rug was about six feet across, but at intervals, strips of rug about two feet wide had been laid out, projecting from the rug.

Molly and Claire came closer.

The roof of the attic sloped, and Molly and Claire kept their heads down as they crept closer.

It looked like...

"It's a campsite," Molly said.

"What?"

"It just looks like one," she said. "But why..." she handed Claire the flashlight and dropped to her knees with a *whump* on the carpet. She looked back at the edge of the carpet and the extended pieces, and, putting her elbows down on the carpet, let her legs extend. Her legs stuck out from the carpet, but the extensions gave her knees and toes something to rest on.

"Claire, try this," she said.

"I don't want to get down on…"

"Come on."

Claire harrumphed and got down on the carpet, taking a spot at a ninety-degree angle from Molly, extending her feet on the carpet. She put the flashlight down and rested on her elbows. "Okay."

"Look down," Molly said.

She did.

At first, she couldn't see it. And then as her eyes adjusted, she saw dim light flickering through the floor. There were holes drilled through the attic floor and the sitting room ceiling, just about an inch wide and long, a series of them in a circle, with holes in the rug that matched them perfectly.

She stared through the holes in the carpet. What she saw below was the sitting room, now sloshing with a foot of water at least.

Molly put her hands down flat, her thumbs together on the carpet as she looked through, like Hitchcock in pictures Claire had seen in their drama book.

Molly breathed in, out. Finally, she spoke. "He's been watching us."

"Who?"

Molly looked up at the close, tilted ceiling of the attic and Claire shined the light.

She saw photos, group shots, Polaroids, newspaper articles. And each of them had neat little labels hand-written in pen:

TERRY

MARGARET

FRAN

… with the oldest photos farthest right, starting in the early 50s, and then newer ones added to the left, a growing collection across the ceiling. But they stopped in the 60s, as far as Claire could tell.

"Not us," Claire said. "Not us specifically. He watched the girls before us. For years."

Claire crouched as she moved along the ceiling, until finally she reached a group photo.

The photo showed the girls of the dormitory, a long white border at the bottom carrying a legend of those pictured. Molly joined Claire as they looked. The girls were all fresh-faced, standing on the mall in front of the dorm in the fall of 1953.

At the center of the girls was a man, the headmaster. And next to him was a woman, her face scraped away with a knife or file. And next to this faceless woman was a little boy, probably nine years old.

The legend told the names. "Assistant to the Headmaster Beatrice Tarrant," Molly read. "That's Mrs. Tarrant. And the little boy is named Peter Tarrant."

"Mrs. Tarrant had a son?"

"Has a son," a man's voice said. They spun around. A man in white coveralls stood by the ladder with something in his hands. Claire didn't recognize it at first.

Then he fired it with a soft *whirp* and Claire didn't see the harpoon that shot out until it stuck her hand to the attic wall. Pain sang nastily through her as she saw her dainty hand impaled against the class of 1967.

More Mrs. Tarrant with a scratched-off face, Claire realized. And she screamed in pain.

She had been holding the flashlight in her other hand and it rolled on the floor, casting light and shadow. Molly didn't even take a moment to think. She ran for the stranger in the dark.

Claire watched Molly move as the stranger took a step forward to meet hand to hand. They tumbled and then both of them howled as Molly and the stranger crashed to and right through the attic floor.

6.

Claire screamed in pain. Her free hand shook as she reached up with instinct to her stuck hand and screamed again when she touched it, every nerve and bone in her hand throbbing with pain.

What, what, what do I do, what do I do...

The spear running through her hand was about a quarter inch wide and had punched right through the center of her palm. Even as her mind swam with images of what the inside of a hand, what a skeleton's hand, looked like, she had no idea if it had broken anything except muscle and skin. The spear was about a foot long and embedded deep in the plywood of the attic's roof. It seemed to be made of fiberglass and was about two feet long.

She heard Molly and the stranger shouting, jostling below. She heard them in the water as Molly shouted epithets. But that was far away because the pain was louder. She had to get her hand free.

The spear ended in a metal loop about the size of a quarter. She didn't think she could lift her hand over it.

She would have to break off the end. Claire reached for the end of the spear with her free hand and tried to grab it with her hand and apply leverage

FLOODWATER

with her palm, like trying to break a pencil with one hand. The moment she put pressure on it she hissed as pain seared through her once again. She felt the bones of her hand colliding with the fiberglass.

"Claire!" Molly shouted, and then she couldn't be heard again. There was more fighting and then a heavy splash. Kicking.

Claire gritted her teeth and yanked part of her free hand down, breaking the shaft. It splinted in her good palm, but the pain was nothing like that of her impaled one. She counted.

One.

More splashing below. Molly sounded like she was trying to talk.

Two.

And then it stopped.

Three and Claire yanked her hand up the shaft until it was free.

Her hand was a gory mess and she held it awkwardly at her side as she doubled over, stumbling back. She reached the rug and stopped, falling to the floor, remembering there was a giant hole in the floor.

She tried not to sob, tried to control her breath. She didn't hear anything below.

She crawled towards the hole, a four-foot-by-three-foot rectangle where the ceiling of the sitting room had given way. She waited a moment, listening, and dared to stick her head over the hole.

Below, in the dim light of the flooded sitting room, she didn't see the stranger at all. All she saw was Molly, face down in the water, floating at the edge of the couch.

Molly's white shirt clung to her back as she bobbed in the water. "

No.

Claire jammed her throbbing hand into her stomach as she got up and ran for the ladder.

7.

Claire sloshed through the sitting room, certain that the stranger would pop out at any moment. But she couldn't wait. She cried out as she reached Molly and grabbed the girl's shoulders, pulling her up from behind as Claire sank to her knees in the water.

She knew this. She had seen this. In CPR training, Youth Group, Freling First Baptist Church, Freling, North Carolina. She had trained for this.

Claire had Molly under the arms and slapped at the girl's face with her good hand. She couldn't find any breath.

Claire struggled to get to her feet, dragging Molly. *Here do we go,*

209

where do we go?

She laid her on the coffee table, which was just barely out of the water.

"Come on, Molly, please," she said. She started to put her hands on Molly's breastbone and could barely take the pressure on her own hand.

And it didn't matter.

Heart attack, she remembered her youth minister saying. If someone's drowned, they need breath.

She turned Molly's head to the side. Water dribbled out. Then she turned Molly's head back, tilting it, and clamped her mouth over Molly's. Pinched her nose.

Breathed hard, four times.

Claire stopped, listening to Molly's mouth. The pain in her hands was far away, replaced by the thrumming of the rain.

Could she hear breath? Anything.

Checked for a pulse. There was one.

She blinked back tears and clamped down again, breathing, breath, breath, breath—

Molly shook like a bronco, bashing Claire's nose with her forehead as she bounced, spattering water out of her mouth. The girl sucked in air and coughed, vomiting water over the side and scrambling all her limbs at once.

"Oh my God, Molly, I'm here, oh my God."

Molly slid over into the water and grabbed onto the couch, laying her head on the soaked cushion. She coughed and looked at Claire. "Jesus what happened."

"That man, I think he drowned you…"

"No…" she coughed, gesturing weekly towards Claire's bloody hand, which she held against her stomach."

"It's…" she blinked back tears. "He harpooned my hand."

"What did you do?" she asked, coughing.

"I had to break it." She held her hand out over the water. The sloshing, murky river that was the sitting room was so filthy that she didn't want to think about what it might be doing to her. "The harpoon, I mean, I broke it and… you know, jerked my hand off of it."

"And then you saved me." Molly struggled to her feet. She rolled her shoulders, coughing. "Jesus you're a tough bitch."

"Yeah." She shrugged. "But I don't know where he went."

Molly looked down and then said, "Hey… is it me or is the water still rising."

"No, it is," Claire said, as she realized the water was now up over the couch. Distantly she was aware that the dam must have breached, and they were in a hole that was filling up. "We have to go back up."

Moving slowly and painfully and then quicker as they heard the rush of water and rain, the girls made their way once more up the steps.

"I don't understand," Claire said as they climbed once more to the main attic. "So that guy was watching us…"

"I don't think he ever watched us," Molly said. She turned to Claire on the stairs, running back her hair as they climbed. "That little voyeur nest he had was old. All the pictures were too. I think he was in that ambulance that overturned. I think he came home and did what he always wanted to do."

They climbed the ladder into the main attic and looked out a tiny window at the end. The water was rising. What were they going to do?

They stayed there, talking. They talked about all the things they planned to do when they got warm and dry.

"I'm not doing anything here," Molly said. "I'm going home."

"Please don't," Claire said. Outside, she saw a potted plant roll by in the water and collide with a tree.

"I thought you didn't want me here."

"If I didn't want you here," Claire said, "I would have left you in the sitting room."

They saw a sweep of lights; the source of which Claire couldn't pinpoint. "What is that?" It swept across the polluted water outside and glanced at the window.

"It's a chopper," Molly said. "It's a helicopter." She threw the window open and thrust out her hand, waving it around and crying, "Heyyy!"

Then she pulled back, looking around. "We need to get on the roof. Find an axe or… anything."

They scurried through the attic, kicking over old decorations, looking for tools. They didn't find an axe or hammer.

Claire found an old dress form, though, armless and legless, black-cloth-covered mannequin with a heavy brass knob for a neck. Together they used it to batter all hell out of the attic roof until finally one of the pieces of plywood gave way.

They stacked up boxes and climbed and Molly used the dress form and then both arms to push a rectangular piece of the roof up, tiles ripping out of the way as she grunted and shoved.

Molly climbed up first and then she reached down, grabbing Claire's wrist under her bad hand and pulling on the good one, until Claire and Molly flopped out onto the roof together. They got up immediately, waving as a white helicopter zoomed away, pitched up, and started back. They jumped and waved as the searchlights hit them.

The helicopter was so loud that Claire couldn't even hear the rain. A pair of guys in the side of the helicopter, alien-like in their helmets and goggles, waved signals at them and rolled down a ladder. It swung this way and that until finally, Molly grabbed it. The rungs were red and heavy plastic. She thrust the ladder towards Claire. "You first."

"No, you!"

"You got a hurt hand," Molly said. "You first."

Claire grabbed the ladder and put her feet on it, and began to climb, using her elbow to try to hold it as she started to spin. Molly caught the ladder below her and kept it steady and then suddenly there were men grabbing her and dragging her up.

Molly was below on the ladder and Claire looked out. The water was at the level of the roof now, lapping over the tiles. Molly put one foot on the ladder and then as her other foot dangled, she smiled.

And then a man emerged from the hole and grabbed her foot. It was the stranger, pulling. Molly's face was a rictus of rage as she gripped the ladder, putting her arm through the rungs so that she wasn't going anywhere. Claire heard Molly shout something as she kicked the stranger viciously with her heel, and he fell free.

The stranger in the white coveralls disappeared into the attic, and the water flowed after him as the helicopter lifted off.

As they flew away, the medics asking questions the girls didn't hear, Claire crawled back to the big open side and put her arm around Molly. As it shrank in the distance, the dormitory protruded from the deluge less and less, and then was swallowed whole. ♜

⇒ CONTRIBUTORS ⇐

JEREMIAH DYLAN COOK is a horror writer whose work has appeared on The NoSleep Podcast, in Castle of Horror Anthology Volumes 4, 5, and 7, in Ghost Orchid Press's *Hundred Word Horror: Cosmos and Beneath* anthologies, and on the Lovecraft eZine's Patreon page. His work has also won first prize in Purple Wall Stories February 2021 Writing Competition, and in the Ligonier Valley Writers 2018 Flash Fiction Contest. In addition, he is a published Lovecraft Scholar with an essay appearing in Hippocampus Press's Lovecraftian Proceedings No. 4. While pursuing his bachelor's degree at St. John's University, he received the Mario Mezzacappa Memorial Award for Outstanding Achievement in Poetry and Prose. He completed his master's degree in Writing Popular Fiction at Seton Hill University, and he is a member of the Horror Writers Association. You can learn more about Jeremiah at jeremiahdylancook.com, or you can find him on twitter @ jeremiahcook1. He is always especially delighted to discuss board games, David Bowie, Tolkien, or Resident Evil video games.

DENNIS K. CROSBY is a San Diego based indie author and speaker with an MFA in Creative Writing from National University. Originally from Oak Park, IL, he is the award-winning author of the Amazon bestselling urban fantasy novel, *Death's Legacy*, released November 2020, and its follow up *Death's Debt,* released November 2021. The bourbon loving Chicago Cubs fan and deep-dish pizza connoisseur is currently working on the third book in his Kassidy Simmons series and writing weird and creepy short stories in his spare time. To keep up with his journey, check out: denniskcrosby.com
And you can follow him on Twitter and Instagram: @denniskcrosby

KATYA DE BECERRA is the author of genre-bending, critically acclaimed speculative novels, *What the Woods Keep* and *Oasis*. Her next book, *When Ghosts Call Us Home*, is forthcoming in 2023 with Page Street. Her short fiction appeared or is forthcoming in various anthologies and literary magazines. She is a co-editor of a curated horror anthology *This Fresh Hell* (Clan Destine Press, 2023) which reimagines old horror tropes in new and unexpected ways. Katya has a PhD in Cultural Anthropology from the University of Melbourne; for the past ten years she's been working in academia as an educator and researcher. You can keep up to date with Katya's writing and updates through her website katyadebecerra.com, newsletter (katyadebecerra.com/newsletter), Instagram, Twitter and Facebook (@ katyadebecerra).

JASON HENDERSON is a *Locus* Best-selling author (for the first *Highlander* novel), WGA Screenwriting Award nominee, and a Texas Lone Star List recipient for his series *Alex Van Helsing*. He is the host of the Castle of Horror/Castle Talk Podcast, which regularly features genre stars like Elvira and Rob Zombie. Jason's *Young Captain Nemo* series reached #1 on multiple lists. With In Churl Yo, he co-publishes Castle Bridge Media.

HENRY HERZ's speculative fiction short stories include "Out, Damned Virus" (*Daily Science Fiction*), "Bar Mitzvah on Planet Latke" (*Coming of Age*, Albert Whitman & Co.), "The Magic Backpack" (Metastellar), "Unbreakable" (*Musing of the Muses*, Brigid's Gate Press), "A Vampire, an Astrophysicist, and a Mother Superior Walk Into a Basilica" (*Three Time Travelers Walk Into...*, Fantastic Books), "The Case of the Murderous Alien" (*Spirit Machine*, Air and Nothingness Press), "The Ghosts of Enerhodar" (*Literally Dead*, Alienhead Press), "Maria & Maslow" (*Highlights for Children*), and "A Proper Party" (*Ladybug Magazine*). He's written twelve picture books, including the critically acclaimed *I Am Smoke*.
Blog: henryherz.com
Twitter: twitter.com/HenryLHerz
Facebook: facebook.com/Henry.Herz
Instagram: instagram.com/henry_herz/

WILL MCDERMOTT has published eight novels and 18 short stories, and helped create innumerous worlds, characters, and stories for card, board, and video games. His fiction is often set in gaming universes, including *Magic: The Gathering*, *Warhammer 40K*, and *Mage Wars*. His most recent novel, *Strangled by Death*, is a tale of *Carl Kolchak: The Night Stalker*. Will has written a second *Night Stalker* novel, which should be published in 2022. Find out more at willmcdermott.com. Follow Will on Instagram at @w_mcdermott.

ROB NISBET admits to being old enough to remember the 80s and claims to be not yet senile enough to have forgotten them. He remembers being so wowed by the *Blade Runner* film of 1982 that he has devoured most of Philip K. Dick's writing. He is eking out the few books he has not yet read for his old age.
Rob has contributed to many anthologies and magazines including three previous Castle of Horror collections. He has written several audio

scripts produced by Big Finish for their *Doctor Who* range and has recently completed a few murder mysteries featuring Sherlock Holmes. He has won four international short story competitions with prizes ranging from a welcome amount of cash to a t-shirt and a mug.

JOHN PRITCHARD has been fascinated by horror films and supernatural stories for as long as he can remember. At school his English teacher told him he had a morbid imagination and he's been putting it to good use ever since, writing the horror novels *Night Sisters, Angels of Mourning* and *The Witching Hour,* the fantasy epic *Dark Ages,* and several spooky Doctor Who audio dramas for Big Finish, two of which were nominated for Scribe Awards. He still enjoys his day job in hospital administration and likes reading about history and current affairs in his spare time. He tweets about movies, ideas, and pleasing paragraphs at @MissFury1.

 The Donjon was inspired by Michael Mann's film *The Keep* and F. Paul Wilson's source novel, as well as by a vignette in David A. Bell's book *The First Total War,* and a location in Victor Hugo's great novel of the French Revolution, *Ninety-Three.*

CHARLES R. RUTLEDGE is the author of *Dracula's Return* and three novels in the Griffin & Price series, written with James A. Moore. His short stories have appeared in over thirty anthologies, and he has co-edited several anthologies as well. Charles owns entirely too many editions of Dracula, keeps soil from Transylvania in an envelope on his desk, and is seldom seen in daylight.

New York Times bestselling author **ALETHEA KONTIS** is a princess, storm chaser, and adventurer. She has written over 20 books and 50 short stories, including *AlphaOops: The Day Z Went First, Enchanted,* and *Prince Phillip's Birthday Waltz* (Disney). Alethea is the recipient of the Jane Yolen Mid-List Author Grant, the Scribe Award, the Garden State Teen Book Award, and two-time winner of the Gelett Burgess Children's Book Award. She has been twice nominated for both the Andre Norton Nebula and the Dragon Award. Alethea also narrates stories for multiple award-winning online magazines and contributes regular YA book reviews to NPR. Born in Vermont, she currently resides on the Space Coast of Florida with her teddy bear, Charlie. Find out more about Princess Alethea at aletheakontis.com.

HEATH W. SHELBY grew up a child of the 1980s. The movies, the television shows, the music, the video games, the fashion, the pop culture… in his heart, Heath is still smack dab in the midst of that glorious decade. In

215

real life, Heath lives in the present in Searcy, Arkansas, where he is the father of two incredible kids (his son Collin and his daughter Caitlynn) and his Maltizhu, Leia. When he's not writing or reminiscing about the 80s, Heath is the Program Director/Music Director/On-Air Personality for Crain Media. In his free time, you will find Heath cruising in his red Mustang; visiting his inspirations, his parents; Rokken with Dokken; hanging out at the nearest Margaritaville, scarfing down a Cheeseburger in Paradise or three; and praying that somehow, some way his beloved San Francisco 49ers will win at least one more Super Bowl during his lifetime.

Facebook: facebook.com/heathwshelby
Instagram: the_heath_shelby
Twitter: @heath_shelby

JIM TOWNS is an award-winning filmmaker, writer, and artist.

His feature films include *Prometheus Triumphant, House of Bad, State of Desolation* and the upcoming *The Beast Inside.* His short fiction has been published in print and online by Burial Day, *Switchblade Magazine,* Dead Fern Press, *Castle of Horror,* Hellbound Books, and many more. His first nonfiction book *American Cryptic* was released in 2020 by Anubis Press, and his debut novella *Bloodsucker City* is available through Castle Bridge Media. 2022 will see the publication of his follow up to *American Cryptic, American Boogeywoman.*

He lives in San Pedro, CA, with his wife and several mysterious cats.

IN CHURL YO has served as an editorial director and an award-winning creative consultant to several magazines during his career. Amazing Stories called his debut novel *Isonation* "a fast-paced post-pandemic story where nothing turns out to be quite what it seems." His follow-up novel *Austinites* offers readers a literary nostalgia-infused trip through 1990's Austin. *Something Doesn't Make It True,* a poetry collection, is out now. Born and raised in Texas, where he graduated from the University of Texas at Austin with a degree in Marketing, he made the move to cooler and greener climes out West with his wife and two children. He is Co-Publisher with Jason Henderson at Castle Bridge Media. Follow him on Twitter @inchurlyo.

BRYAN YOUNG (he/they) works across many different media. His work as a writer and producer has been called "filmmaking gold" by The New York Times. He's also published comic books with Slave Labor Graphics and Image Comics. He's been a regular contributor for the *Huffington Post, StarWars.com, Star Wars Insider magazine, SYFY, /Film,* and was the founder and editor in chief of the geek news and review site *Big Shiny*

Robot! In 2014, he wrote the critically acclaimed history book, *A Children's Illustrated History of Presidential Assassination.* He co-authored *Robotech: The Macross Saga RPG* has written two books in the BattleTech Universe: *Honor's Gauntlet* and *A Question of Survival.* He teaches writing for Writer's Digest, Script Magazine, and at the University of Utah. Follow him on Twitter @swankmotron.

CASTLE BRIDGE MEDIA RECOMMENDS...

If you liked *The Castle of Horror Anthology Volume 8: Thinly Veiled: The 80s*, you might also enjoy reading the following titles from Castle Bridge Media available on Amazon or by order at your favorite book store:

Austinites
By In Churl Yo

Bloodsucker City
By Jim Towns

THE CASTLE OF HORROR
ANTHOLOGY SERIES
Volume 1
Volume 2: *Holiday Horrors*
Volume 3: *Scary Summer Stories*
Volume 4: *Women Running From Houses*
Volume 5: *Thinly Veiled: The 70s*
Volume 6: *Femme Fatales**
Volume 7: *Love Gone Wrong*
Volume 8: *Thinly Veiled: The 80s*
Edited By Jason Henderson and In Churl Yo
*Edited By P.J. Hoover

Castle of Horror Podcast
Book of Great Horror:
Our Favorites, Top Tens
and Bizarre Pleasures
Edited By Jason Henderson

Dream State
By Martin Ott

FuturePast Sci-Fi Anthology
Edited by In Churl Yo

GLAZIER'S GAP
Ghosts of the Forbidden
By Leanna Renee Hieber

Isonation
By In Churl Yo

MID-LIFE CRISIS THRILLERS
18 Miles From Town
By Jason Henderson

Nightwalkers: Gothic Horror Movies
By Bruce Lanier Wright

THE PATH
The Blue-Spangled Blue
By David Bowles
The Deepest Green
By David Bowles

SURF MYSTIC
Night of the Book Man
By Peyton Douglas
Dark of the Curl
By Peyton Douglas

Yesterday's Tomorrows: The Golden Age
of Science Fiction Movie Posters
By Bruce Lanier Wright

Please remember to leave us your reviews on Amazon and Goodreads!

THANK YOU FOR SUPPORTING INDEPENDENT PUBLISHERS AND AUTHORS!
castlebridgemedia.com

www.ingramcontent.com/pod-product-compliance
Lightning Source LLC
Chambersburg PA
CBHW051949220626
47052CB00004B/871